## Erle Stanley Gardner and The Murder Room

**>>>** This title is part of The Murder Room, our series dedicated to making available out-of-print or hard-to-find titles by classic crime writers.

Crime fiction has always held up a mirror to society. The Victorians were fascinated by sensational murder and the emerging science of detection; now we are obsessed with the forensic detail of violent death. And no other genre has so captivated and enthralled readers.

Vast troves of classic crime writing have for a long time been unavailable to all but the most dedicated frequenters of second-hand bookshops. The advent of digital publishing means that we are now able to bring you the backlists of a huge range of titles by classic and contemporary crime writers, some of which have been out of print for decades.

From the genteel amateur private eyes of the Golden Age and the femmes fatales of pulp fiction, to the morally ambiguous hard-boiled detectives of mid twentieth-century America and their descendants who walk our twenty-first century streets, The Murder Room has it all. **>>>**

## The Murder Room
### Where Criminal Minds Meet

**themurderroom.com**

T0373041

**Erle Stanley Gardner (1889–1970)**

Born in Malden, Massachusetts, Erle Stanley Gardner left school in 1909 and attended Valparaiso University School of Law in Indiana for just one month before he was suspended for focusing more on his hobby of boxing that his academic studies. Soon after, he settled in California, where he taught himself the law and passed the state bar exam in 1911. The practise of law never held much interest for him, however, apart from as it pertained to trial strategy, and in his spare time he began to write for the pulp magazines that gave Dashiell Hammett and Raymond Chandler their start. Not long after the publication of his first novel, *The Case of the Velvet Claws*, featuring Perry Mason, he gave up his legal practice to write full time. He had one daughter, Grace, with his first wife, Natalie, from whom he later separated. In 1968 Gardner married his long-term secretary, Agnes Jean Bethell, whom he professed to be the real 'Della Street', Perry Mason's sole (although unacknowledged) love interest. He was one of the most successful authors of all time and at the time of his death, in Temecula, California in 1970, is said to have had 135 million copies of his books in print in America alone.

*By Erle Stanley Gardner*
(titles below include only those
published in the Murder Room)

**Perry Mason series**

The Case of the Sulky Girl
   (1933)
The Case of the Baited Hook
   (1940)
The Case of the Borrowed
   Brunette (1946)
The Case of the Lonely
   Heiress (1948)
The Case of the Negligent
   Nymph (1950)
The Case of the Moth-Eaten
   Mink (1952)
The Case of the Glamorous
   Ghost (1955)
The Case of the Terrified
   Typist (1956)
The Case of the Gilded Lily
   (1956)
The Case of the Lucky Loser
   (1957)
The Case of the Long-Legged
   Models (1958)
The Case of the Deadly Toy
   (1959)
The Case of the Singing Skirt
   (1959)

The Case of the Duplicate
   Daughter (1960)
The Case of the Blonde
   Bonanza (1962)

**Cool and Lam series**
*First published under the
pseudonym A.A. Fair*

The Bigger They Come (1939)
Turn on the Heat (1940)
Gold Comes in Bricks (1940)
Spill the Jackpot (1941)
Double or Quits (1941)
Owls Don't Blink (1942)
Bats Fly at Dusk (1942)
Cats Prowl at Night (1943)
Crows Can't Count (1946)
Fools Die on Friday (1947)
Bedrooms Have Windows
   (1949)
Some Women Won't Wait (1953)
Beware the Curves (1956)
You Can Die Laughing (1957)
Some Slips Don't Show (1957)
The Count of Nine (1958)
Pass the Gravy (1959)
Kept Women Can't Quit (1960)

Bachelors Get Lonely (1961)
Shills Can't Count Chips (1961)
Try Anything Once (1962)
Fish or Cut Bait (1963)
Up For Grabs (1964)
Cut Thin to Win (1965)
Widows Wear Weeds (1966)
Traps Need Fresh Bait (1967)

## Doug Selby D.A. series

The D.A. Calls it Murder (1937)
The D.A. Holds a Candle (1938)
The D.A. Draws a Circle (1939)
The D.A. Goes to Trial (1940)
The D.A. Cooks a Goose (1942)
The D.A. Calls a Turn (1944)

The D.A. Takes a Chance (1946)
The D.A. Breaks an Egg (1949)

## Terry Clane series

Murder Up My Sleeve (1937)
The Case of the Backward
  Mule (1946)

## Gramp Wiggins series

The Case of the Turning Tide
  (1941)
The Case of the Smoking
  Chimney (1943)

Two Clues (two novellas) (1947)

# The Case of the Backward Mule

## Erle Stanley Gardner

An Orion book

Copyright © The Erle Stanley Gardner Trust 1946

This edition published by
The Orion Publishing Group Ltd
Orion House
5 Upper St Martin's Lane
London WC2H 9EA

An Hachette UK company
A CIP catalogue record for this book is available from the British Library

ISBN 978 1 4719 0948 1

www.orionbooks.co.uk

# 1

AS THE big steamer eased her way through the Golden Gate, the western sun highlighted the sides of San Francisco's buildings until the city seemed to be all white, rising in stately splendor from the blue water.

Terry Clane, returning from the Orient, fought back an impulse of exultation.

Steeped in the philosophy of those wise men who dwelt in hidden monasteries where studies might be pursued in peace, Clane knew that triumph and defeat were both impostors, that success and failure were but different facets of the same jewel. Yet he knew also that here in San Francisco there was work to be done—dangerous work, and he was eager to get at it, eager to see once more his native land.

Standing at the rail, the wind ruffling his dark wavy hair, he watched the changing scenery of the shore line until the vessel glided smoothly in to the dock.

The sun had now set and a new moon hung over the city.

It was a delicately arched new moon, slender, graceful and promising, the moon which Chinese call "The Moon of the Maiden's Eyebrow."

Seeing that moon, Terry Clane thought of Sou Ha, the Chinese daughter of Chu Kee, thought also of Cynthia Renton. Cynthia would doubtless be there at the dock to meet him, and following that meeting . . .

The gangplanks were run aboard and for the next thirty minutes Clane was busily engrossed with the formalities of disembarking. Finally, his baggage having been inspected by customs, Clane moved toward the fence-like structure which separated the incoming passengers from those who had come to greet them.

Through the openings in the fence Clane saw his trusted confidential man, Yat T'oy, sitting calmly on a bench, hands folded in his lap, waiting. Clane caught Yat T'oy's eye.

His smile brought no answering gleam of recognition. Yat

1

T'oy looked at him with wooden-faced indifference, turned calmly away, not too hurriedly, not too slowly.

Clane, perplexed, looked around for Cynthia Renton. She was nowhere in sight.

Clane emerged from the narrow passageway, caught the eye of a newsboy, flipped him a quarter and took one of the late papers, which he folded under his arm. He started toward Yat T'oy, proceeding cautiously now, knowing that Yat T'oy's wooden-faced indifference masked some warning which the ancient Chinese servant dared not give.

And now Clane was conscious of eyes that were resting upon him with more than casual interest. A man by the door, another by the baggage truck, a third at the gate.

Clane walked past the bench where Yat T'oy was seated, taking care not even to look at the old man.

Yat T'oy took a cigarette from his pocket, fumbled awkwardly for a match. *"Gie heem,"* he said as though merely muttering some imprecation at the failure of the match to light the cigarette.

Clane hardly needed the Chinese warning of danger. He walked casually away from Yat T'oy, stood by the gate waiting for his luggage to be brought out.

The three men kept their eyes on him but made no move.

Clane yawned, thought of the newspaper under his arm, unfolded it and snapped it open.

The action might have been a signal. The three men converged on him at once, almost frantic in their haste.

"You're Clane?" one of the men said. "Terry Clane?"

"Right."

The man took his right arm, another took his left. "Just a minute, buddy, it'll only take a minute. Someone wants to ask you some questions."

"What about?" Clane asked.

"We wouldn't know," the man said and firmly removed the newspaper from Clane's hands.

"But look here," Clane began, "you can't . . ."

"Take it easy, buddy, take it easy," the men said.

The third man was behind now and they were moving steadily forward.

2

Clane held back.

The pressure from behind increased and the pace was accelerated. He was rushed into a big black sedan, doors slammed, a motor throbbed to life and almost instantly a siren wailed into a low-voiced demand for the right of way, a wail which soon became a screaming, insistent command as the car rushed into speed.

Clane, settling back against the cushions, surrendered to the inevitable, but in the back of his mind he filed one fact for reference. These men had been watching him to see what he would do, to see with whom he would speak, where he would go. Yet one thing had forced their hands, one thing which had evidently been carefully agreed upon in advance. Clane was to have no opportunity to glance at the evening newspaper. The minute he opened that newspaper, the men had gone into action.

It was an interesting fact to which Clane gave due consideration so that that which was to happen next would not come as too great a surprise.

## 2

TERRY CLANE lit a cigarette, settled back comfortably in the chair. Across the desk, Police Captain Jordon adjusted a combination desk lamp and ash tray so that it was midway between them, a gesture apparently intended to make the ash receptacle mutually convenient.

Terry Clane, however, noticing the peculiar grilled sides of the light stand, realized that there was a microphone concealed within the metallic base, and that by placing it exactly between them, Captain Jordon had assured himself that the conversation would be duly recorded on wax cylinders.

"Mr. Clane," the police captain said, "I'm not going to take more than a few minutes of your time. I realize how anxious you are to be free to see the city, so I'll be frank—and abrupt."

"Thank you, Captain."

"You've just returned from the Orient, Mr. Clane?"

"Yes. Your men were waiting for me when the boat docked."

"I take it you know why."

"Frankly, I do not."

"You have been in the Orient for some time?"

"Yes."

"War work?"

"Yes."

"And before that you were an old hand in the Orient?"

"I had lived in China, studied there."

"I believe you once specialized on the art of concentration in some Chinese monastery?"

"Yes. I spent two years in study."

"You became adept in the art of concentration?"

"I was a novice. I learned a little."

"Learned to concentrate for some specified period of time?"

"Yes."

"How long?"

"A little over four seconds."

*"Four seconds, Mr. Clane!"*

"Exactly."

"Surely you are joking! I have never studied concentration, but I frequently find myself concentrating for several minutes, sometimes an hour."

Clane kept the smile from his lips. Only his eyes showed amusement. "You have, as you so aptly state, never studied concentration."

"You mean that you doubt my word?"

"Not at all. We merely use the word concentration in a different sense. In the way the word is used in the Orient it means contemplation, with every bit of mental energy brought to bear upon that which is being contemplated; every bit."

"Well, that's the way I do it."

"Does the ringing of the telephone interrupt your concentration and make it difficult for you to return to a contemplation of the problem?" Clane asked, innocently.

"Indeed it does. Sometimes my wife rings up when I'm concentrating and . . ."

Clane's smile caused the police captain to break off in mid-sentence.

"In the Orient," Clane said, "one who would *hear* the ringing of a telephone bell would be held not to be concentrating. Only when the contemplation becomes so absolute that no external disturbances can distract the attention is concentration even considered as having been begun."

The police captain looked skeptical, then suddenly changed the subject. "All right," he said crisply, "we'll let all that go and get down to business. Before you left for the Orient this last time you were either engaged to Cynthia Renton, a portrait painter, or were very well acquainted with her. You had also known her sister, Alma Renton, for some years. After you left, rumor has it that Cynthia was pretty much broken up for a while, then she took up with a chap named Edward Harold. Did you ever meet him?"

"No."

"You've seen him?"

"Never."

"You know about him?"

"Yes. In a way. I was not engaged to Cynthia Renton when I left. I had been engaged to her. I suggested that she had better be free when I had to leave on this war work. My mission was highly dangerous. The chances were good against my ever returning. I wanted her to be free to meet other men on the basis of becoming interested in them. Otherwise the engagement would have dragged along and then inevitably have been broken. It's only human nature to crave companionship, and Cynthia is very much alive, a bundle of dynamite, or she was the last I saw of her."

"Exactly. Now about Harold's trouble. What do you know about that?"

"I knew that he had been arrested for the murder of Horace Farnsworth, tried, convicted, sentenced to death and had appealed. The trial took place just as I was leaving China."

"How did you know of the verdict, the sentence and the appeal?"

"By wireless."

"From Cynthia?"

5

"Yes."

"She appealed to you for help?"

"She hoped I'd get back from the Orient in time to be of some help, yes."

"You knew Farnsworth?"

"Yes. He had some money of Cynthia's which he was investing for her. He was also a partner in the Eastern Art Import and Trading Company. I knew the others in that company: Stacey Nevis, Ricardo Taonon and George Gloster. Farnsworth had, I believe, been in the Philippines for a while, investigating some gold-mining properties near Baguio. Naturally, I don't think Harold was guilty."

"Why?"

"I don't think he did it. I think he was framed."

"Yet you don't even know him?"

"Except through Miss Renton's letters."

"You would, perhaps, do a great deal to see that he was not executed?"

"Don't misunderstand me, Captain. I'd do anything in my power, regardless of the cost, to see that sentence of death was never carried out."

"Exactly. Where were you last night?"

Clane showed surprise. "On the boat, some two hundred odd miles offshore."

"You didn't leave that boat by plane or otherwise?"

"Heavens no. Of course not. I couldn't possibly have done so even if I'd had the opportunity. Why do you ask?"

"Because last night Edward Harold was being taken by automobile from the county jail to San Quentin prison where the death sentence was to be carried out. His appeal was, of course, pending, but it is customary for criminals convicted of felonies to be taken to the penitentiary to await the disposition of their appeals."

Clane sat, rigid, attentive, waiting for that which he felt was to come. The desire to keep him from seeing the newspaper could have but one explanation.

"And," Jordon went on, "at approximately ten-thirty last night the car had what appeared to be an ordinary blowout. Later on police found that heavy roofing tacks had been sprinkled all over the road. While the officers were making a first somewhat dejected appraisal of the flat tire, two masked men stepped from the bushes by the side of the road. They were heavily armed and, inasmuch as the surprise was complete, they were able to rescue Mr. Harold. The officers were handcuffed with their own handcuffs. Harold was taken away with these masked men."

Clane sucked in a quick breath. Beyond that he showed no emotion.

"Do you know anything about this affair?"

"Only what you have told me. This is the first I have heard of it."

"Did you have any part in it—any part in the planning of it?"

"Definitely not."

"And you have absolutely no idea where Mr. Harold might now be hiding?"

"None whatever."

Captain Jordon pushed back his chair, said casually, "Rather a peculiar, interesting law point is involved, Mr. Clane. The Supreme Court will dismiss an appeal taken by a person who is a fugitive."

"You mean that if a person is convicted of a crime in an illegal manner; simply because he has escaped from jail, the Supreme Court would impose a penalty?"

"Come, come, Mr. Clane. That's loosely stated. The Supreme Court doesn't impose a penalty. The man is already under sentence of death and the Supreme Court merely assumes the position that it is the height of impertinence for a criminal who is hiding from the law to seek to invoke the benefit of the law."

"I take it that's all?" Clane asked.

"Just one more point, Mr. Clane. If we should consider it necessary, would you have any objection to repeating your statements to a polygraph operator?"

"None whatever," Clane said.

And no sooner had the words left his mouth than he realized by the expression on the face of the police officer that the trap into which he had walked had been the sole object of this preliminary phase of the examination.

"Excellent," Captain Jordon said. "We consider it necessary for you to do so. It will only take a few moments. Right this way, please, Mr. Clane."

# 3

THE room was entirely free of the taint of the Inquisition. It wasn't particularly cheerful, but on the other hand there was none of the hostile atmosphere so frequently found in rooms at police headquarters. The place might well have been an office, furnished plainly but efficiently. The machine, of course, dominated the room just as the electric chair dominates the execution chamber; but the chair in which Clane was placed was comfortable and, once the various electrodes and gadgets had been adjusted, the machine itself seemed trying to be friendly. It looked perfectly innocuous, something which might have been a radio waiting to be turned on.

There was only one man in the room, in itself a disarming factor; and this man seemed anxious to put Clane at ease. Moreover, the manner in which he went about doing it showed that he was a good student of psychology.

"Of course, Mr. Clane," he said, "with a man of your intelligence we don't try to pull any hocus-pocus. We simply ask your cooperation in taking the test. We know that if it weren't voluntary on your part you wouldn't be here. Naturally if you had anything to conceal, knowing that you weren't obligated to take this test, you would have refused it. So, in a way, our examination becomes something of a matter of form."

Clane nodded.

"And," his interlocutor went on, "in view of the fact, we don't try to conduct the examination the way we would that of a suspected criminal, for instance."

"I see," Clane said.

"Now, of course," the man went on, smiling, "I've got to turn in a record which will show the examination has been effective. In other words, it will show your emotional reaction to questions. There's no use trying to persuade a man of *your* intelligence that that isn't what we're after. You know as well as I do that's the sole object of the machine."

Clane nodded again.

"By the way," the man said, "my name's Maynard—Harry Maynard."

"I'm very glad to meet you," Clane said. "I presume you not only have my name but my fingerprints as well."

Maynard laughed. "Oh, hardly that, Mr. Clane. I understand you've had some very interesting experiences in the Orient in connection with psychology."

Clane merely nodded again.

Maynard laughed. "I'm not even going to look at the needles on the recording devices, Mr. Clane. With you I think it's an idle gesture, but you must realize that in order to turn in a record showing a fair test, I have to first get some normal reactions."

Again Clane nodded.

"And," Maynard said, smiling, "it doesn't need any glance at the machine to tell me that you're indignant, that back of the mask of your cold courtesy you are angry at the police for subjecting you to this indignity, perhaps a little angry at yourself for having consented to do something which would prolong the interview and delay getting you settled in your hotel."

"I don't think a man needs much knowledge of psychology to reach *that* conclusion," Clane said.

Maynard threw back his head and laughed heartily. "After all, Mr. Clane, I merely work here."

Clane smiled.

"So," Maynard said, "we can't do anything until you relax, Mr. Clane. If you'll just have enough confidence in me to relax and forget about this machine and all the inconveniences to which you have been subjected and chat for a few moments, I'll then be in a position to go on with the test. And please believe me, Mr. Clane, when I tell you that I won't try to take any unfair advantage of you. I'll tell you when the test is starting."

"The machine is running now, is it not?"

9

"Naturally. The object of the test is to first get the witness in his normal frame of mind. Then we get the normal reactions. In other words, when I feel that you are sufficiently relaxed, I'll tell you that the test is about to commence. Then I'll ask you routine questions to which we know the answers. I will ask you when you left the Orient. I will ask you whether you were on board a certain ship. I will ask you whether you docked at a certain time. I will ask you if you know certain people."

"And then try to startle me?" Clane asked.

"Well, to be perfectly frank with you, Mr. Clane, I'll start mixing the questions up. I'll ask you rather suddenly if you knew Edward Harold. And, of course, we'll expect the machine to show that when I suddenly bring up his name there will be a certain rise in your blood pressure. That's only natural. After all, you know that's the information the police are after. You'll realize we're getting close to the nerve of the matter then. You'll brace yourself, mentally."

Clane nodded.

"And then I'll ask you various other questions," Maynard went on. "And you certainly are enough of a student of applied psychology to realize that those questions will alternate. In other words, I'll try to ask you the key questions at unexpected moments and when your mind is occupied with something else, so that I'll get your normal reaction. Now that's the program, that's what I have to do. It's what I'm being paid to do; it's part of my job. The questions and answers will be recorded on wax records, the readings of the polygraph will be recorded on a synchronized sound strip. The result will be checked over as a matter of routine, and filed. And that's all there is to it. Now then, the sooner you relax and get to chatting with me just as you would with some acquaintance in a club, the sooner you give me completely normal reactions, the sooner we can start the test, and the sooner it will be over."

Clane tried to keep the reflexes of his mental efforts from showing in his eyes. Dammit, the man was clever. That business of saying exactly what he was going to do, apparently putting the cards all on the table, and then casually saying that he would suddenly switch the questions to Edward Harold.

What had the needle on the machine shown when Maynard had suddenly pulled that? Had the needle given a jump? It had been done cleverly. All the more so because Maynard had asserted that the test had not yet commenced. Had Clane betrayed himself? Was there any way of beating the machine?

"Could you," Maynard asked, "tell me something of your studies in the Orient while we're waiting?"

"The Chinese mystics believe that everything is accomplished through concentration," Clane said. "The difference between man and the lesser animals is that man has the ability inherent within himself to control the thought stream of his consciousness and direct it to certain objectives."

"That's *very* interesting. I certainly envy you your opportunities. As you must realize, Mr. Clane, in order to qualify for a job here it's necessary for a person to have devoted quite a bit of time to the study of psychology."

"I can understand," Clane said.

"And, as such, I think I am perhaps far more curious about the methods by which the Orientals develop their powers of concentration than the police are in this merely routine test."

"I see."

"So," Maynard said, smiling disarmingly, "I don't mind telling you, Mr. Clane, inasmuch as I'm supposed to get your mind for the moment off the fact that you're taking a lie detector test, I'm going to pump you purely for selfish reasons."

"Go right ahead."

"The power of concentration is consciously developed among these Orientals?"

"Certainly."

"Can you explain a little more of what you mean by that?"

Clane said, "First there is the question of the degree of concentration. A person first tries to concentrate with *all* of his faculties for even a fleeting instant. If he gets so he can do that, then gradually the opportunity is given him to increase the time of concentration. After a while, he gets a period of perhaps one second, then two seconds, or three seconds. Or perhaps with exceptional pupils, four or five seconds."

"Four or five *seconds!*" Maynard said. "You surely mean minutes, Mr. Clane."

11

"I don't mean minutes," Clane said.

"But good heavens, to concentrate for a matter of seconds . . . Why, we all of us do that every day. You aren't by any chance spoofing me?"

"Not in the least. Take, for instance, a person suddenly confronted with danger. Suppose you're driving an automobile and another car unexpectedly comes around a mountain curve, headed directly toward you. There's a moment—a brief flashing interval—during which you are concentrating so intently on the thing to do that for that one brief instant you are actually using all of the mental powers which you possess. Then the reaction sets in and your period of concentration is over."

"You mean the mental reaction?"

"No, the physical reaction. You are first concentrating on what to do. Then the brain orders the muscles to respond. The reaction time is measured in fractions of a second. Once the muscles begin to respond, the mind has ceased to use *all* of its powers on a contemplation of the mental problem."

Maynard said, "Until you started pointing out the principles of concentration to me, I would have sworn that I could have concentrated for ten minutes at a time quite easily."

"Try concentrating on the tip of my finger for just *two* seconds," Clane said. "Let me know when you're ready by moving your right hand just an inch or two."

Clane took a watch from his pocket. "Are you ready?"

Maynard stared intently at Clane's extended finger. "Just a moment," he said.

There was silence in the room for as much as ten seconds, then slowly Maynard moved his right hand.

Instantly Clane pocketed his watch.

"Well?" Maynard asked.

"Will you be perfectly frank with me?" Clane asked.

"Yes."

"You waited to move your right hand until you had banished all extraneous thoughts from your mind, didn't you?"

"Naturally."

"And when you moved your right hand, you felt that you had brought every bit of mental power to bear upon the tip of my finger."

12

"Exactly."

Clane said, smilingly, "Of course, it wasn't a test, Mr. Maynard. It was merely a demonstration. I was taking an unfair advantage of you."

Somewhat nettled, Maynard said, "I don't think you did. As a matter of fact, Mr. Clane, I think I concentrated on the tip of your finger for a full two seconds at least."

Clane said, "It wasn't what they would have called concentration in the Orient, for even as much as a millionth of a second. But as a matter of fact, according to your own definition of concentration, it didn't last for as much as a tenth of a second. I timed it."

"I beg your pardon," Maynard said almost angrily. "How did you know when I ceased concentrating? You put your watch away almost the moment I moved my right hand. You didn't wait for a full two seconds."

"You're certain?"

"Absolutely. The minute I moved my right hand you suddenly snapped your watch back into your pocket."

"Then you noticed the time element, that it lacked the full period?"

"Yes."

"Then a portion of your mind was thinking about the watch in my hand and about the period of time which had elapsed."

"Well, I think that's only natural."

"It's only natural," Clane said, "but surely you must realize that a mind which is thinking about a watch and trying to determine the passing of a time interval is hardly concentrating all of its faculties upon some other matter."

Maynard frowned, then abruptly laughed. "You win," he said. "I must devote more time to studying this Oriental concept of concentration."

"You won't find it in books."

"Where will I find it?"

"In yourself."

"But *you* went to the Orient. You spent several years in study for the purpose of learning to concentrate for a matter of seconds."

"That's right."

Maynard said, "Well, it certainly is most interesting. It's something I'd like to discuss with you further, Mr. Clane, but I think you have now sufficiently relaxed so we may proceed with the test. You'll remember that I told you that I'd be fair with you, that I'd tell you when I was ready to start the test."

"Thank you, that's appreciated."

"And now if you're ready we'll begin on the test, Mr. Clane?"

"Quite ready," Clane said and then added smilingly, "able and willing."

"You're acquainted with Cynthia Renton?"

"Yes."

"How long have you known her?"

"Quite a few years."

"You have recently arrived in this city?"

"Yes."

"Just a few hours ago?"

"Yes."

"You knew that Edward Harold had been convicted of the murder of Horace Farnsworth?"

"I did."

"Did you know that he had escaped from custody?"

"Not until Captain Jordon announced it to me a short time ago."

"You have had correspondence with Cynthia Renton in which she has told you something about Edward Harold's troubles?"

"Yes."

"Did it surprise you that she didn't meet you at the boat?"

"Frankly, it did."

"Then there must have been some extraordinary reason for her absence?"

"Perhaps."

"And did it occur to you that perhaps the reason she was absent was that she was with Edward Harold?"

Clane realized now the deadly web which was being spun about him. It wasn't only a question of learning what he knew, but these men with the aid of this machine were intent upon reading his mind, upon using his own mental processes

14

to trap Cynthia Renton. There must be some way of beating a machine of this kind. Clane had read somewhere that the thing could be done by surreptitiously moving a foot, provided it was done at just the right time. That would give a slight rise to the blood pressure. The thing to do was to watch carefully and do it at just the right question. It wouldn't do to have the blood pressure rise on one of the danger questions. It must be done on one of the minor questions so that the record would be thrown off the normal pattern. Clane waited, feeling certain that Maynard, having probed his mind as far as he felt was feasible on that point, would ask a few casual questions to relax the witness. But Maynard asked one more pertinent, highly dangerous question. "Do you have any idea where Miss Renton might be now?"

Clane said, "No." But even as he spoke, he felt certain that the machine had betrayed him. There was only one thing to do and that was move his foot on the next question.

"Could you tell us approximately how long Cynthia Renton has been acquainted with Edward Harold?"

"I think about two years."

"Oh, I'm sorry, Mr. Clane," Maynard said. "You moved your foot slightly. I forgot to caution you about that. The thing to do is to remain perfectly relaxed and not twitch or engage in any voluntary muscular motion. You see, we have a device on the machine now which registers voluntary muscular motions but that doesn't prevent the needle from giving a slight rise in its reading. It used to be that people could confuse our readings by slight, almost imperceptible twitches of the leg or wiggling of the big toe. So in order to compensate for that it was necessary to arrange to show when some voluntary muscular motion threw our readings off."

"I see," Clane said smiling. "I'm glad you told me. You see, I don't know too much about these machines."

"They're very fascinating. Sometime I'll explain them in detail to you in return for a little more of that interesting explanation of the Oriental development of the mind."

"Sometime when we both have more time," Clane said.

"Exactly."

Abruptly Clane thought back to the time when he had been

captured by bandits, when the suave Oriental who led the bandit gang had been about to chop off a finger to send with a ransom demand. By conscious effort Clane held that experience in mental abeyance, just back of the threshold of consciousness.

Maynard's voice went on smoothly, switching to a routine question. "Do you know any of the circumstances in connection with the murder of Horace Farnsworth?" he asked.

Abruptly Clane threw a mental image of these bandits into his consciousness, and so well did he do it that for a moment he experienced emotional tension all over again. Then he let the image fade from his mind.

"No," he said. "I was, of course, out of the country at the time he was murdered."

Maynard started to ask another question then checked himself, frowning for a moment in puzzled perplexity.

Clane knew then that the man was so seated that he could study the recording needles of the machine and that Clane's mental gymnastics had been successful in sending the needle shooting upward into the zone which marked sudden emotional tension.

"You weren't in this country at the time of Farnsworth's murder?" Maynard asked.

"No."

"Are you certain, Mr. Clane, that at that exact time you hadn't perhaps been here in the United States, in some other part of the country perhaps, but nevertheless here?"

Once more Clane's mind flashed back to the bandits. "No," he said shortly.

Maynard shifted his position, then abruptly switched to other things. "You had a pleasant trip across?" he asked.

Clane knew that in order to complete his ruse, he needed to register great relief now that the subject of the questioning had left the murder. He brought to his mind the feeling of triumphant peace he had known when he had learned of the ending of the war. "The boat was rather crowded, of course, but it was a pleasant voyage."

"You have been in Honolulu?"

"Oh, yes."

"And have spent some time in Japan?"

"Yes."

"You consider the philosophy of the Chinese superior to our own?"

"I think the Chinese philosopher is able to accomplish comparatively more than the Caucasian philosopher."

"In what way?"

"He makes a more practical application of his philosophy."

"You mean he turns it into money-making?"

Clane smiled. "That is the very thing he wishes to avoid. I think you will find the tendency of the Western philosopher is to use his knowledge to monetary advantage. The Chinese is so anxious to avoid doing that that when he takes up philosophy he deliberately courts poverty, living in the most primitive surroundings in the most simple way."

For a moment Maynard hesitated and Clane felt certain that the next question would be a sudden flashback to the Farnsworth murder so he held his mind in readiness. There had been the time when he was caught in a typhoon in the Straits of Formosa in a Chinese junk and . . .

"Did you see Horace Farnsworth shortly before he was killed?"

Clane concentrated on the memory of that typhoon, the surging waves rising abruptly upward only to have their tops sliced off by the wind as neatly as though some invisible knife had trimmed the mountain of water to a level-topped mesa, the labored creaking of the timbers in the old junk, the shriek of the wind through the rigging.

"No," Clane said shortly and then added, "I've answered questions about that half a dozen times. I don't like to have my word doubted. I was in China at that time."

"We have to ask questions in that way in order to make a fair test," Maynard explained suavely. "Many times I have to make what might amount to false accusations in order to evaluate the readings of the machine."

"I see," Clane said with frigid formality.

Abruptly Maynard produced a map of the city and held it in front of Clane's eyes. "I'm going to ask you a few questions about this map, Mr. Clane," he said. "I don't want you to answer those questions; just listen to them."

17

Clane mentally braced himself. This was the thing which had worried him. If Cynthia Renton had been in serious trouble, if she had arranged for the rescue of Edward Harold, she would have gone for sanctuary into the depths of Chinatown, to the apartment of Chu Kee, a wealthy, wise Chinese whose business was as mysterious as his personality, but whose friendship had been given to Terry Clane and some years ago through Terry Clane to Cynthia Renton.

That friendship had been extended through Sou Ha, Chu Kee's Americanized daughter, a sparkling, vivacious young girl who had superimposed the education of a Western college upon an Oriental background. The result had been a startling mixture of psychological oil and water.

Terry Clane dared not betray the location of Chu Kee's apartment, not at any rate until after he had scouted the premises.

"Now then," Maynard went on, "I would like to have you orient yourself on this map, Mr. Clane. You will see that it is a map of the city. We are at the present time located right here. And here is the dock where you landed. This is the main business district; over here is the vicinity of the swank shops; and the best hotels are around generally in this district. This is waterfront; over here is Chinatown; and then there is an exclusive residential district in this vicinity. Do you get the general picture?"

"Yes."

"You will note that the map is divided by heavily inked red lines into four quarters. Then you will notice that each of these quarters is in turn subdivided by blue lines. And then if you will notice closely, the blue lines are further subdivided into fine red squares which are numbered. Do you see all that?"

"Yes."

"For instance, Miss Renton's apartment is located in this second quarter of the city, in this blue square, and in the very small red square within that blue square, which is numbered twenty-two. Do you follow me?"

"I do."

"Very well," Maynard said. "Now I will ask you, Mr. Clane, if you wanted to find Cynthia Renton, or if perhaps you

18

thought that Edward Harold was hiding in the city, where would you look for him?"

Clane laughed. "You must think I have some magical powers, Mr. Maynard. After all, I just arrived. . . ."

"I understand," Maynard said. "It's just an experiment. Would you look in this quarter? Or this quarter? Or this quarter? Or this quarter?"

In turn, Maynard's finger indicated the four quarters of the map.

Clane had been ready for this question. He chose the exclusive residential district for the place where he would register the sudden upswing of the needle on the machine, and as Maynard's finger touched that spot on the map, Clane's mind reverted to one of the few times he had engaged in a fistic encounter.

Maynard indicated that his ruse had been successful by referring to the third quarter. "In this exclusive residential district," he said, "are there any of these blue squares which would intrigue your attention? For instance, this one, this one, this one, or this one, or . . ."

By turn, Maynard's finger covered each one of the blue squares.

Clane let his mind concentrate upon an emotional disturbance when Maynard's finger touched the seventh blue square.

"Directing your attention to this blue square number seven, Mr. Clane, let's examine the red squares in turn."

There were thirty-five small red squares within this blue square, and with the point of a pencil Maynard pointed to each in turn.

Feeling that it would be dangerous to carry the matter further, Clane let his mind remain at ease while the pencil touched each one of the red squares.

Maynard apparently was puzzled. "If you don't mind," he said, "we'll go over this once more."

Once more his finger pointed out each of the quarters into which the city had been divided. Once more Clane made a conscious effort to recall an experience of danger when Maynard's finger touched the third square. Once more they went down to the numbered blue squares. Once more the trail was hot until Maynard's pencil started pointing out the individual red squares, and then Clane permitted himself to relax, serene in the consciousness that he had now diverted Maynard's attention to a part of the city which meant absolutely nothing.

Maynard said, "Well, I guess that's all."

Clane was aware of this trap, a premature announcement of the completion of the test designed to lull the victim into a false sense of security.

Then abruptly Maynard opened a drawer and pulled out a small wooden figure. "Does *this* mean anything to you?" he asked.

To save his life Clane couldn't overcome the emotional impact that the figure aroused in his mind.

"I see that it does," Maynard said dryly.

"Indeed it does," Clane admitted.

Maynard said, "It seems to be a figure of a very aged Chinese on a horse. The peculiar thing is that he is seated backward."

"It isn't a horse," Clane told him. "It's a mule."

"Can you tell me something about the figure?"

"He's Chow Kok Koh, if one uses the Cantonese. Or Chang Kuo-lao, if one prefers the Mandarin designation."

"Well, let's stick with the Cantonese since that seems a little easier for me to pronounce," Maynard said. "Just who is Chow Kok Koh?"

"He is one of the eight Chinese Immortals."

"Can you tell me anything more about him than that?"

"He is supposed to have supernatural powers of magic. He can make himself invisible at will. The white mule which he is riding can be folded up and put away. You will note that he carries a sunshade and has on his back, carried by a sling, something which looks like a small bag of golf clubs."

Maynard nodded.

"That," Clane said, "is *yuku*, a musical instrument consisting of a bamboo tube. The things which look like golf clubs are two rods with which the bamboo tube can be beaten. It is a primitive musical instrument, particularly associated with Chow Kok Koh."

"But surely, Mr. Clane, there is nothing about the symbology of this figure which would account for the very strong emotional reaction which this figure aroused when I produced it."

Clane made a wry face. "I'm afraid this machine is reading my mind."

"Perhaps you can assist us by telling us the reason for that emotion."

"I think," Clane said, "the particular figure which you are holding in your hand is a figure which I gave to Cynthia Renton just before I left on my last mission to China."

"Would you mind telling me why you gave it to her?"

"It was a gift."

"It had some particular significance?"

"Yes."

"Can you tell us what that is?"

"I would prefer not to."

"Why?"

"It doesn't have anything to do with the murder," Clane said. "It goes into some very secret Chinese philosophy. Properly understood, the figure of Chow Kok Koh represents the Oriental acquiescence in the course of life's stream which we mistakenly refer to as 'fatalism.' "

"And why should you hesitate to tell me about that?"

"Because it is something rather fine, something rather sacred. It is knowledge which is closely guarded. Those who will tell you about Chow Kok Koh are usually the ones who don't know. Those who do know give their information only to the person whose mind has been prepared to receive it."

"You think perhaps it would be too deep for my intelligence?" Maynard asked, with a patronizing smile.

"I am not certain that your mind is ready to receive the information."

Maynard accepted defeat. He put the figure back in the drawer of the desk, unfastened the bands which held electrodes and pressure-measuring devices to Clane's arms. He regarded Clane moodily, thoughtfully.

"Well?" Clane asked.

"I don't understand it." Maynard said. "Either there is

something in connection with your thought processes which I haven't accurately diagnosed, or else . . ."

"Well?" Clane asked. "What's the rest of it?"

"Or else," Maynard said calmly, "you surreptitiously returned to this country and murdered Horace Farnsworth. That's all, Mr. Clane. You may go now."

# 4

A TAXI deposited Terry Clane in front of a downtown office building, for the most part dark and silent now, only an occasional lighted window marking the late labors of some harassed executive trying to catch up in his business affairs by working long after the staff had gone home.

A call bell summoned the janitor, who brought the elevator up from the basement.

"Who do you want to see?"

"Stacey Nevis."

"Six hundred and two. He expecting you?"

"Yes."

The janitor indicated the night register. "Sign here. Your name, the office you're going to, the name of the man you're going to see."

Terry Clane filled out the record. The janitor shot the elevator up to the sixth floor.

"Do you know if he's still in?" Clane asked as he left the elevator.

"Think he is. Think he's got another man with him. You the man they're waiting for?"

"I believe so."

"Okay."

The door clanged and the cage slid down into the silence, leaving Terry Clane standing in the dimly lit corridor down which the echoes of his steps seemed to precede him until he came to the lighted oblong of ground glass which bore the legend in gilt letters: STACEY NEVIS, *Investments*. ENTER.

Terry Clane tried the door. It was unlocked and he entered

the outer office, its stale aftermath of the day's business contrasting with the fresh night air on the outside.

The door of the private office was propped open and two men facing each other were seated in chairs that had been drawn close together. They were smoking and there was that about their posture which indicated a low-voiced exchange of confidences.

The man who was facing the door jumped up as Clane entered. He was smiling affably with his hand outstretched. "Well, well, at last," he said. "We'd about given you up."

"I was detained," Clane said, shaking hands.

Nevis, a tall loose-jointed man in the late thirties, managed somehow to keep himself clothed with an air of rustic simplicity despite the expensively tailored garments which he wore.

George Gloster, the other man in the room, some seven or eight years older than Nevis, stocky, quick, intense, nervous in his motions, rose from his chair, crossed the office with quick strides, pushed out his hand, but his smile was perfunctory. The dark glittering eyes seemed to be taking a cautious inventory. He said, "I'm afraid I haven't much time left."

"That's all right," Clane said, "it won't take long for me to say what I have to say."

"Have a nice trip?" Nevis asked.

"So-so."

"Boats pretty crowded, I presume?"

"Very."

"All right, let's sit down and get going," Gloster said, and dragged his chair over the office carpet so that it was at the far corner of Stacey Nevis's desk, which left Nevis virtually no alternative but to seat himself somewhat formally in the swivel chair behind the desk, leaving Terry Clane to take the chair in which Nevis had been sitting when Terry Clane had opened the door.

That left the men seated in a triangle, grouped about the desk, and there was that in Gloster's manner which invested the gathering with all the formality of a directors' meeting. Clane, who had wished for an informal visit, found himself outmaneuvered by Gloster's trick with the chairs.

"Where is Ricardo Taonon?" Clane asked.

"He had other plans for the evening," Nevis said.

Clane said, "Well, we can get along without him. As I understand it, Farnsworth was trustee for Cynthia Renton. He was her investment manager and I believe he had about ten thousand dollars of her money."

"I believe that's right," Nevis said.

"I am wondering if some of that money didn't go into the Eastern Art Import and Trading Company, a partnership composed, as I understand it, of Farnsworth, you two, and Ricardo Taonon."

"I don't think it did," Nevis said.

"I'm wondering. I'm going to try to unscramble some of Farnsworth's financial affairs, which, I understand, were pretty badly mixed up."

Nevis ran a big clumsy hand over the top of his head, scratched the hair at the base of his neck. "Hang it, Clane," he said, "there's something strange about Farnsworth's financial affairs. He put ten thousand dollars into the Eastern Art Import and Trading Company all right. He always insisted that was his own. Cynthia Renton's money went into an oil deal that didn't pan out. But he offered to take that off her hands any time she wanted to handle it that way.

"Shortly before his death he told us all about it and asked us to let him have ten thousand bucks out of the partnership and charge it to his account.

"We understood how it was and Ricardo told him he could have it any old time he needed it."

"He had some gold-mining stuff up around Baguio in the Philippines," Clane said.

"We sent him over there," Gloster said. "The partnership."

"I heard that was on his own," Clane said.

Gloster shook his head. "Ricardo engineered that whole deal. He wanted to keep it under cover and it was given out at the time over there that it was Farnsworth who was making the mining investments. It was all partnership. Farnsworth's signature's on the agreement, all signed before a notary."

"That's right," Nevis said. "The trust stuff for Miss Renton is another story. That went into the oil stock. He was willing to take that off her hands. He knew you were coming back, and Ed Harold had been asking questions, so Horace arranged for the ten thousand dollars to pay Miss Renton back her money in cash if she wanted. I guess the oil stuff is worth maybe six or seven thousand, but it's apt to go up. Horace left twenty thousand in insurance, payable to his estate, so no- body's going to lose anything. And, as I say, he'd arranged to draw ten thousand from the partnership any time he needed it for Miss Renton."

"Leave a will?" Clane asked.

"No will. No near relatives. There's a half sister in the East somewhere. I guess she'll take the estate."

"Who's handling the estate?" Clane asked.

"The Public Administrator."

"Did Horace leave any detailed account of the trust investment?"

"Yes. He left a statement of trusteeship and a statement that his investments with the trust funds were in this oil business, and that he felt he was partially to blame the stock wasn't worth more. Therefore he said that if anything happened to him he was giving the beneficiary the option either to take over that investment or to take the cash."

"Signed by him?"

"Signed before a notary."

"Rather strange a man would make a statement like that unless he anticipated he wouldn't live long. He didn't have any premonition, did he?"

"Not that we knew about, Clane. He was peculiar. Given to morose periods of silence. That oil investment worried him. He thought when he went into it he was going to make a million for Cynthia Renton."

Clane said, "Well, I'm here. I'm going to look into a lot of things. I wanted you to know. You can either cooperate or not. It'll make a difference whether you want to . . . in the way I play things."

"We want to," Nevis said.

Gloster was silent for a moment, then blurted, "I don't see just where it's . . . well, any of your business."

"I'm making it my business," Clane said. "Is that plain?"

25

"Plain enough," Gloster said. "Go right ahead. I'll be in favor of giving you what information you're entitled to, but I'm not going to open any partnership books to you. And you can bet Ricardo won't either."

Nevis said, "After all, we have to account to the Public Administrator, George. Why couldn't we . . . ?"

"Because we aren't going to and we don't have to," Gloster said, interrupting. "Business is business. Clane comes barging back like the knight in shining armor and sends us a wireless telling us to meet him here on a matter of great importance. Shucks! I'm busy. I don't intend to be pushed around. Facts are facts, and the facts are there in writing. As far as Horace is concerned, the killing wasn't over money. It was just plain damn jealousy. Ed Harold thought he was sort of a guardian for Cynthia Renton, and he resented Horace having anything to do with her. And Horace wasn't at all certain but what Ed Harold was taking altogether too keen an interest in Cynthia Renton's money rather than in Cynthia herself. And that's your murder, right there in a nutshell."

Nevis nodded. "George is right, Clane."

"And the documents showing this partnership gold deal in the Philippines are all signed by Farnsworth?" Clane asked.

"Before a notary," Nevis said.

"Look here," Gloster said. "I don't give a damn about Cynthia Renton's money or about Horace Farnsworth. If Horace used part of Cynthia's money to put into this partnership, then she's entitled to his share, and that's a nice little melon. If he didn't, she can get her ten thousand bucks back. Farnsworth told me Cynthia's money went into the oil, and it worried him. He also put that in writing. I guess that's enough. If you don't like it, go talk with the Public Administrator. If you don't like that, Cynthia Renton can get herself a lawyer. And if you'll take my advice, don't go messing around in something that's none of your business. Edward Harold did that, and where is he now?"

"I guess that's what the police want to know," Clane said.

"That's right. He escaped last night," Nevis said. "It was a fool move. He can't get away with it. They'll nab him sooner or later and any chance of a commutation of sentence from the Governor's office is out the window now. It's a shame. He isn't a bad sort, but he's hotheaded and he's bullheaded. Not a good combination."

Gloster said, "I've got things to do. I'm going home."

He moved over to the coat closet, put on his hat and coat, casually opened the door of the private office, called back over his shoulder, "Good night," and went out.

Nevis made an awkward attempt to be friendly. "George never liked Harold," he said, "and . . . well, you know how it is. He's just, also he's dour and crabby. Everyone who knows George knows he's honest as the day is long."

Clane nodded, said after a moment, "I'd like to talk with Ricardo."

"He'd have been here if he could," Nevis assured him. "I guess he knew what you wanted. Guess we all did as far as that's concerned. If I can help you any, why, let me know. If Cynthia Renton can show any of her dough went into this partnership, she's certainly welcome as far as *I'm* concerned. It would be a nice piece of cash."

"What is Farnsworth's share worth?" Clane asked.

"You could guess it as around a hundred thousand bucks," Nevis said. "And his investment was exactly ten grand. That, of course, is a coincidence. It might be a good one for you. But Horace told me that Cynthia's money went into the oil deal. He told George the same thing, and it's in writing. I don't think you can beat that. *We* don't care who gets his share."

"Thank you," Clane said, shaking hands. "I wanted to get the facts first hand. If Horace signed those statements, I guess that's all there is to it. Cynthia wants cash to pay for Harold's lawyers and to finance his appeal. I wanted to get the low-down here."

Nevis said, "I, for one, am mighty glad you're back, Clane. Anything I can do to help you get settled?"

"Not a thing," Clane told him.

"Well, if I can . . . You know, *anything,* just let me know."

Clane thanked him and walked out.

# 5

AS CASUALLY as though he hadn't heard that Cynthia Renton was not to be found at her apartment, Terry Clane directed a taxi to her apartment and rang the bell. When he turned away after receiving no answer, he was conscious of the car which had pulled up to the curb. There were two men sitting in that car. The one on the right-hand side opened the door.

"Hi, buddy."

"Good evening," Clane said.

"Looking for someone?"

"Yes."

"She ain't there."

"Apparently not."

"Guess we'd sorta better check up on you. Name maybe, and perhaps a driving license and a social security card. You know, just a routine check-up."

"How would a passport do?" Clane asked.

The officer frowned. "Well, now, I guess that's all right."

Clane produced a passport. The officer made notes. "You been in China?"

"That's right."

"When did you get back?"

"About three hours ago."

"Oh, oh, and came right here?"

"Not directly here, no."

"Where ya been?"

"At police headquarters."

"Huh?"

"That's right."

"How'd you happen to go there?"

"I was escorted."

"By whom?"

"Detectives who met me at the boat."

The officer grinned. "Okay," he said. "On your way."

28

Terry Clane found Alma Renton, Cynthia's sister, in her studio apartment. She opened the door to his knock, took a quick backward step as though to get him at proper perspective. Then with a glad cry, she flung herself into his arms. "Terry, oh, Terry!" she sighed.

She gave him tremulous lips, her eyes fluttered shut. For a moment she relaxed. Then she was laughing half hysterically. "Oh, how I've been waiting for you, Terry," she said. "I didn't dare to meet the boat. Detectives were there. The most terrible things have been happening . . ."

"I know," Clane said.

"The officers are absolutely furious. If they could get Edward Harold, I think . . . gosh, Terry, I think they'd *kill* him. Do they do that sometimes? You know, claim a man was resisting arrest?"

"I wouldn't know," Clane said, and then added reassuringly, "and I doubt if anyone else would. You probably hear lots of rumors, but you can take them with a whole barrel of salt."

"Apparently an escape was the last thing on earth they were looking for. It's made the police seem inefficient and exposed them to a lot of censure. They're absolutely furious. It's a deadly cold fury. They're leaving no stone unturned. I'm scared."

"Who engineered the escape?" Terry asked.

She lowered her voice to a whisper. "Cynthia and a friend of Ed Harold's, a man named Bill Hendrum. You don't know him. He's one of these barrel-chested he-men who believe in direct action. It was a crazy thing to do and I'm just sick over Cynthia. They'll catch her, of course, eventually—and when they do, they'll throw the book at her. The officers told me that. They said I could tell her in case she communicated with me. They're absolutely furious. And they said orders were out to get Ed Harold alive or dead. Oh, Terry, I'm just limp with fright. You know Cynthia. Her idea of loyalty and all that. She told me she'd kill herself the day they executed Harold, a sort of protest to society. She isn't . . . oh, Terry, why *couldn't* you have got here sooner!"

"I did the best I could. I tried for a plane, but they red-taped me to a steamer, and if I'd missed that they'd never have let me go. You see there were some things they wanted me to check on en route. It was that or nothing. You've heard from Cynthia?"

"Not a word. Of course, Terry, I'm hoping she's playing it smart, that she'll either show up with an alibi, or else just sit tight and let them try to prove it on her. But I'm afraid she and Ed have gone away to hide as long as they can and then shoot it out with the officers.

"There's nothing one can do except go on living the same as though nothing had happened. They're shadowing every move I make. They'll be following you, too, I guess."

"Well, the best thing we can do is pretend to carry on our regular routine. How about dinner?"

"It's a date. How soon?"

"Soon. I've been thinking of a good thick steak with baked potatoes and lots of butter ever since we left Hong Kong."

"Did you stop in Honolulu?"

"No, we came right through."

She said, "I wrote you care of the boat in Honolulu. I didn't know whether it would stop or not. I guess you didn't get my letter."

"No."

"Did you know anything about . . . about the escape before you arrived?"

"No. The police broke the news to me. Did they give you a lie-detector test, Alma?"

"Heavens, no."

"They may do it," he said.

"My gosh, Terry, would I betray myself . . . ?"

"Probably," Clane said. "I'll give you a recipe for making it a little bit difficult for them to evaluate the readings."

"Don't you want a drink, Terry? I'll have to put on a little war paint. It'll take me two or three minutes and I can fix you one as easily as not."

"No, we'll have a cocktail at the café," Clane said. "I'll look around while you get fixed up."

He moved slowly around the studio, studying some of the finished and unfinished paintings. When she joined him some five minutes later, he said simply, "You've improved in your work, Alma."

"Thanks."

"Your technique always has been good. Now you're getting a depth, a certain sweep of power into your work. It's hard to define."

She said simply, "It comes through suffering."

"Suffering?"

"Yes. I've found that out. Suffering is a large part of life, and you can't understand life until you've suffered. I keep thinking of that figure on the mule and the story you told me about it."

"Do we ride or walk?" Clane asked, holding the door open for her. "The police are also interested in that figure. Did it enter into the case?"

"No. Not directly. The case was terrible. Let's walk. It's only a couple of blocks."

"When did you see that figure last?" Terry asked.

"Cynthia had it on her mantel. She was very much attached to it. It was a tie that bound her to you. And then she appreciated the philosophy back of it."

"The last time I saw it," Clane said dryly, "the police suddenly thrust it under my nose. It had blood spots on it."

"Terry! It couldn't have."

"It did," Clane said. "At least the spots looked to be blood."

"Oh, Terry! How did that happen?"

"I don't know. That's what I want to find out."

"I don't see how . . . Cynthia considered it one of her most prized possessions. You wanted to break off with her when you went to the Orient on that dangerous mission. Some crazy idea about giving her her freedom. You shouldn't have done it, Terry."

"Why?"

"Oh . . . because."

"Because she fell in love with Edward Harold?"

"I'm not so certain she is in love with him, Terry."

"If she isn't, she'd better be," Clane said grimly. "She's certainly in a mess now, and I guess he is too."

Alma choked back a sob. "Don't, Terry. You know Cynthia. She isn't like other people. She's wild and impulsive and unconventional. Life is really a cage, a cage of deadly routine, and Cynthia is like a wild thing that can't be caged."

"Tell me what you can about the case," Terry Clane said in a low voice when they were seated in the restaurant. "Cover as much ground as you can before the food arrives, then we'll quit talking about the case and quit thinking about it."

She said, "You know Horace Farnsworth, Terry. He was like an uncle to Cynthia. He simply worshiped the ground she walked on. He was worried about the way Cynthia tossed money around and he wanted to have her take care of it. He said that inside of five years she'd have gone through the fortune she inherited and be absolutely broke."

"So Cynthia turned it over to him?"

"Certainly not. Cynthia is wildly impulsive and unconventional but she wouldn't put all of her financial eggs in one basket. She gave him five thousand to invest and then later on another five thousand."

"Did she keep a close check on where he was making her investments?"

"No. She considered this to be only a drop in the bucket. She gave it to Horace and then forgot about it. She wanted it for a nest egg. And Horace wanted to run it up to a million dollars and surprise her. I think he took some chances with it on that account."

"Go ahead. What happened?"

"Well, after you left for China and told Cynthia you wanted her to be free and that you were going on a dangerous mission and all that . . . Well, the poor child was completely heartbroken for a while and then Edward Harold came along. He was just what she needed to cheer her up. He was as scatterbrained as Cynthia in some ways, and conservative in others. He's strong for the underdog. He appealed to her."

Terry kept his eyes on the tip of the fork with which he was making designs on the tablecloth. "Were they engaged?" he asked.

"Don't be silly," Alma said. "Cynthia was waiting. But she liked Edward and they went places together and he became just absolutely utterly infatuated with *her*. He just worshiped the ground she walked on."

"And became jealous of Horace Farnsworth?"

For a moment there was a long silence, then Alma said, "I don't know."

"You never were very good at lying," Clane said.

She met his eyes then.

"Yes, he was intensely jealous."

"Go on."

"Well, Edward Harold kept wanting Cynthia to get her money back from Horace Farnsworth, or to have him make a detailed accounting. And Cynthia laughed at him and told him Horace was absolutely dependable and honest and skillful. Well, you know how those things build up."

"So Harold went to Farnsworth?"

She said, "Edward Harold did a little investigating. You remember that I wrote you that Horace had gone into partnership with Stacey Nevis, Ricardo Taonon, and George Gloster?"

Clane nodded.

"It was an unfortunate association," she said. "Terry, I distrust that Ricardo more than I can tell you. He gives me the creeps. There's something devious and mysterious about the man."

Clane smiled. "He's a Eurasian," he said. "He's sensitive. He feels his mixed blood. Has enough of the Oriental in him to make him retire within himself when he gets hurt. He's like a cat that wants to crawl away by itself when it's sick. A dog will seek human companionship, but a cat wants only to get away from everything and everybody."

"I know. I try to make allowances for that. But nevertheless the man is a . . . Terry, he's evil."

"Well, we'll pass that for a minute. Tell me what happened. Did Horace Farnsworth put Cynthia's money in the partnership?"

"No. He put it in oil—and it didn't pan out."

The waiter drew aside the green curtain and, with something of a flourish, deposited two dry martinis and a bowl of green olives.

Clane said, "I think you can duplicate these martinis in about five minutes. Okay, Alma, that's enough for now. We quit talking about the case and talk about something else."

They clicked the tips of their glasses together, sipped the drink. Then Clane said, "There's one more question. Has it ever occurred to you that Cynthia might have gone to . . . friends of mine?"

"Chinese?"

"Yes."

"I've thought of that."

"All right," Clane said. "Try *not* to think of it. The police have ways of reading your mind. And refuse to take any lie-detector test in case they ask you if you're willing to do so. Tell them your nerves are too unstrung. And now let's eat."

## 6

WHERE San Francisco's Chinatown separates itself from the rest of the city, the line of demarcation is sharp. It is as though the Chinese, mindful of the fact that a Western author had observed that East was East and West was West and never the twain might meet, had endeavored to offer visible proof of the logic of that statement.

Terry Clane, emerging from the Stockton Street tunnel, found himself surrounded by the atmosphere of the Orient as effectively as though he had stepped from a ship to the wharf at Hong Kong.

Here were expensive shops, beginning to show once more in the windows those objects of Oriental patience which are so inconceivable to the Western mind. Here was a sampan carved from ivory beginning to turn with age, a sampan loaded heavily with sacks of merchandise, peopled with miniature ivory figures bent with the toil of a lifetime of labor, so cunningly fashioned they were complete even to the smallest detail. One could see the wrinkles about the tired eyes of the stooped man who worked the sculling oar back and forth by the aid of a rope so arranged that it kept the blade of the oar turning at just the right angle to yield greatest efficiency. This ivory masterpiece had taken years of work by a clever craftsman. It was so marvelously complete that the observer looking at it might well have felt he was standing on a dock at the Whangpoo, looking through the wrong end of a telescope at one of the typical sampans passing by. Yet the price at which it was to be sold was such that an affluent Westerner could well buy it, place it carelessly on top of the mantel as an ornament and forget about it, little realizing that in the capacity for taking such infinite pains over such a long period of time lay the key to China's indestructibility.

Over these stores were offices, apartments, lodge rooms where the various tongs held their meetings, and down the side streets one could catch glimpses of figures moving silently along the line of shops where merchandise was sold by Orientals only to Orientals; Chinese drugstores where one might find weird remedies concocted from various animals and reptiles; grocery stores where one might find Chinese delicacies, birds' nests for soup, *son keou tow* with its peculiar pungent inimitable flavor that is like nothing else on earth, "petrified eggs" which had been buried in mud until they had solidified into a dark jelly with a flavor that few Occidental palates could appreciate.

Terry Clane moved through these side streets, opened a plain, unmarked door which disclosed a flight of grimy stairs lighted by a dispirited bulb which seemed about ready to give up its inadequate struggle against the dark shadows that were forever closing in upon it.

Terry Clane closed the door behind him, walked with swift sure steps up the dusty stair treads. He came to an upper hallway where his feet echoed from uncarpeted boards, where lines of solid wooden doors remained closed, somber and silent, masking whatever might lie behind them with the inscrutable secretiveness of the Orient.

Terry climbed another flight of stairs, moved down another corridor, paused at a door so old that the varnish on it had turned dark and had granulated, a door which with age had collected all of the grime and dirt of a big city.

Uninitiated fingers could never have found the bell button which was to one side of the door, concealed in the shadows. Clane pressed the button, twice. There was no sound of a signal from within.

Clane waited patiently. The noise of the city did not penetrate to this corridor. So far as any audible evidence was concerned, the building might have been entirely vacant, holding its breath, waiting for a victim to walk into its sinister embrace.

There was a faint, all but imperceptible sound as somewhere a sliding panel moved cautiously backward far enough to enable invisible eyes to appraise the visitor standing there in the dim light of the corridor.

Abruptly from the other side of the door came the sound of a heavy bar being slid back by some smooth-running, electrically propelled mechanism; then the door swung inward on heavy ball-bearing hinges such as are used to support the weight of the steel door of a vault.

That door itself was as interesting and as deceptive as the other surroundings. Back of the layer of cheap, stained wood with its decomposing varnish was a layer of toughest steel, and on the inner side of this layer of steel was a surface of carved teakwood inlaid with intricate designs that were pleasing to the eye.

An old Chinese servant stood on the threshold. His motionless face might well have been carved from old ivory by the same artisan who had fashioned the sampan in the window of the expensive art shop farther down the street. Only the eyes of the old man showed emotion. They were dancing with pleasure.

He bowed deferentially, stood to one side.

"Will you deign to honor this dwelling?" he asked in Chinese.

Clane entered, dropped a hand affectionately upon the old man's shoulder.

"My eyes are being feasted," Clane said in Chinese.

The old servant made no reply, but under his hand Terry Clane could feel the frail body trembling with excitement and emotion.

36

Wordlessly the man turned, led the way down a corridor carpeted with an Oriental rug so soft and springy that the visitor might well have felt that his feet were walking on moss. On each side of the reception hallway were chairs of dark Chinese wood inlaid with mother-of-pearl in artistic scenes of gardens, of figures posing in stately dignity on ornamental bridges across canals. Overhead lights scintillated through purest rock crystal, cut and polished into prisms that transmitted the light in deflected rays to each corner of the room.

The Chinese servant opened a door and stood back to one side. Sou Ha came to meet Terry Clane with outstretched hand and the calm, self-contained dignity of the Oriental. Halfway to him she lost her self-control and ran with a squeal of delight to fling herself in his arms, a trembling, vibrant bundle of silk-clad femininity.

"Terry!" she sighed, and then tilted her head back, her eyes closed. The long lashes swept her cheeks.

Terry Clane bent to the half-parted lips.

Behind them the aged Chinese servant quietly closed the door.

Sou Ha's eyes opened. She smiled in Terry Clane's eyes, then disengaged herself. "I couldn't do it."

"Couldn't do what?"

"Couldn't be Chinese. I tried but I have lived here too long. My emotions got the better of me."

"Meaning that the Chinese do not have emotions?" Terry taunted.

"Don't be silly," she said. "The Chinese have emotions but conceal them. They do not surrender to them. I tried to discipline myself and I lost. I am glad that I lost. The civilization of the Orient is superior to that of the West, but we have lost much by not learning how to kiss."

She laughed up at him. "My father," she said, "would be shocked. But after all, why did he send me to a California college if he didn't want me to learn the ways of your country?"

"Why indeed?" Clane asked, smiling.

She was pure Chinese. Her features held the classic lines which represented a cultured aristocracy that could trace its family back for some three thousand years. But superimposed upon this Chinese background was something that was distinctly Western, a certain jaunty independence, an ability to meet fate upon equal terms and to laugh at life.

"Where's your father?" Clane asked. "And how is he?"

"He's fine. He hoped you'd come tonight."

"I'd have been here sooner," Clane said, "if it hadn't been for the police."

"Over the escape of Edward Harold?"

"Yes."

"But good heavens, you just arrived from the boat. How could you be expected to know anything about that?"

Clane smiled at her.

"Oh, well. I know," she said. "I suppose I'd feel the same way if I were the police. Did they find out anything?"

"I hope not."

"Did you know anything?"

He laughed. "Now you are like the police."

"Terry," she said, "tell me. Did you . . . did you engineer it?"

"You mean the escape?"

"Yes."

"No."

"I thought perhaps you had. It was . . . it was done so adroitly."

"As a matter of fact, I didn't know anything about it until after I was interrogated by the police. They told me."

"Will they catch him?"

"I'm afraid so. They have his fingerprints. They have his photographs. They have suffered humiliation. They want him badly enough. I'm wondering if perhaps they don't want revenge badly enough so they won't catch him too soon, but will wait a while."

"Terry, what do you mean?"

Clane said, "I'm not too certain about the police. Sometimes they are vindictive."

"But I don't understand what you mean about not catching him."

Clane said, "He was convicted of murder. He had perfected an appeal. It might well have been that there were some holes in the case. The Supreme Court might have set aside the conviction. All right, he escapes. While he is a fugitive from justice he has no standing in court. The Supreme Court will dismiss the appeal on proper application."

"You mean the police will try to have the appeal dismissed?"

"Yes."

"And then?"

"And then after the appeal has been dismissed and it is too late for Harold to do anything to save himself, the police might find him. Then he would be whisked away to the death cell with no possible hope for a review of his case unless the Governor should decide to give him executive clemency, and he'd hardly do that to a man who had made the police force lose face by engineering an escape."

"Then the police know where he is and are just going through the motions of trying to catch him until after they can . . . oh, Terry, that seems terrible."

"It's just a thought that I had," he said. "Something to be considered. It doesn't fit in with the facts of the case—yet."

She said, "Come. We must talk with father. He's waiting. He'll know you're here."

She led the way to another door. Turning at right angles, she stood slightly back and let him precede her through the doorway, saying, "Father, he has come."

Chu Kee arose from the straight-backed chair in which he had been seated and hurried forward. The placid calm of his countenance was broken by a smile. For a moment only he paused to clasp his hands in front of his breast, shaking hands with himself in Chinese style. Then he too forsook the impassivity of the Orient to envelop Clane's hand with long sensitive fingers. "My son," he said in Chinese, "it has been long."

"It has been long, my Teacher," Terry Clane said. "But absence has made the reunion all the more pleasant."

"Pain," Chu Kee admitted, "is but the appetizer which makes pleasure the more palatable."

Clane laughed and said in English, "You have a proverb for everything. Don't I remember that at one time you said pleasure was but the sleep of life, that progress was made through overcoming hardship and learning to endure pain?"

Chu Kee's eyes twinkled. He continued to talk in Chinese. "The snow-capped mountain may seem a jagged crag from the north, while it looks as a soft snowball from the south. Yet it is the same mountain. Only the viewpoint has changed. Will it please you to sit down and tell me about what you did in China?"

Chu Kee escorted his guest over toward the row of ceremonial seats which graced the wall of the room, then suddenly smiled and said, "Perhaps you would be more comfortable in the cushioned chair?"

Terry Clane shook his head. "I have learned to enjoy the things of China," he said and permitted himself to be seated in one of the straight-backed inlaid chairs, chairs which to the average white man would have been unendurably hard and uncomfortable.

"Really," Clane went on, "when you get accustomed to them, they're much better than the cushioned chairs. You're sitting upright in these chairs and with your back straight, not slouched down on the end of your spine. You are well, my Teacher?"

"Life has given this unworthy one health," Chu Kee agreed. "And you, my son?"

"Never better."

The servant brought tea in Chinese cups that were more like covered bowls nestling in doughnutlike saucers.

"You have accomplished that which you set out to do?" Chu Kee asked blandly.

"I am hopeful that my trip was a success."

"Others thought it so?"

"Yes."

"That is well."

There was a period of silence during which they sipped their tea, then Chu Kee said abruptly, "Your friend, the Painter Woman, where is she?"

Clane looked at him with startled surprise. "You don't know?"

"I do not know," Chu Kee said gravely.

"But I thought . . . well, in a jam like that, I thought she'd come to you."

"I too thought she would come to me," Chu Kee said. "As one who is close to you, she also is close to me. That which is mine is at the disposal of a friend of yours."

Terry Clane sat in silence, digesting that information.

"You have not heard from her? There has been no message?"

"There has been no message."

"There will be one," Chu Kee said in a tone of quiet assurance. "She knows what boat you were on?"

"Yes."

"She will read that it has arrived and will get some word to you."

"That would be exceedingly dangerous," Clane said. "The police are looking for that very thing to happen. They will try to intercept any message she sends."

"The Painter Woman is clever," Chu Kee said as though that effectively dismissed the possibility of police intercepting her message.

They were silent for the space of several seconds. Then Chu Kee, picking up his cup of tea, held it in his clasped hands, letting the heat of the liquid warm his long sensitive fingers. "There is gossip," he said at length.

"About what?"

"The Eastern Art Import and Trading Company."

"And what is the gossip?"

"I do not hear it all, but evidently there has been much loss and much profit. These men play at politics in the Orient."

"I have heard they are interested in the Philippines," Clane said.

"One hears many things," Chu Kee murmured.

"This was supposed to be authentic."

"Many profits and many losses," Chu Kee went on almost dreamily. "First there was a great loss, then there was a period of recovery, and of late there has been a big, a very big, profit. These men are becoming powerful because one of them is shrewd."

"One of them, my Instructor in Wisdom?"

"This Ricardo Taonon, the Eurasian," Chu Kee answered obliquely after the Chinese custom, "is a man of great wile. His mouth says that he is a great friend of China."

"Empty words?" Terry Clane asked.

"Words, certainly," Chu Kee said gravely. "The significance of those words is not yet known. I have men who are investigating. They are shrewd men—and they are puzzled. The man is deep. He plays a game which does not appear on the surface."

After that there was a period when there was no talk. Silence enveloped them in an aura of friendship where each drew strength and pleasure from the presence of the other, sitting there in a row on straight-backed cushionless chairs sipping the hot pale amber of tea which is only for the palate of the connoisseur.

This tea had been grown at a certain elevation above sea level. A hundred feet higher or lower produced tea of a different quality. Only leaves of a certain tenderness were picked at a very particular time, gathered by the most attractive maidens in the village who selected each leaf with the care that a diamond merchant would bestow in choosing a stock of gems, inspecting each carefully for flaws and blemishes. To drink such tea rapidly is a crime against good taste. Such tea is to be sipped carefully in small quantities so that the delicate aroma penetrates to the nostrils. The flavor is nectar to the tongue.

The silence endured for three minutes, for five, for ten.

Clane finished his cup of tea. Sou Ha made a motion toward the teacup to refill his cup but Clane bowed and smiled. "It is enough, Sou Ha. I have work to do."

"There will be a message," Chu Kee said confidently.

"And in a message is danger."

"This Ricardo Taonon," Chu Kee cautioned. "You knew him in China?"

"I met him in Hong Kong, yes."

"Did you learn, perhaps, anything of his connections?"

"No. He seems to know everyone but he has no close friends. Apparently he's on friendly terms with everyone, particularly the influential people, and there it ends."

Chu Kee said, "My own men found him very difficult to appraise in Hong Kong. He is an interesting man. You will walk very carefully, my son, and keep to the middle of the street."

Clane bowed his leave-taking, gently shook hands with himself after the Chinese custom. "I will walk slowly and carefully," he said, "and keep to the middle of the road."

Sou Ha showed him out, her soft pliable hand resting on his arm. "It is better," she said, "that you leave by another door than the one through which you entered."

Clane nodded acquiescence.

She led him along soft Oriental carpets, past rooms which flanked the long corridor, whose perpetually closed doors were merely a front of poverty to conceal the luxury of that which lay behind. "You will be careful, First-Born?" she asked.

"As careful as can be, yes."

"My father thinks you are in danger."

"Why?"

"He does not always confide in his daughter. Tell me, you have no idea where the Painter Woman is?"

"No."

"Then she is with this man who has escaped," Sou Ha said. "She has decided to live with him so long as he lives and to die with him when he is . . . I am so sorry, my friend, have I hurt you?"

"No."

"You still love her?"

"I gave her her freedom when duty called on me to return to the paths of danger, paths that would take me far from civilization, far from the contact of mail."

"And did she desire this freedom which you gave her so lightly?"

"I explained to her that it was out of the question for her to come with me, that I would be gone for years."

"Oh, you *explained*," Sou Ha said and then laughed musically.

Clane looked at her.

She guided him to a door. "In my country," she said, "there are many very wise men. You have studied under these men,

First-Born. You have learned to concentrate, you have acquired much knowledge. And by meditation you have ripened that knowledge into wisdom."

Clane looked down at her, his eyes questioning.

"Go on," he said.

"But these wise men," Sou Ha went on, "steeped in the lore of their wisdom, know nothing of women. Therefore, they can teach nothing of women."

She pressed a button. An electric mechanism shot back steel bolts on the inside of the door.

"And how does one go about acquiring this knowledge of women?" Terry Clane asked.

Her eyes laughed up at him. She came close to him. "You may kiss me again."

A few moments later Terry Clane stepped out of the quiet luxury of that sumptuous room into the carpetless poverty of a dusty corridor illuminated by a single unshaded incandescent which dangled down from twisted green wires, faded and fly-specked.

The door behind him swung noiselessly shut and Clane could hear the whir of the electric mechanism as the heavy steel bars were shot home.

The kiss of the Chinese girl tingled against his lips. The touch of her hand was still warm upon his cheek and her words still ringing in his mind. These wise men with their knowledge which had been gleaned through the ages, their secrets of meditation by which knowledge might be transmuted into wisdom, could teach nothing about women because they knew nothing about women.

And how did one learn about women?

He saw once more her laughing eyes, the red of her warm lips. "You may kiss me again," she had said.

And Terry Clane, sure of himself when he had been within the fastness of a monastery high in the seclusion of snow-capped mountains, suddenly felt the tranquillity of his mind vanish into nothing as he walked along the bare boards of the corridor and descended the narrow flight of stairs toward the smelly side street of San Francisco's Chinatown.

## 7

Y AT T'OY, Terry Clane's man of all work who had been
sent on to San Francisco two months in advance with
instructions to secure, furnish, and provision an apartment
or some suitable flat, was still in the waiting room at the pier,
sitting just as he had been when Terry left. When Clane returned, the man was occupying the same hard wooden bench
with motionless calm. The waiting figure was steeped in a
patience so infinite that it could only have been the heritage of
centuries. This patience is the passive side of action, which
recognizes that infinity is not an intangible something which
begins with death, but is an ever-present reality that sur-
rounds the philosopher with the calm consciousness of cease-
less time.

Yat T'oy expressed no surprise and no emotion as Terry
Clane entered the waiting room. He rose and said, "I have
baggage all together. You wish go to home now?"

There was no curiosity as to where Clane had been during
the intervening hours, no question as to how Clane had known
where Yat T'oy could be found. The Chinese servant had
simply waited until Clane had come. Clane had arrived, and
that was all there was to it. The master had his own affairs.
If the master chose to confide in the servant, that was well.
If he did not so choose to confide, that also was equally well.
All of which didn't mean that Yat T'oy's inscrutable eyes
didn't take in everything and his active mind didn't know
virtually everything which touched upon Terry Clane's life
or might conceivably affect his happiness.

Yat T'oy would have committed murder on behalf of his
master without even so much as a moment's hesitancy. He
would have only needed to know that something stood in
Terry Clane's way to do his utmost to see that the obstacle
was removed. And while he knew and respected Clane's desire
to remain within the letter and the spirit of the law, nevertheless Yat T'oy placed great reliance upon an eight-inch

dagger which reposed in a cunningly concealed sheath harnessed to the back of his shoulder blade. Yat T'oy was an expert in the use of the razor-bladed weapon. However, Yat T'oy knew enough of the temperament of his master to say nothing about those occasions when Yat T'oy, sharing the anxiety which came from being in a tight spot, due to some personal enemy of his master, knew secretly that the cause of that anxiety had been permanently and skillfully removed.

His creed was one of deep-seated unswerving loyalty. All other things were minor.

Yat T'oy was small of stature and he had been shrunk by age and hard work. His face was wrinkled and dried, but his eyes were as bright and alert as those of a bird. There was nothing that missed the comprehensive gaze of Yat T'oy, and that which he saw he remembered in detail and duly reported to his master.

"Place to live very hard find," he said in staccato English.

"But you have a place, Yat T'oy?"

"I have place."

"Good place?"

"Not number one. Perhaps by'm'by later one get more better."

It was characteristic of Yat T'oy that when he talked with Terry Clane in the pidgin English of the treaty ports, he was in no mood to be interrogated in detail and so Clane didn't press him, but hailed a cab, watched Yat T'oy supervise the stowing of the baggage, then climbed in and let Yat T'oy give the cab driver the address.

When they arrived at the four-flat building where Yat T'oy had secured a big flat on the south half of the second story, Clane was agreeably surprised. "Why, Yat T'oy, this is perfect! I had heard it was almost impossible to get anything here in San Francisco. How on earth did you do it?"

Yat T'oy's face brightened under Terry Clane's approval. He spoke now in Cantonese. "The man who is the janitor of this building is of my family."

Clane nodded silently, knowing that Yat T'oy referred to a relationship for which there is no exact counterpart in the

Western world. The nearest that one can approach it is to say "alle same my cousin."

"People who live this flat have much trouble," Yat T'oy went on, grinning. "Cook stove make trouble alle time, trouble with electricity, burn out radio machine."

Yat T'oy had reverted to English once more as he contemplated the trouble he had getting the apartment.

"What happened?" Terry Clane asked, fighting to keep back a smile. "What did the janitor have to do with it?"

"Flat leased by very rich, very greedy woman," Yat T'oy said. "She owns stock big hotel but too greedy stay there."

"I don't get it," Clane said.

"Has very fine rooms, four, five, six rooms in big hotel," Yat T'oy said. "Hotel rooms become very easy to rent. She very greedy. She makes all five rooms into bedrooms and leases flat here. Rent on hotel rooms for one week pays rent on flat for one month. Always same, rich people try get more money. Americans very rich, never so rich have plenty. Always want more."

"And I take it she has gone back to live in the hotel now?" Clane asked.

"Alle same gone back. Very damn fast gone back."

"What happened?"

"Much trouble with flat. Electricity makes big blue flame, burns out fuses, burns out tubes in radio, radio tubes very hard get. Much trouble with stove, much trouble with radiators, make noise all the time, leak water on carpet, very bad."

"I see," Clane said gravely, "and so she preferred the conveniences of the hotel?"

"She move."

"Soon?"

"Two weeks. She make trouble, then move."

"And how about us?" Clane asked gravely. "Will we have trouble with the radiators? Will there be short circuits in the electric wires? Will there be blowing out of radio tubes?"

"No trouble," Yat T'oy said shortly and began unpacking Terry Clane's bags. "Janitor alle same my cousin."

Clane prowled around the place. Much of the furniture was that which he had left in storage, valuable Chinese pieces which Yat T'oy had reconditioned with great care. For the rest, the Chinese, with that shrewd sense of values which is inherent in his race, had picked up here and there and at auctions and in second-hand shops luxurious furniture of prewar quality. Furniture which had been built to last and needed only reconditioning under the cunning touch of Yat T'oy's skillful fingers to be as good as new.

There was about the apartment a comfortable lived-in atmosphere, and so familiar had Yat T'oy made himself with the tastes of his master that things were arranged exactly as Terry Clane would have arranged them had he been there.

Clane settled down into the luxury of a deep-cushioned chair, reached out mechanically and found that Yat T'oy had placed a humidor with his favorite mixture of tobacco and a pipe rack at his hand.

Clane tamped moist tobacco into the pipe, lit a match and puffed contentedly. Yat T'oy watched him solicitously. "Have eaten already?"

"Have eaten," Clane said.

"Brandy?"

"Good brandy, Yat T'oy?"

"Number one."

Clane nodded. Yat T'oy brought him a snifter glass and Clane spun the golden liquid about, watching the oily streaks which clung to the sides of the polished glass.

"Where did you ever find brandy like this, Yat T'oy?"

"China boy work in liquor store," Yat T'oy said. "Alle same my cousin."

Clane let the aroma of the brandy seep to his nostrils, settled back in the chair, his eyes lazy-lidded with contentment, his muscles relaxed.

"Edward Harold escaped from the police officers, Yat T'oy."

"I read in newspapers."

"Cynthia Renton disappeared the same night that Edward Harold disappeared. She has not been in touch even with her sister."

Yat T'oy's eyes rested briefly on Clane's face, then slithered away, then returned once more to his master's countenance.

He blinked attentively, turned his eyes away once more. He said nothing.

"She will try to get in touch with me. She knows that I am due to arrive at about this time and the newspapers will report that my boat has docked. Do we have a telephone, Yat T'oy?"

"Have telephone."

"Be careful in case anyone should call to leave a message. Be sure that you get the message exactly right. It is possible the police will listen in on the wire."

"Janitor who is alle same my cousin very smart," Yat T'oy said. "Police no listen in."

Clane said, "The police are very smart too."

"China boy more smart."

Clane smiled. "Perhaps," he said, "the message will be in the newspapers. Do you have the newspapers?"

"Today's newspapers already here. Also newspapers about escape from policemen of Edward Harold. Also newspapers about murder."

"You mean you have back copies telling about the murder of Horace Farnsworth?"

"Have got."

"How on earth did you get them?"

"China boy works in Red Cross where collect old papers," Yat T'oy said.

"And I suppose he is alle same your cousin."

"Alle same."

"It must have taken much work to go through that mass of papers in order to find the ones you wanted," Terry Clane said.

"My cousin help me, I help him. We work at night, not much work."

Clane settled down to reading the newspapers.

Yat T'oy stood for a few moments in the doorway watching him. Then he said, "Bell by your chair. You want me you ring a bell."

He noiselessly vanished, leaving Terry Clane to concentrate on what had been reported in the daily press of the murder of Horace Farnsworth, the subsequent trial of Edward Harold, the conviction, and then Harold's dramatic escape.

According to the evidence as reported in the press, Edward Harold on the day of the murder had called on Horace Farnsworth. Harold, testifying in his own behalf, had insisted that had been at Farnsworth's request and that when he had called on Farnsworth, he had found the latter very uneasy, even to the point of being despondent, perhaps frightened. Apparently Farnsworth had wanted to confide in Harold and, according to the defendant, had changed his mind between the time he had telephoned and the time Harold had arrived.

After some conversation which Harold had described from the witness stand as "pointless," Harold had brought up the subject of certain investments Farnsworth was making for a mutual friend, a Cynthia Renton—thinking that perhaps this had been the thing about which Farnsworth wished to consult him.

Farnsworth, however, had stated that he invested in some securities and hadn't liked them. He had arranged matters so Miss Renton could get her original capital out of the investment or, if she desired, hold it for a speculative profit.

But the place where Harold had trapped himself and the testimony which, when proven false, had brought about his conviction of murder in the first degree was his assertion that he had not, after that first visit, returned to Farnsworth's house.

The first visit had concededly taken place about five o'clock in the afternoon. Apparently it had lasted until around five-twenty. It was the contention of the prosecution that about six o'clock Harold had returned. He swore that he had not done so; but a neighbor had seen him hurriedly emerge from the front door of Farnsworth's house, almost run down the street, jump into a car and drive away. The identification was positive and absolute. Another person who had known Harold for years had seen him at a minute or two past six driving his car along the road within a block of Farnsworth's house. Yet Harold had, at first, sworn positively he had not returned to Farnsworth's house after that first visit. Then confronted with the statements of these other witnesses, Harold had lost his head, become angry and sullen. He had suddenly refused to answer further questions concerning that second visit on the ground that the answers might incriminate him. After that there had been nothing to it. The jury had retired and reached a verdict of first-degree murder with a deliberation of less than an hour.

The body of Farnsworth, discovered at six-twenty-five by one Sam Kenyon, Farnsworth's house man, cook, chauffeur, valet, and man of all work, had been carefully examined by a police surgeon who had arrived before seven o'clock. He had sworn that the time of death was between five and five-thirty.

Sam Kenyon had spent some two hours during the afternoon with friends. He had purchased a pair of shoes and a necktie, walked home somewhat leisurely since Farnsworth required only a light supper in the evening. On entering the kitchen, Kenyon had been impressed by something which struck him as highly unusual. There was a kettle of furiously boiling water on the electric stove. The burner under the water had been turned on to its hottest adjustment and the water in the kettle had boiled down until only an inch or two remained.

Because this indicated Farnsworth had wanted hot water for something and had then forgotten he had put the kettle on the stove, Kenyon had gone at once to Farnsworth's study. He had found him lifeless, sprawled on the floor, and the servant had immediately telephoned the police. The call had been relayed to a radio car and police had arrived within five minutes to find Farnsworth's lifeless body—and the kettle still furiously boiling away in the kitchen.

At this point, police, making a further investigation, found the oven of the stove had been heated until its highest temperature had been reached on the built-in thermometer in the oven door. They opened this door, found Farnsworth's uncovered wrist watch in the oven, bearing traces of water in the mechanism and stopped at five-twenty-six.

Apparently Farnsworth had in some manner got his watch filled with water, had gone to the kitchen, put on a kettle of water, turned on the heat in both burner and oven, had removed the back from his wrist watch, put it in the oven to dry out, returned to the study, and almost immediately met his death.

How had he got his watch partially filled with water? Why had he wanted boiling water? The police considered these interesting but incidental questions.

Studying the reports of the case, Clane realized that the evidence linking Harold with the actual crime of murder was weak and circumstantial. It had been the man's unfortunate attitude on the witness stand, his attempt to cover up that second trip, his deliberate perjury, which had convicted him.

It had been the theory of the prosecution that Harold had killed Farnsworth on the occasion of the first visit, but that after he had returned home, Harold had realized he had left at the scene of the crime some evidence which would betray him and that he had returned to remove that evidence— a very nice, very logical contention, but there had not been the slightest shred of evidence to substantiate it.

Viewing the case from the viewpoint of a jury, irritated at Harold because of his attempt to conceal that second trip, angry at the man's clumsy attempt at lying, it was only natural that a first-degree verdict would have been returned. Looking at it from the calm, dispassionate viewpoint of a reviewing tribunal, it would be seen at once that Harold's conviction was on circumstantial evidence; that while he had apparently lied about making a second trip to Farnsworth's house, yet it could be claimed by a shrewd lawyer that Harold, having returned to Farnsworth's house on a second visit, a visit which related to some matter so private he did not wish to disclose it to anyone, had entered the house, found the man murdered, and acting upon a sudden surge of blind panic had decided to keep out of it. Having been trapped into a denial that he had made that second trip, he had sought to stick to his story.

Since it was elemental that circumstantial evidence alone should not be considered by a jury as sufficient to warrant a conviction unless there was no reasonable hypothesis other than that of guilt consistent with the evidence, there was every chance the Supreme Court would reverse the verdict.

This possibility made the evidence of that kettle of boiling water and the waterlogged wrist watch in the oven more important than ever. Had Farnsworth had some other visitor and decided to heat a kettle of water because of something this visitor had proposed?—such, for instance, as steaming open the flap of a sealed envelope? If so, who was that visitor? Had he left any clues? And had the wrist watch got waterlogged while the kettle was being filled in too big a hurry? It was an interesting field for speculation, one that the Supreme Court might well enter into; and, having embarked upon such speculation, would possibly feel the case had not been really solved until the mystery of the steaming kettle and the waterlogged watch had been explained.

Therefore, Harold's escape became a second major tactical blunder in a case which had been ineptly handled from the beginning.

Terry Clane folded the papers, replaced them on the table and devoted his thoughts to the case against Edward Harold, a case in which a mere surmise of the police, virtually without anything to back it up other than circumstantial evidence, had resulted in Harold's conviction. The gun with which the murder had been committed had never been found. There was some weak and inconclusive evidence that it was Harold's gun. It was conceded that he owned a .38 caliber revolver. The murder had been committed with a .38 caliber revolver. When called upon to produce his revolver, the one which he admittedly owned, Harold had been unable to find it. The gun had apparently vanished from a bureau drawer in which it had been kept. But, as Harold had tried to point out to the police, he simply kept the gun there wrapped in oiled rags. He had had no occasion to look for it or to use it for a year. During that time, he had experienced the usual turnover in help, during a time when labor, restless and prosperous, had made it almost a universal habit to take jobs, work on them for a few weeks and then drift to other jobs.

In one of the other rooms Clane could hear the steady insistent ringing of a telephone bell. Then he heard Yat T'oy's muffled voice answering the instrument, and a few seconds later Yat T'oy, shuffling into the room, said, "Man who say name alle same Gloster must talk very important. I tell him maybe so you not home I go find out. You home? You not home?"

Clane gave the matter swift consideration. "I'm home," he said.

"Very well," Yat T'oy said. "You sit still. I bring telephone."

Yat T'oy shuffled out. A few moments later he returned with a telephone instrument which he plugged into a socket near Clane's chair.

Clane said, "Hello, Gloster. What is it you wanted?"

Gloster's voice seemed tense with emotion. "Clane," he said, "I know it's late, but I want to see you. I have something to tell you. There are reasons why I can't go to your apartment. Could you come to the warehouse of the Eastern Art Import and Trading Company?"

"Why there?"

"Because there's something here I want to show you, something I want you to see, and then I want to make a statement to you. It's important, damned important."

"I'll be there," Clane said. "What's the address?"

Gloster gave him the address, asked him to come at once.

"I'll be there as soon as I can get there," Clane said and hung up.

He found Yat T'oy's eyes registering disapproval, but no remonstrance came from the lips of the old servant. He merely shuffled to the closet, brought out Clane's coat, hat, scarf, and gloves.

It wasn't until Clane was halfway to the street that he realized the thing he had thought was a cigarette case in the side pocket of his overcoat was in reality a small automatic which Yat T'oy had thoughtfully slipped into the pocket.

# 8

TERRY CLANE emerged from the door of his apartment, turned up the collar of his overcoat against the chill fog which was swirling in and started walking briskly down the pavement toward the hotel where he felt certain he would find a taxicab waiting.

A dark coupé across the street showed a little pinpoint of red light glowing brightly, then fading.

Momentarily Clane slackened his pace. That would be someone puffing on a cigarette, probably some dumb cop who had been given the job of watching his apartment and who failed to realize that eyes which had been trained in China to observe the most minute details would instantly pick up the glowing end of a cigarette.

Terry dismissed such espionage as being too clumsy to be worthy of his attention. He heard the car motor start into life. From the corner of his eye, he saw the car make a U turn in the middle of the block, still without the lights being switched on.

Not until the car had completed the turn and was coming up behind him, did the dim parking lights come on. Then abruptly the car gathered speed and drew alongside.

For a brief moment Clane was startled as he realized that this was no shadowing job. The car was speeding to a point directly abreast, then it slammed to a stop. A door swung open and a rough voice commanded, "Get in."

Clane glanced over his shoulder, saw somewhat to his surprise there was only one person in the car, a huddled, shapeless figure that sat behind the steering wheel. Nor was there any indication of a weapon. The cigarette had been tossed away and he could see only the vague outline of the shadowy figure.

Clane glanced up and down the street. At that hour of the night there was no one in sight.

"Come on," the voice said gruffly. "Get in."

55

Clane's ears picked up something incongruous in the command, a vague, indefinite something which clamored at the threshold of his attention for recognition. There was something wrong with that voice, something . . . suddenly he had it. It was the voice of a woman.

Clane turned abruptly, walked to the curb.

"Oh, Owl," the voice said with sobbing anxiety, "please. I didn't want to shout who I was."

"Cynthia!" he exclaimed under his breath and jumped to the running board, slid into the seat beside her, and pulled the door shut. "What in the world are *you* doing *here?*"

She instantly switched on the lights, slammed home the gear shift, and eased her foot back on the clutch pedal. The windshield wiper fought back fog-bred moisture. "Waiting for you," she said. "And I've been there so long I'm chilled to the bone. I thought you would never come out."

"Why didn't you send a message? Why didn't you telephone?"

"I was afraid to. I thought the police would have your line tapped. I was waiting where I could see you at the boat. I saw them pounce on you, and I was afraid. I ran away."

"How did you find my flat?"

"Through Yat T'oy, of course. I'd been up there several times, helping him arrange things. And then . . . this . . ."

Clane placed his hand on her shoulder. "Take it easy, Cynthia."

She said, "Look, Owl, I can't drive and talk. I'm going to swing around on a side street some place where we can park. We have lots to talk about and I want to be where I can look at you without being guilty of what the speed cops have insisted is negligent driving."

"I'm on my way to meet someone, Cynthia. It may be rather important."

"Oh, bother that someone. You haven't anything in your whole life that's half as important as this, Terry."

Abruptly she concentrated her attention entirely on driving the car. Clane felt the same thrill he had always felt when riding with her, the deft sure touch of her hand on the wheel, the daring abandon with which she slammed down the throttle to the floor board and zipped through traffic. Now she made time through the deserted streets.

"Don't be picked up for speeding," Clane cautioned. "It might be embarrassing."

"I'm watching my rear-view mirror and the side streets," she said. "Here's a good place where we can talk."

She swung the car in an abrupt turn and almost in the same motion selected a parking place near the curb, guided the car adroitly to its berth between painted white lines, switched off the ignition and headlights, squirmed out from behind the steering wheel, swung to face him, and raised her lips.

Clane put his arms around her, felt once more the oft-remembered warmth of her body, the fragrance of her hair. Her lips, warm and eager, were hot on his; and her arms twined around his neck, strained him to her.

"Terry," she breathed after a moment, and as she turned her cheek, Clane felt the moisture of her tears.

"Cynthia, you're crying."

"You're damn right I'm crying," she said. "My gosh, I thought you'd *never* get here."

"Cynthia, what ever possessed you to do it?"

"What?"

"Arrange Harold's escape."

She was silent for several seconds, then she said suddenly, "Let's talk about it in order, Owl."

"Where do we begin?"

She said firmly, "We begin with when you went away and were so damn noble that you wouldn't marry me before you went."

"I couldn't have taken you with me, Cynthia, and the chances were twenty to one that I'd never come back. I wanted you to be free and . . ."

"Oh, I know all about that," she said impatiently. "You made it plain enough when you left."

"And," Clane went on keeping his eyes on the fog-shrouded sidewalk, "it turned out that I was right. You became interested in Edward Harold."

For a long time she said nothing. Clane, looking out through

57

the window, suddenly realized that she would say nothing
until he had turned to meet her eyes. He swung his head. She
was looking at him and there was enough light from the
ornamental street lights to show the tears glistening on her
cheeks.

"And now," Clane went on, "you've done something that
was typically Cynthia. You've done the impulsive thing, the
thing that takes everyone by surprise. Who were your ac-
complices, Cynthia?"

She said somewhat angrily, "Is that all you have to ask?"

"What else could there be?" he asked in surprise.

"Nothing," she said sharply and wriggled back behind the
steering wheel.

"I've gone over the newspaper accounts of the case," Clane
said. "When you stop to analyze the evidence that connected
Harold with the murder, it was all circumstantial evidence, and
not what you would call a robust case. The thing that brought
about Harold's conviction was the way he told his story, his
denial that he had gone back to see Farnsworth."

"Perhaps he didn't go back," she said with fierce loyalty to
the absent friend.

"The evidence doesn't indicate it."

"Oh, hang the evidence! People have been mistaken on
identifications before."

"Not this time, I'm afraid, Cynthia."

She said abruptly, angrily, "All right, you have an appointment. I'll drive you to where you want to go."

"Cynthia," he said, "we've got to straighten this out. I
want to know where Harold is."

"Why?"

"Because he has to give himself up."

"Give himself up to be executed," she said. "He'd rather
die first and I'd rather have him. It's better to be out in the
open, shooting it out with a bunch of cops and going down
with a chestful of bullets than to be dragged out of a cell like
a cur being hauled out of a cage, placed in an airtight execution room, and have people leering at you through windows
while you listen to the hissing of the cyanide tablets dropping
into the acid and forming the gas that you'll presently inhale.

58

And all the time those leering eyes of the morbidly curious, looking at you through the glass slits. You, chained there to a chair, surrounded by this ring of curious eyes that can't even give you enough privacy to meet your end decently. To hell with it! Edward would rather hole up in a building somewhere and shoot it out with the cops, and I don't blame him."

"There's yourself to be considered," he said gently.

"And I don't count either," she said. "The trouble with you is you're so damn right."

"You don't act like it now."

"I'm not talking about now. I'm talking about when you went to the Orient. I was happy-go-lucky and impulsive, and everything in life seemed a joke. And you told me that I couldn't live life that way, that life was serious, that it would get me down in the long run. Damn it, you're right! But I'm not going to yield to life without a struggle. I'll fight it all the way. I hate being logical and careful and safe and conservative and cautious and conventional. I hate the whole damn business. Do you hear me, Owl?"

"Life doesn't care particularly whether you hate it or not," Clane said. "Life exerts a steady pressure. You learn that causes build effects, which in turn become causes, until you have a wheel."

"Not that, Owl. I won't let life get away with all that. Why not just laugh at life and throw out your chips? It's a gamble anyway. I think you develop as much character by gambling as you do by the patient, slow, plodding, mathematical way of trying to live life. Life isn't anything that can be hoarded. It's a force. It's something you're spending even when you're trying to save it. You . . . you might just as well go along with it."

"But," Clane pointed out, "you were trying to tell me that I had been right and that life had got you down."

"On account of . . . on account of you, Terry Clane."

"In what way?"

"When you went away, my life was . . . All right, we won't talk about it. You want to talk about the murder case. You want to talk about the circumstantial evidence and all that. Go ahead."

59

"The point is," Clane explained patiently, "the Supreme Court will review the case and consider that it was a case of purely circumstantial evidence, that the jury were probably unduly prejudiced by Harold's manner on the stand and his clumsy attempt at denying that he had returned to Farnsworth's house."

"So what?"

"So they're apt to set aside the conviction and give him a new trial."

"All right. Let them do it."

"But the point is," Clane said, "that under the law a defendant has no right to press an appeal unless he is abiding by the law. If he has escaped and is holding himself in defiance of the law, he loses the benefit of it. He can't carry an appeal to the Supreme Court while he is a fugitive from justice. The district attorney is planning to go into court tomorrow morning and move for a dismissal of the appeal. You know what that will mean. Once the appeal is dismissed, all hope is gone. When Edward Harold is captured, he'll be sent directly to the death house—only the intervention of the Governor can save him. And it's hardly possible that the Governor will exert himself to save the life of a man who has escaped from the custody of officers at the point of a gun."

"I tell you they won't ever take Edward alive."

"All right," Clane said. "What I want is for Edward Harold to surrender."

"Never."

"I want him to walk into jail and give himself up, and I want to go ahead and work on that case. I want to help with the appeal. I want to try and unearth some new evidence."

"Edward doesn't intend to give himself up."

Clane went on patiently, "We have to be very careful. We've got to arrange things so that it's done dramatically and spectacularly. We must smuggle him right up to the doors of the jail so that he can walk up and surrender. Or else go to one of the newspaper offices and surrender to the newspaper. But you can see what will happen if he can't do one of these things cleverly enough. If some officer catches him while he's on his way to the jail to surrender himself, no amount

. of protestation on the part of Harold that he was going to give himself up would be of any avail. The officer will pull the old publicity stuff. Newspaper reporters who like to keep in good with the officers will dish out the usual tripe that while Patrolman John Doe was walking to the bus line after his shift on duty he kept his eye on passing pedestrians, mentally checking off each face against the wanted list, which he studied daily, a practice which he had diligently followed for some twenty years. And last night it paid off in a big way because among the hurrying pedestrians John Doe found the face of the one man whom police were seeking more diligently than . . ."

"Owl, stop it," she commanded.

"You see what I mean, Cynthia. He has to surrender. It has to be accomplished in such a manner that . . ."

"I tell you he isn't going to surrender. He'll never surrender. He prefers to die fighting. The mockery of it all! The judge forcing the prisoner to stand up, going through all that rigmarole of asking him if he has anything to say why sentence should not be pronounced, and telling him that he's going to die. I hate it. I hate the damn hypocrisy of it—the smug lawyers, careful to keep their faces turned at just the right angle so that when the photographers shoot pictures of the courtroom scene, they'll get Mr. District Attorney and Mr. Attorney-for-the-Defense in a properly impressive pose. I tell you, Owl, he'll never give himself up. Never, never, never."

"And then of course there's your own position in the matter to be considered."

"*Not* to be considered," she said.

"What sort of a chap is Edward Harold?" Clane asked.

"He's a man who fights against injustices," she said. "He's always sympathized with the underdog, always tried to do what he could for the man who was down. And it makes him furious whenever he hears of cases of oppression. He loves life. He loves liberty. He says that the one thing he asks of life is freedom of choice. And imagine a man like that in a scrape like this."

"You love him very, very much?" Clane asked.

She abruptly snapped on the ignition.

"Where's your appointment?" she asked.

"Don't bother to drive me there. Take me to where I can get a cab."

"No, I'll take you there."

She had taken off the emergency brake and was easing the car into motion as Clane gave her the address.

Abruptly her foot slammed down the brake pedal. She turned to him as though he had struck her. "Terry, *what* are you doing?"

"Giving you the address of the place I want to go."

"What are you trying to do? Are you playing with me as a cat plays with a mouse, doing that old stunt of yours of reading people's minds . . ."

"Take it easy, Cynthia. What's all the commotion about? I simply am going to this address to meet George Gloster. I think it's the warehouse of the Eastern Art Import and Trading Company."

"And George Gloster is going to meet you there."

"Yes."

She released her foot from the brake, slammed the car into gear, shot out into the middle of the street, took the corner in second, slapped the gear-shift lever back into high as she straightened out on the boulevard.

"We're not going to a fire," Clane said.

Her lips were pressed together in a firm, straight line. "That's what you may think," she said.

"What," Clane asked, "is the idea?"

She flung words at him over her shoulder, her eyes watching the fog-shrouded street intersections as the car went screaming by. "Edward Harold," she said, "has been concealed in the Eastern Art Import and Trading Company's warehouse. You can see what will happen if George Gloster goes there. How long has he been there?"

"I don't know. He telephoned me to meet him there just before I left the apartment and . . ."

"You don't know whether he was there then or just going there?"

"No."

Cynthia choked back something which could have been a sob. "And all the time we've been talking," she said, "Edward Harold has been there and . . ." She didn't finish the sentence.

She didn't need to.

# 9

THE warehouse was dark, a gloomy, forbidding building which fronted on a narrow street near the waterfront. Down here the fog had settled until the headlights of Cynthia's car seemed boring through a tunnel of watered milk.

Cynthia swung the car into the narrow side street, braked it to a stop, pushed open the door on her side and was out almost before Clane had his door open.

She didn't wait for him but started running toward the entrance to the warehouse.

"Take it easy, Cynthia," Clane cautioned, moving along behind her with long swinging strides. "Let's try and find out first what . . ."

His words were wasted. She was running.

Clane's hand, dropping to the right-hand coat pocket, found the automatic which Yat T'oy had so thoughtfully put there. His left hand encountered a small pocket flashlight.

The entrance of the building was shrouded in darkness, but the beam of Clane's tiny flashlight showed that the door was slightly ajar; and through the swirling, thick fog he could dimly make out the bulk of an automobile parked at an angle, pulled up off the road and across the sidewalk, an automobile which seemed comfortably ensconced off the right of way and on private property, as though it were resting in a familiar parking place.

Clane called through the crack in the doorway. "Hello in there. Is anyone home? This is Terry Clane, Gloster. You there?"

There was no answer, no sound save water dropping from the eaves of the building.

Cynthia, heedless of Terry Clane's warning, pushed open

the door, groped for a light switch. Terry Clane's flashlight furnished an illumination which enabled her to locate the switch. She clicked it on and lights disclosed the interior of the warehouse.

It was a small one-story warehouse. The front part contained a room which could be used as an office, and behind this was the warehouse proper. Here were tiers of packed cases wrapped with braided strips of flexible bamboo bearing Chinese characters and the stenciled label "Eastern Art Import and Trading Company, San Francisco, U.S.A." There was about the place the peculiar mingling of the musty smell of a warehouse with the smell of the Orient.

Terry Clane walked to the doorway of the office while Cynthia walked out toward the back of the warehouse, and his eyes, trained to take in details, photographed upon his mind the things which he saw.

The office had been cut off from the rest of the warehouse building by a partition, and occupied the entire east side of the building. The warehouse door was on the north. Opening it, one entered the main warehouse. A few feet farther on and to the left was a door which opened into the partition dividing the warehouse and the office. In the southeast corner of that office room was a wall telephone. On the south side of the room, moved out a few feet from the wall, was a table. Three or four chairs were scattered about the place. In the center of the room was another small table covered with old magazines. On the northwest side of the room and directly back of the door from the warehouse was a washroom, the door standing open. It contained a wash bowl and a toilet. Back of that and in the northeast corner of the room was an army cot, a folding canvas affair, on which were several army blankets. Another blanket had been folded over so as to serve as a hard makeshift pillow. On the floor were canned goods piled against the wall so that the labels were plainly visible—soups, fruit juices, canned beans, canned meat, vegetables, canned milk, and a big glass jar of coffee. A big wastebasket was partially filled with empty tins. Over on the table at the south end of the room was a portable electric plate, a small aluminum frying pan, some knives and forks, a can opener, a cup and saucer, and a coffee pot.

Clane took another step, then came to a startled halt.

Just to the east of the table, lying so that the feet were pointed toward the door to the warehouse and the head toward the southeast corner of the room, was the body of a man, lying face down. And from that body a pool of thick blood seeped slowly in an ever-widening circle.

"Cynthia," he called over his shoulder, "this way, quick. Don't touch anything."

He kept his eyes busy while he waited for her to join him.

The tall oblong windows in the office were so covered with dust and cobwebs as to make it almost impossible to see out of them. They were all closed with the exception of a window in the southwest corner, which was raised wide open and through which the damp, fog-filled atmosphere penetrated into the room, giving the place a dank, clammy chill.

Clane turned as he felt the pressure of Cynthia's body against his back, saw her peering over his shoulder. "Terry . . . Terry, what is it? . . . Oh, for God's sake, is . . ."

"Take it easy," Clane cautioned. "There's a body on the floor."

"Of course there is. I . . . Terry, let me past, let me in there, I say!"

Terry pushed her back.

"Terry, if that's Edward, if . . ."

"Get back," Clane commanded.

"Terry, I must. I have to . . ."

"You don't have to do any such thing. Keep your hands at your sides."

"Why?"

"Because you can't afford to touch anything. You can't afford to leave a single fingerprint here. Do you understand?"

The expression on his face, the earnestness of his words, carried conviction. "Oh Terry," she said, "I have to . . . Let me go to him."

Clane shook his head. "Take a careful look, Cynthia. Is that Edward Harold?"

"I . . . I can't see from here. Oh, Owl, is he dead?"

"I'm going to find out," Clane said. "You stand right there. Don't touch anything. Don't move out of that doorway. Above all, don't touch any object."

Terry Clane, on the other hand, exercised no care to keep from leaving fingerprints. He rested his hand on the back of a chair, moved around the little square table, then walked over to stand by the larger table where he could look almost directly down on the body.

"It's George Gloster," he called out.

Cynthia said, "Oh!" and that was all.

Clane bent over the table now, looking down at the knife and fork, the spoons, the cup and saucer, the cooking utensils. They were all clean and polished, indicating that they had been carefully washed and dried after they had been used the last time. On a corner of the table was a small ash tray, fairly well filled with cigarette ends and burned matches. Beside the ash tray was a pocket-size magazine, opened and placed face down on the table as though the reader had wanted to mark the place from which he was reading.

Near by on the table was the end of a cigarette and a long groove was burned in the finish of the table. A chair had been pushed back from the table and was almost against the wall, separated by some two feet from the edge of the table. It was, Clane noticed, the only chair which had a padded seat.

On the desk was a clean, oblong desk blotter and impressed upon the buff unstained freshness of this blotter were the prints of four fingers, marked in what seemed to be grimy oil dust, the sort of dust which would accumulate over the years in a city warehouse. The print of the index finger was broader than the others, that of the little finger so small as to be little more than a dot.

Clane turned, walked back to Cynthia, said, "Okay, Cynthia, this is where you get out."

"And what do *you* do?"

"I notify the police."

"Terry, you can't. You keep out of this . . . You . . ."

"There is every possibility," Clane interrupted, "that the police have my telephone tapped. In that event they know George Gloster asked me to meet him here. For you to be

66

here would be suicidal. Police would claim that you had secreted Edward Harold here, that Gloster surprised you, and you shot him to keep him from notifying police."

"Oh, Owl. Why, that's a nightmare."

"A nightmare," he said, "that will come true if the police ever know you've been here. You should never have arranged that escape. Now you have a murder case of your own on your hands."

"Owl, you'll have to let me tell you all about this, how it happened that I . . ."

"Not now," he interrupted impatiently. "Get on your way. I'll give you ten seconds and then I'm going to notify the police."

"Owl, I can't. You mustn't. We . . ."

Clane gravely took her elbow, piloted her out toward the door that led from the warehouse on the north. "Did you touch anything after you came in?"

"I don't think so. Yes, the doorknob on the inside. I . . ."

Clane took his handkerchief, carefully wiped the inner surface of the doorknob, held it open and escorted her to her car. He held the car door open, helped her in, then slammed the door shut. "On your way," he said.

"Look, Owl, can't you . . ."

Clane turned and deliberately walked away. Cynthia watched him a moment, then switched on the ignition. Clane heard the whir of the starting mechanism, then the pulsing of the motor. A moment later the lights came on and the car slipped smoothly away into the fog-filled night, leaving Clane standing in the deserted side street surrounded by the buildings of the warehouse district, dark, forlorn, gloomy buildings from the eaves of which the fog moisture dropped to the ground in a steady cadence of mournful dripping.

Clane walked over to examine the car which was parked off the road. It was a closed car, a two-tone club coupé. The fog moisture had collected in beads on the windshield and on the hood. Two little rivulets of water, fed by this moisture, had dropped down the windshield and down the hood, trickling to the ground in vertical lines. Clane noted the license number of the automobile. He dared not open the door to look at the registration certificate.

He gave Cynthia Renton a full five minutes. Then he walked back into the warehouse, switched the lights off and on, entered the office, was careful to avoid the pool of blood as he tiptoed his way around to the telephone.

As he was about to pick up the receiver, he noticed near the telephone a fresh sliver where the wood had been marred by some recent injury.

Clane bent for a closer inspection.

He saw that a bullet, apparently of .38 caliber, had struck the wall and slightly embedded itself. From the size and shape of the hole, Clane would have said that the bullet had been somewhat battered before it had penetrated the wood.

Clane moved over, picked up the telephone receiver and said, "Police Headquarters, please. Get me the Homicide Department. I want to report a murder."

## 10

INSPECTOR Jim Malloy of Homicide greeted Terry Clane with the cordial enthusiasm that one customarily shows toward a rich relative.

"Well, well, well, if it isn't Mr. Clane," he said, wrapping Clane's hand with thick powerful fingers. "I suppose you remember me all right. I worked on that Mandra murder case— a most interesting . . ."

"I remember you perfectly," Clane said.

"Well now, that's nice of you. That's interesting, the idea that a man like you would remember just a dumb cop. Now, of course, with me, I remember you because it's my business to remember people. And then, of course, we don't ordinarily meet people like you, but you're meeting average people like me every day, lots of them. And now you say you have another body down here?"

"A body, not another body."

"That's right, that's right. You'll pardon me. I was thinking of that other case. And this body, do you happen to know who he is?"

"George Gloster."

"Gloster, Gloster. Now I've heard that name. . . . Let's see, this is a warehouse, isn't it?"

"That's right. Eastern Art Import and Trading Company."

"Well, well, well, I knew I'd heard the name Gloster before somewhere. Now this man Horace Farnsworth that was murdered a while back—he was a member of this Eastern Trading Company, or whatever you call it, wasn't he?"

"I believe he was."

"Well now, let's just go take a look," Inspector Malloy said. "I take it you didn't touch anything? Of course, you wouldn't —you've been all through this before. It isn't like talking with an amateur, so to speak."

"I touched the telephone," Clane said, "because it was the only chance I had to get the police department. There aren't many phones around here. You could walk for miles in this district without finding a phone."

"You could for a fact," Malloy said. "Well, we'll just discount that then. Your fingerprints on the telephone. Fingerprints anywhere else?"

"I may have touched a chair or two inadvertently before I realized what I was up against."

"I see. Of course, you shouldn't have done that, Mr. Clane, but you'll learn. You'll learn as you have more experience. You'll learn."

"I don't want any more experience."

"Well, of course, of course! Now let's see. We go right in here and the lights are on. Were they on when you came, Mr. Clane?"

"They were not," Clane said.

"You turned them on?"

"I did."

"Well now, are you a member of this Eastern Trading Company?"

"No, I am not a member of the Eastern Art Import and Trading Company. Perhaps, I'd better tell you my story after you've looked around a bit."

"Well, I'll just take a look. Now the light switch is right here by the door. You turned this on?"

"Yes."

"Then that'll account for another fingerprint. You'll have to remember that—your fingerprint on the light switch. Then what did you do?"

"I went through this door here to the left."

"That's right, the door in this room. Oh—there it is. There's the body."

"There's the body," Clane said.

"Just like it was when you arrived?"

"That's right."

"You didn't move anything?"

"No."

"Good boy," Malloy said. "You're learning, you're learning. Well now, let's see. There's a window open over there. You didn't open that window?"

"No."

"It was open like that when you came?"

"Yes."

Malloy turned back to one of the men on Homicide. "Sammy, run around and take a look under that window. Be careful now—you might find a footprint or perhaps the mark of a jimmy on the window sill. Be careful you don't mess things up. Just sort of tiptoe around and give it the once-over. Now let's see, there's the body lying over there, feet toward us, head toward the telephone, lying on its stomach, head turned a little bit to the right, right hand outstretched and about even with the head, left hand doubled back and about even with the man's belt. You can identify him? You say that's Gloster?"

"That's Gloster."

"You went over and took a look?"

"I went over and took a look."

"You shouldn't have done that. You should have identified him after we got here."

"I had to use the telephone," Clane said.

"That's right, that's right. You went over there to use the telephone. See anything else while you were there?"

"I just used the phone, that's all. I did notice where a bullet had embedded itself in the boards."

"A bullet? Well now, that's interesting. You looked at it pretty carefully? Sure it was a bullet?"

"I just saw the end of it. It's a round object that looks like a bullet."

"You didn't touch it?"

"No."

"That's fine. No fingerprints of yours on the bullet then. That'll help. Now if you'll just step outside, Mr. Clane, and let our men get busy here, we'll perhaps find out a lot more things. There's a little fingerprinting to do, and a little checking up. You know how those things are. By the way, here's a pile of canned goods and a cot. Looks as though someone had been sleeping here. Did Gloster live here?"

"I don't know. I shouldn't think so."

"I wouldn't think so either. Hardly a place for a man to live. Perhaps a night watchman has been sleeping here. But there's been a lot of cooking, hasn't there?"

"Apparently."

"Someone lived here, someone who was rather neat. Yes, I'd say neat as a pin. Dishes all washed up nice and clean. Empty cans all stacked in a big wastebasket. Quite a few empty cans there. Apparently the man didn't have much of an opportunity to get out to dispose of his garbage. Now *that's* interesting."

Clane said nothing.

"Very interesting indeed," Inspector Malloy went on. "Now if this here Gloster was a member of this Far Eastern what-do-you-call-it Company, then there's a pretty good chance he knew this Edward Harold that the police are looking for. Don't you suppose he did?"

"I suppose it's a natural assumption."

"Do you know that he did?"

"I think that he did."

"Well now, that's interesting. Now wouldn't it be funny if . . . Well, I guess we won't bother you any more right now, Mr. Clane. You're probably a little squeamish about these

71

things. If you'll just step right out and wait there in the police car, you'll find one of the boys there to talk to you."

"And see that I don't get away?"

"Oh no, heavens, no, nothing like that! Why should *you* want to get away?"

"I thought perhaps you thought I wanted to get away."

"And why should I be thinking anything like that, Mr. Clane? What have you got to get away for?"

"Nothing."

"That's right, nothing at all. Why, no, we wouldn't consider for a minute that *you* wanted to get away. No, no, you'll just sit there, and I know you won't mind waiting to tell us your story. Let's see now, you felt it was pretty deserted down here and a person would have a hard time getting to a telephone. That's why you decided to go over and use that particular instrument to call us."

"That's right."

"Well, if this neighborhood is so isolated, how did *you* happen to get down here?"

"In a taxicab."

"And then you let the cab go?"

"That's right."

"You should have kept it waiting. You might have had some difficulty getting another one."

"I thought that Mr. Gloster would take me home."

"Oh, you knew Mr. Gloster was here?"

"Naturally."

"Well, we'll find out all about that later on, Mr. Clane. If you'll just go out and sit in the car now, I'll get to work and do the chores here. Just a lot of routine, you know, covering things with powder, looking for fingerprints. And, by the way, I guess you'd better give the boy your fingerprints out there. Just a little messy, you know, gets the ends of your fingers smeared up with ink; but it's one of the things we have to do. You've been in this room and you've left fingerprints here and there and of course we want to be able to identify those fingerprints of yours when we find them. Wouldn't want to find some real good latent print and think we had the print of the murderer, and then after a while find out that it was the fingerprint of Mr. Terry Clane. That would be embarrassing, wouldn't it, ha, ha, ha!"

"Very embarrassing," Clane agreed.

"All right, just step out there. Fred, would you mind taking Mr. Clane's prints? Then you can sit out in the car with him and talk to him. He's an interesting chap to talk to. Isn't interested in baseball and prize fights and the things you'd ordinarily talk about. He's interested in Oriental philosophy. Don't try to talk with him about that because you don't know anything about it, but perhaps you can get him to talk with you while you listen. And don't ask him any questions about the case. Leave that for me. I wouldn't want him to have to repeat what he has to say. I'll be out just as soon as I can get things going here. Now if you boys will set up the cameras there, we'll get some pictures first rattle out of the box. You can plug into that outside socket and string your wire in for your floodlights. And we might start taking some measurements of the position of the body and the location of the furniture. The district attorney will be wanting a map of the place. You know how he is, Clane. Lawyers have a certain rigmarole they go through with and the district attorney will want something he can produce as People's Exhibit Number One. All right, Fred, just take Mr. Clane out in the car and try to keep him interested, keep him talking."

Clane followed the officer out to the car where he was duly fingerprinted and then given a rag on which he could wipe off the surplus ink from the tips of his fingers. The manner in which the officer whom Inspector Malloy referred to as Fred tried to keep up a conversation, coupled with what Malloy had said, made Clane realize that these officers were trying to keep him from having a chance to think up some good story. They wanted to keep his mind thoroughly occupied.

Fred asked Clane all about China, all about the Chinese people, about the Chinese religion, about Clane's trip across on the boat, about a hundred and one incidental things. Some of the questions were searching and intelligent, some of them were just questions; but there was a continuing stream of questions. Clane had no opportunity whatever to relax into thoughtful silence. He was peppered with verbal question

73

marks, coming with what at times seemed to be the unceasing rapidity of hail falling on a tin roof. But Clane, realizing that this was part of Malloy's test and that any attempt on his part to become silent would be duly reported to the Inspector and considered as a suspicious circumstance, kept his good nature and answered the questions, for the most part making his answers brief so that the burden of carrying on the conversation fell upon Fred. But at the end of fifteen minutes Clane was forced to admit that this was a game at which Fred was adept. Evidently he had done it before. Clane had a shrewd suspicion that the officer was hardly listening to his answers but was using the period during which Clane was talking to formulate some new question.

At the end of twenty minutes Inspector Malloy came barging out of the building, his genial bluff good nature a mask behind which his busy brain went about its business.

"Well, well, well, Clane," he said, "I can see that Fred's been pumping you to find out all about the Orient. I should have cautioned you about Fred. He's after information all the time. Too bad you don't know more about baseball. Fred's an expert, can tell you everything about any player in any of the leagues. You get to talking with him about baseball and he'll be betting you money first thing you know, and you won't stand a chance, Mr. Clane. But I suppose Fred's an expert on the Orient now. Now if you wouldn't mind stepping right in here, Mr. Clane, and . . . But before you do that, perhaps you'd better show us just what happened. Now you came here in a taxi."

"That's right."

"Now where did you get that taxi?"

"It was one I just happened to find cruising along the street."

"Lucky, that's what you are," Malloy said. "You know, lots of people would be prowling around the street looking for a taxicab for an hour or so and wouldn't get it. But you just pop out of your apartment and bang, there's a taxicab right there. That right?"

"Not right there, I had to walk two or three blocks."

"Walk two or three blocks. Well, well, well, think of it, stepping out and finding a taxi within two or three blocks.

That's marvelous. That's really wonderful. I guess you're just lucky. Perhaps it's a good thing you *didn't* talk baseball and get a bet out of him, Fred. Mr. Clane's lucky enough so he might have won just on sheer luck, ha, ha. Now right this way, Mr. Clane. But before we do that, let's pause here just for a moment. Your taxi swung around and made a turn. Yes, I can see it did. Here's some tracks that must have been made by the car you came down in. So the taxi stopped about here and let you off."

"That's right."

"Then what did you do?"

"I walked toward the door of the building."

"Tut, tut, tut, Mr. Clane," Malloy said. "You mustn't do that."

"Mustn't do what?"

Malloy was grinning at him. "Mustn't cheat your cab driver out of his fare," he said. "You told me you let the cabby go."

"That's right. I did."

"Then you must have paid him off."

Clane smiled. "I overlooked that."

"You mean you overlooked paying him off?"

"No, overlooked telling you about it."

"Come, come, Mr. Clane, you mustn't do that. Now as I remember it, you've had quite a bit of rather unusual mental training?"

Clane said nothing.

"Seems to me I heard once that you knew all about concentration. I recall that in the Mandra case the district attorney told me to watch out for you. A man with a trained mind that way mustn't forget those little things. Now, don't misunderstand me, Mr. Clane, I want you to tell me everything you did, absolutely everything. Understand?"

"I understand."

"Nothing is too trivial. Nothing is too small. I want you to just show me what you did and tell me what you did. Now you were standing right here when you got out of the taxicab?"

"Well, about over in here," Clane said.

"All right, you were standing over there. Now you reached

down in your pocket and took out some money and paid the cab?"

"That's right."

"How much was the amount of the bill?"

Clane suddenly realized the trap into which he had been led. Inspector Malloy would subsequently check up on the exact distance from a point within two or three blocks of his apartment to this warehouse. Clane, having recently arrived from the Orient, being unfamiliar with present taxicab rates and not knowing the distance, would be certain to blunder in case he had not come in a taxicab.

Clane's mind raced to meet the situation. He answered Malloy's question with no apparent hesitancy. "I don't know, Inspector. I gave the man a bill and told him to keep the change."

"A bill?"

"That's right."

"What kind of a bill? Dollar bill? Two-dollar bill? Five-dollar bill?"

"A two-dollar bill."

"Well, well, well, well," Inspector Malloy said. "That's generous of you. The fare probably wouldn't have been that much."

"I didn't think it would be, but didn't know."

"You didn't look at the meter?"

"No, I didn't. I was thinking about something else and just got out and handed the man a two-dollar bill."

"Well, now, that's a point, Mr. Clane. You see now why I told you that no detail was too small. We might have had some trouble finding the cab driver who drove you down here. But the way you handed him a two-dollar bill and told him to keep the change, we shouldn't have any difficulty. Lots of people consider two-dollar bills bad luck, you know. A cabby wouldn't refuse to take it, but he'd change it into something else first chance he had. That's a break for us, Mr. Clane. A two-dollar bill, and told him to keep the change. That shows how it is in this game. You just can't overlook anything, no matter how small it is. You see what you've done? You've given us an excellent means of finding that cab driver. That'll

THE CASE OF THE BACKWARD MULE

be a break for you because he'll substantiate your story. Now you gave him a two-dollar bill and told him to be on his way?"

"That's right."

"Now why did you come here in the first place?"

"Because Mr. Gloster asked me to meet him here."

"Asked you to meet him here? Now that's strange. Rather a peculiar place for an appointment, isn't it?"

"I thought it was after I arrived."

"That's right. The lights weren't on, you said?"

"No, they weren't on."

"District was all dark?"

"Yes."

"And you were certain Gloster had told you to meet him here?"

"That was the address he had given me."

"And how did he ask you?"

"Over the telephone."

"Over the telephone. Know what time that call came in?"

"No, I don't. It was some time after eleven."

"About how long before you got here?"

"Oh, within say twenty minutes."

"Within twenty minutes. Now where was he telephoning from?"

"He didn't say."

"But you assumed he was telephoning from here?"

"Well, I didn't know. He had told me to meet him here and I told him I would."

"Quite friendly with him, were you?"

"No, I was not friendly with him."

"Not hostile to him, were you? Surely you didn't have anything against the man?"

"No."

"Just more or less indifferent?"

"More or less."

"Well, which is it? More? Or less?"

Clane laughed and said. "It's neither. I was just indifferent to the man."

"But you knew him?"

"Yes, I knew him."

"And you'd got off the boat from China this afternoon, I believe?"

"That's right."

"And then had a session with the police. That was unfortunate. I'm sorry about that. Do you know the first thing I said when I heard that they'd grabbed you at the dock and taken you up for questioning? I said, 'That's too bad. That really is. Here's Mr. Clane just arrived from China. He's been away from this country for a long time and there are people he wants to see and . . . well, it's just too bad, that's all.' "

Clane waited, knowing that Malloy would give him no respite from the flow of seemingly innocent questions which were, nevertheless, designed to trap Clane into such a position that the incongruity of his statements would soon become apparent.

Knowing Inspector Malloy's technique from previous experience, Clane sought to take advantage of every second's lull in the conversation to think ahead.

"So you got off here and found that this man Gloster wasn't here and paid off the cab."

"That's right."

"Didn't the cab driver ask if you wanted him to wait?"

"Yes."

"And you told him no?"

"That's right."

"You're a brave man, Mr. Clane. But then I suppose you've been in lots of tough places in your life, and a dark section of a big city doesn't hold any particular terrors for you. But as you so aptly pointed out, a person would have to walk perhaps for a mile or two in order to find any telephone down here, and it's pretty dark and deserted. Not the sort of district you'd pick out for an evening stroll, is it?"

"No."

"And yet, despite the facts that you had an appointment with Gloster, that Gloster apparently wasn't here to keep that appointment, that twenty minutes had elapsed from the time Gloster had telephoned you and he still wasn't here, and the building was dark, and the district seemed to be deserted, you let the cab driver go?"

"That's right. You see, I felt certain Mr. Gloster would be here."

"You knew he was a man of his word, eh?"

"I thought he'd be."

"A great deal of confidence to have in a man you hardly knew. I believe you said you hardly knew him?"

"I knew him. I wasn't particularly friendly, but I wasn't unfriendly. I just knew him."

"Just a matter of indifference, I take it."

"That's right."

"We've been all over that before, haven't we? Ha, ha. We keep going around in circles. Well, let's get away from that circle. Now did you notice this automobile parked over here when you drove up?"

"I did."

"Did it occur to you that that might be Gloster's automobile?"

"I didn't think very much about it one way or the other."

"Well, it's his automobile."

"Yes, I assume now that it must have been. Unless Gloster came here by cab."

"That's right. That's Gloster's automobile. It was parked there, right in that same position when you arrived?"

"Yes."

"Well, that's fine. Then we know that Gloster must have been here and lying dead in that office while you were out here paying off the cab driver. Giving him a two-dollar bill and telling him to keep the change. That's right, isn't it, Mr. Clane?"

"That's right."

"Well, then we may assume that the cab bill was less than two dollars. Probably less than a dollar seventy-five. If it had been more than a dollar seventy-five, the cab driver would have told you about it. He'd have wanted more than a two-bit tip. Well, perhaps more than a dollar and eighty cents. So we'll assume that from the place you came to this place the bill was less than a dollar and eighty cents, and you let the cab driver go. All right, we're that far. Now you watched the cab drive away, didn't you?"

"No, I didn't."

"You didn't?"

"No. I started right for the door of the Eastern Art Import and Trading Company here."

"Started right for the door?"

"That's right."

"Despite the fact that the building was dark and the man you expected to meet apparently wasn't here, you started for the door?"

"That's right."

"Well, now isn't that a bit unusual, Mr. Clane, for a person to try to enter a dark building where apparently no one . . ."

"I didn't say I tried to enter the building."

"But you did enter it, didn't you?"

"Yes."

"Then do you want me to understand that you entered it without trying? Ha, ha, ha! That's rather illogical, Mr. Clane."

"Perhaps," Clane said, "you'd better let me go ahead and give it to you in narrative form the way it happened."

"Oh, we're doing very well by this question-and-answer method. It enables me to keep right on the subject. But let's see now. You walked toward the entrance of the building, but you didn't intend to enter. Is that right?"

"I intended to stand in the doorway of the building, waiting for Mr. Gloster. There was no particular reason to remain standing here in the middle of the street."

"Well, that's right. It's not the middle of the street. It's pretty much to one side of it, but I can see your point. You went over intending perhaps to sit down on the doorstep there?"

"That's right."

"Well, looking at it that way, that's perfectly logical, Mr. Clane. So you went over and sat down on the doorstep?"

"No, I didn't."

"You didn't?"

"No."

"But I thought you told me that's what you intended to do?"

"It is."

"Then something changed your mind. You must have seen

something. You must have noticed something a little out of the ordinary."

"That's right."

"What was it?"

"When I got over here, I saw that the door was partially open."

"Well, now that's something, Mr. Clane. That's a very fine point, a very fine point indeed. The door was partially open. You see how we're getting things just by having you go over every detail of what happened. That door being partially open may be quite a clue. You're sure the door was partially open?"

"That's right."

"So you walked right in?"

"No," Clane said, "I called first."

"You called. What did you call?"

"I said, 'Oh, Gloster!' "

"And got no answer, I take it?"

"That's right."

"So then you walked right in in the dark."

"No," Clane said, "I didn't. I had a little flashlight in my pocket."

"A little flashlight," Malloy said. "Well now, that's something. You really go prepared, Mr. Clane. You really do. When you go to call on a person, you take a flashlight with you."

Clane said, somewhat angrily, "It's not an unreasonable precaution. When I was in the Orient, I never went out without . . ."

"That's it. That's it," Malloy said, his voice showing relief. "I'd forgotten about your being in the Orient. Of course, that explains it. Here a person ordinarily wouldn't take a flashlight in going to pay a sociable visit. But you've been in the Orient. Streets are narrow and dark, and . . . why, certainly, that accounts for it. You'll pardon me, Mr. Clane. Go right ahead. You had a little flashlight so you took the flashlight out and walked into the office . . ."

"No," Clane said. "Remember I told you about the light switch. I took the flashlight out and stepped inside the door and looked around for a light switch. I found the light switch right there by the door. Apparently it's a master switch that turns on all the lights in the building."

"Of *course*," Malloy said, his voice indicating that he was disgusted with himself. "I remember you told me you turned on the lights. You used your flashlight to look for a light switch, and then you found the light switch and turned on all the lights and then you put the flashlight back in your pocket."

"That's right."

"And oh, by the way, you were alone, Mr. Clane? I didn't ask you specifically about that, but I gather you were alone."

"If there had been anyone in the taxicab with me, I'd have told you," Clane said.

"I'm satisfied you would. I'm satisfied you would. But you know the way things are, Mr. Clane. I'm just an inspector and I'm supposed to make a report, and I'm supposed to cover *everything* in that report—absolutely *everything*. Now go right ahead. You were in the building here all alone. The lights had snapped on and you could see the entire warehouse and that door over there to the office? Now let's just go stand right in the position where you were when you turned the lights on. All right. You were standing right here. Now you put the flashlight back in your pocket, I take it. There was no need for having a flashlight after the lights came on."

"That's right."

"Then you put the flashlight back in your pocket and stood there with the lights on. Now how about this door into the office here? Was that open?"

"It was slightly open."

"So you walked right in."

"I paused and called out Gloster's name."

"I see. And then you pushed the door open."

"That's right."

"And what was the first thing you saw?"

"I don't know. I just saw the room generally."

"You didn't see the body right away?"

"Not right away. No."

"Now did it occur to you, Mr. Clane, that you'd gone rather far? That you'd gone to a perfectly strange place, one

82

in which you had no interest, had turned on the lights, and entered the place?"

"Not right at the time," Clane said. "One step sort of led to another rather naturally."

"I see. But later on it occurred to you that your actions were . . . well, shall we say, just a bit unusual?"

"Not unusual, I would say. But the culminating effect of those actions was, of course, to leave me standing in this room."

"Exactly. And you put that rather cleverly, Mr. Clane. Rather unusual for a man who was meeting a man who wasn't even a friend, a man to whom he was more or less indifferent. You just walked right in, didn't you?"

"Well, when I saw the open door, I stepped inside. And then I looked for a light switch and then I saw the light switch and saw this other open door, and stepped in here."

"Yes, I can see when you put it that way that one thing sort of led to another. Now go ahead, Mr. Clane. You saw the body."

"That's right."

"And what was the first thing you said when you saw the body, Mr. Clane?"

"Why I didn't say anything."

Malloy looked at him in surprise. "You didn't *say* anything, Mr. Clane?"

"Nothing."

"Why, why not? Didn't it impress you as being unusual to find a body lying here?"

"Naturally."

"And yet you didn't mention it, didn't say a word?"

"To whom would I have addressed the remark?" Clane asked.

Inspector Malloy slapped his thigh with his palm. "Of *course,*" he said, "you were alone. I'd overlooked that for a minute. Wasn't anyone with you? A woman perhaps?"

"I think we've already gone over that."

"So we have, so we have. But I just wanted to be certain. That's right. You didn't say anything because there wasn't anyone with you to say it to. You're not the type of person who would be apt to go around talking to yourself. So you saw the body, and then what did you do?"

"Well, I stepped back out of the room and started to switch the lights off. Then I realized that I would have to notify the police and that I was in a very peculiar position when it came to notifying the police. I hardly wished to go out looking for a telephone."

"Of course you knew you shouldn't touch anything, Mr. Clane."

"Of course. I understood that as a general proposition," Clane said. "But I also knew that I would be supposed to notify the police *immediately* of finding the body of a murdered man this way, and I didn't want to leave the place."

"Well, I can see your point. There's a good deal to that. Yes, I can see the point. You felt that there might be quite a delay in getting to a telephone."

"And," Clane went on dryly, "in case there should be a watchman around I didn't want to be placed in the position of having someone seeing me switch out the lights and leave a building in which there was the body of a freshly murdered man."

"A *freshly* murdered man? Then you thought the shooting had just been done, Mr. Clane?"

"I didn't know. I assumed that it might have been."

"Well, yes, I can see your point. Yes, it might have been very embarrassing if someone had seen you leaving the building and then before you got to a telephone a discovery had been made and people would have said, 'That Mr. Clane now, he must have been the last man to see Gloster alive.' Yes, yes, I can see your point. Very embarrassing position for you to be put in, Mr. Clane. So you went right over to the telephone and called the police."

"That's right."

"And asked for Homicide?"

"Yes."

"Well, now that seems to cover the situation. By the way, did you notice this cot over here that has the blankets on it and the canned goods? And the wastebasket with the empty cans? You must have if you were prowling around enough to have noticed a bullet."

"I wasn't prowling around," Clane said.

"But you did notice the bullet?"

"Yes."

"That's rather a small object."

"It had plowed up a fresh sliver there in the woodwork. Naturally I noticed it. It was right by the telephone."

"That's right, that's right," Malloy said apologetically. "I'd forgotten about that, Mr. Clane. You'll pardon me for what I said about prowling around. Of course, you went over to use the telephone and naturally noticed that fresh sliver there. Of course you would, I should have realized that. It's natural that you would have noticed it. But let's get back to this cot and the canned goods and the cooking utensils. You noticed those?"

"Yes."

"Yes, naturally you would have. A man who is trained to notice details like a bullet certainly would have noticed a whole stack of canned goods. I was just wasting your time and mine asking the question. Now what impression did that make on you, Mr. Clane?"

Clane said, "I assumed that someone had been living here."

"Someone. Now did you have any idea who that someone might have been?"

"No."

"Well now, you know it's a very peculiar thing, Mr. Clane, but here's Edward Harold, who murdered one of the members of this here Chinese art company, and he's just as apt as not to have taken some keys from the body of the man he murdered. Keys, let us say, which would fit the warehouse. Did that ever occur to you?"

"No."

"And, of course, the way we've been watching things—the hotels and rooming houses and apartment houses—and getting reports from any new transient that showed up, it almost stands to reason that this man Harold had to be hiding somewhere in a place just about like this, doesn't it?"

Clane said, "I'm afraid, Inspector, that the ideas of an amateur would be of no value to you on a case of this kind.

It's rather late and I'd like to tell you what I saw and then get back to bed. I've had a strenuous day. I don't feel very much like speculating on what might or might not have happened."

"Yes, yes, of course," Inspector Malloy said. "I understand exactly how you feel, Mr. Clane, but what I'm trying to get at is whether perhaps the thought didn't flash through your mind that this man Harold had been hiding here?"

"I see nothing to indicate to me that the man who was living here was Edward Harold. After all, Inspector, you must remember that I don't know Edward Harold. I've never met him."

"You haven't?"

"No."

"Well, well, well, that's a new angle. That's something I hadn't considered. Interesting too, the way you get around. You arrive here from China and the first thing you know you're all mixed up in this murder case. Well, well, let's see. You want to get home and I'll just ask you a few more routine questions. Now you're certain that you didn't know that Harold was here when you came to call and you didn't come to call on Harold instead of this man Gloster?"

"I have told you," Clane said with dignity, "that Gloster telephoned to me. He was the one who suggested that I meet him at this address."

"That's right, that's right. And you're certain you came alone?"

"Yes."

"There wasn't a woman in that taxicab with you?"

"Absolutely not."

"Well now, that's strange, that is indeed. You didn't carry anything with you that belonged to a woman, did you?"

"Certainly not."

Malloy suddenly turned to one of the men and said, "Let me have the bag."

The man handed him a woman's black handbag.

One look at it and Clane realized that it was Cynthia Renton's handbag. The purse she had been carrying with her that evening.

"Now here's a handbag or purse, whichever you want to call

it," Inspector Malloy went on, "that seems to have been brought here by a woman. The driving license in there is in the name of Cynthia Renton and there's twenty-five hundred dollars in twenty-dollar bills. You wouldn't know anything about that, would you?"

Clane shook his head.

"You didn't bring it with you?"

Again Clane shook his head.

"About what time would you say that you arrived here?" Malloy asked.

Clane looked at his watch. "Well, let's see. I would say that I arrived here—oh, around midnight. Perhaps four or five minutes before twelve."

"That's your best guess?"

"Yes."

"And you didn't see anything of a woman here?"

"No."

"Now you know this Cynthia Renton?"

"Yes."

"Quite well?"

"Yes."

"A very close friend of yours?"

"Yes."

"You were going with her? You were pretty much wrapped up in her when you were here last, weren't you?"

"Yes."

"And you're quite certain she wasn't here visiting this Edward Harold and she asked you to come and see her and she was the one who telephoned and not George Gloster?"

"I've answered that several times."

"I know you have, Mr. Clane, and you'll pardon me for asking it again, but I want to be absolutely sure that there couldn't have been any mistake. It was Gloster who telephoned you?"

"Yes."

"And you know Gloster?"

"Yes."

"You talked with him?"

"Yes."

"When was the last time you saw him before the murder?"

"Earlier this evening."

"Earlier this *evening?* Well, well, well! Now isn't *that* something? It just goes to show what happens when we bring out all these little details. Now what was the occasion of meeting him that time, Mr. Clane?"

"I had an appointment with Mr. Gloster, Stacey Nevis and a man by the name of Ricardo Taonon. Taonon didn't show up. I met the other two."

"Indeed, and why did you meet them?"

"I had a business matter to discuss with them."

"Now aren't those the men who are the partners in this here Oriental art company?"

"You mean the Eastern Art Import and Trading Company?"

"That's it. I'm always getting these business names mixed up. My memory isn't as good as it once was. But aren't those the men who are partners in that company?"

"I believe so, yes."

"And you wanted to see them?"

"Yes."

"You had an appointment with them?"

"Yes."

"And you saw this man Gloster and Nevis?"

"Yes."

"Where?"

"At the office of Stacey Nevis."

"And you talked with these men?"

"Yes."

"For about how long?"

"Oh, ten or fifteen minutes."

"Well, now, isn't that interesting? And then the next rattle out of the box Mr. Gloster telephoned you at some unusual hour of the night. What time would you say it was?"

"Oh, about eleven—perhaps ten minutes past."

"And Gloster asked you to come down here?"

"Yes."

"And you came right away?"

"Not right away," Clane said, sensing the trap. "I told him

that I would be down shortly, and I dressed. I was lounging around in a dressing gown and pajamas."

"I see, I see. You told him you'd be down. You didn't tell him just how soon?"

"No."

"You told him perhaps right away?"

"I may have given him that impression," Clane said, aware of the fact it was quite possible the police had had his line tapped and knew all about that conversation.

"But you *didn't* get here right away."

"No."

"You say you got here around twelve?"

"Yes."

"And you found a cruising taxicab very shortly after you'd left your place?"

"Yes."

"And came here right away in it?"

"Yes."

Inspector Malloy abruptly pushed out his hand, grabbed Clane's hand once more in a bone-crushing grip and pumped his arm up and down. "Thank you ever so much, Mr. Clane. Thank you very much indeed. You've been a real help, you really have. You have no idea how much help you've given me. I don't think you fully appreciate how much you've helped me out. And I won't detain you any longer. I know you're sleepy, I know you've had a hard day. Freddy, will you take Mr. Clane home? Drive him right to his apartment. He'll give you the address and you drive him there *by the shortest route*. Get him home just as soon as you can. And good night, Mr. Clane. That is, good morning. I hope you sleep tight."

"Thank you," Clane said.

Inspector Malloy started back for the warehouse. Freddy took Clane's arm, and with official thoroughness piloted him over toward the police car.

At the door of the warehouse Inspector Malloy called out as though it had been only an afterthought, "By the way, Freddy, take a look at the trip mileage, will you? Find out just exactly how far it is from here to Mr. Clane's apartment down to a tenth of a mile, and drive slowly, don't use the siren, keep within the legal limits. Drive just about the way you would if you were a taxi driver, and make a note of just how far it is and just how long it takes you to drive it. Good night, Mr. Clane—that is, good morning, and thank you very, very much."

# 11

TERRY CLANE, trying the bathroom door the next morning, found it locked. And then to his surprise, a feminine voice called out cheerfully, "Just a moment."

Before Clane had entirely recovered from the effect of that shock, he heard the bolt turn on the inside and Cynthia Renton, wearing a pair of his pajamas and carrying a toothbrush in her hand, smiled cheerfully at him, said, "Good morning," and walked on past as casually as though she had been sharing his apartment for untold years.

"Hey!" Clane called. "What's the big idea?"

She paused, looked back over her shoulder with surprise. She said, "I'm indebted to you for one toothbrush. Lucky for me that you were just moving in and Yat T'oy had bought all new supplies. He found a toothbrush for me without any trouble."

"How long have *you* been here?" Clane asked.

Her eyes widened. "Why, ever since last night."

"What time last night?"

"I came here when you were waiting for the police at the warehouse."

"I don't get it," Clane said.

She said, "Well, go in and take your shower and we'll discuss it over breakfast," and she went slipslopping away down the corridor in a pair of Terry Clane's slippers which were several sizes too large.

Irritated, Clane summoned Yat T'oy.

Yat T'oy's explanation was ready and his face was as bland as the surface of a lake on a calm evening. "Missy say she come spend night. I think you send."

Clane said angrily, "When it comes to certain people, you seem to take a great deal for granted."

"No savvy," Yat T'oy said, his face not changing expression by so much as a flicker of a muscle, but his eyes twinkling with hidden amusement.

Clane pushed his way into the bathroom and pulled the door shut behind him.

Cynthia was bubbling with good humor at breakfast. "Dear, dear, Owl, don't tell me that you had a woman spending the night with you and didn't know it! And for heaven's sake, don't try to tell that to the police."

"The police," Clane said, "will probably tell it to me. Suppose you answer a few questions."

Her innocence was wide-eyed, her manner demure. "Why, certainly, Terry. Anything you ask."

"Just how did you get in here?"

"Why, I walked in."

"I know. But just what caused you to honor me?"

"Well," she said, "I was out there in the warehouse when you discovered the body and called to me, and I had previously put my purse down on the edge of a packing case. I left it there when I joined you in the doorway of the office and ... well, what I saw in there just completely took my mind off it until after I had got in my car and driven away. And then I didn't dare to go back. I knew that you'd called the police. I felt there was a good chance you might find my purse and hide it."

Clane said, "I didn't even see it. I went outside and waited for the police."

"Well," she said, "there I was. I had a five-dollar bill in the top of my stocking for mad money and that was all. Everything else was in the purse."

"Including a big wad of money?" Clane asked.

"Oh sure. You know how it is. I thought I might be sort of on the dodge for a while. Or how do they say it in the underworld, Owl? I guess it's *on the lam*—that's what I mean. If I'm going to be a fugitive from justice, I *must* brush up on my underworld slang."

"So you'd drawn all this money out of the bank?"

"Some out of the bank, some out of an emergency fund that I keep in my safe for things I might need in a hurry."

"So what did you do?"

"I came to see you, Owl. I wanted to borrow some money. I was in a spot. Well, I left the car I was driving in the private garage where I'd been keeping it. You may have noticed that it's not my car. It belongs to a friend who loaned it to me.

"I took a cab and came here. Yat T'oy let me in. I waited for you, but while I was waiting, Yat T'oy scouted around to see that the coast was clear. Well, Owl, it wasn't.

"After I arrived and before you came home, a whole flock of plain-clothes men came driving up. I guess the only word for it is 'debouched.' Anyhow, they scattered all around the neighborhood so they could keep a watch on this flat. And there I was.

"Yat T'oy reported to me and we decided we'd better sleep on it."

"They'll search this place then."

"They have already. As soon as Yat T'oy told me about them I felt certain they'd make some excuse, so I went out to the back service porch and hid in the broom closet. Sure enough, a man came up with the janitor to inspect a leak in the gas pipes. They prowled all around and then left. Yat T'oy came and got me—and here I am."

"How long do you think you can get away with this—staying here?"

"I don't know. I do know that I can't leave. I'm trapped here. Honest, Owl, I didn't plan it that way. I just wanted a loan and to talk with you and see if you'd found my purse or if the police had. And then after I got here, the police—how is it we say it in the underworld?—oh yes, they 'sewed the place up.' "

"It's a mess," Clane said.

"I know. But it's nice, isn't it, Owl?"

"What?"

"Being a fugitive from justice this way. It's sort of a battle, matching your wits with the police."

Clane said, "Snap out of it, Cynthia. You can't kid your way out of this mess."

92

"Sometimes," she said, "I think you're right. But at least I can try and it's lots of fun trying."

"Back of that mask of facetious indifference," Clane said, "you're frightened. You know it and I know it. Why keep up the pretense? Why not give me the low-down?"

"I guess I'm keeping your morale up," she said airily. "But you can see how nice it is, Terry. The police are looking for me all over the city. I haven't any money and they have my purse and driving license. Damn them, they even have my lipstick. And that hurts. You don't realize what it means to be a woman and have no pockets, only a purse. And then lose that purse. Tell me, Owl, were you ever alone on the cold streets of a hostile city with the police looking for you and the fog making your nose run and you didn't have a handkerchief?"

Clane grinned. "You make it sound inviting. What are your plans?"

"Why, I'm going to stay with you for a while, of course. The police have got everything else sewed up and this is the only place left."

"They'll find you here."

"I don't think so. They're going to keep a watch on your apartment night and day from now on. They'll know everyone who comes and goes. But it won't ever occur to them that I got here first. Particularly after that inspection of the gas leak."

She nodded with a self-satisfied little smile, said, "You know, Owl, we *must* practice talking out of the sides of our mouths. If we're going to be outlaws, we want to look the part. Heavens, you can't tell. They might want us for the movies some day; and if you talked out of the front of your mouth, people would think you couldn't have amounted to much after all. I mean as a criminal, you know."

"Well," Clane said, sighing, "I guess you've made a criminal of me all right. One thing's certain—Inspector Malloy never will believe your story about how you happened to get here."

"Tell him to make up one of his own," Cynthia said.

Clane raised his eyebrows.

"Let him do the explaining for a change," she said. "He's

the one who had his man frisk the apartment and decided there was no one in it. Then he put men out to watch everyone who came and went. If he thinks he's so damn smart, let *him* tell *you* how I got in here."

"It's an idea," Clane said. "But unfortunately the talking will have to be done in front of a jury."

"Not unless they catch you, Owl."

Clane sighed, knowing that when Cynthia had one of her irresponsible streaks there was very little that a man could do about it.

"All right," Clane said. "Let's begin at the beginning. I want to know exactly how Edward Harold escaped and who rigged it up for him; what your part in it was, how you happened to hide him down there in that warehouse."

"But, Owl, I didn't."

Clane settled back in his chair, tapped a cigarette on the edge of his thumb nail. "Want one?"

"Not now, thanks."

"Did you engineer the escape, Cynthia?"

"No. I didn't."

"Didn't what?" Clane asked.

"Didn't anything."

"You mean you didn't engineer the escape?"

"No."

"You didn't hide him down in that warehouse?"

"No."

"How did you know where he was then?"

"Owl, I wish you wouldn't shoot questions at me like that."

"Why?"

"Because you sound sort of official and . . . I don't know. It makes me want to lie to you."

"Why?"

"I've always been that way. I want to tell people what I want to tell them and when I want to tell it to them. And when people start shooting questions at me, it makes me just . . . well, I feel they're opening the door and walking in without knocking. And I hide."

"Behind lies?"

"I suppose so if you want to put it that way."

94

"Lying," he said, "is negative."

"Not the way I do it, Owl. It's artistic. It's wonderful. I don't just tell a lie and then wait and get caught. But I tell a lie and I embellish it into a beautiful story; and when I get done with it, it's so much more beautiful than the truth that I'm darned if I don't sometimes believe it myself."

Clane said, "Keep playing around with that philosophy and the police are going to nab you."

"I suppose so. I guess they're going to nab me anyway. You have to admit I'm giving them a merry chase."

"Are you going to tell me or am I going to ask you questions?"

"If you ask me questions, I'll lie."

"Do you want to tell me?"

"Yes. If you aren't so darned eager about it. You look as though you are ready to grab the words before they even hit the roof of my mouth."

Clane settled back and watched the smoke eddying upward from the cigarette. There was a long interval of silence.

Cynthia sighed. "The first thing I knew of his escape, Owl, was when I heard it over the radio."

"So what did you do?" Clane asked, not looking at her but keeping his eyes on the cigarette smoke and making his tone sound casual.

"I didn't want the police to find him. And I thought the police would start looking for me, thinking I might be mixed up in it; and if they could find me right away and find I didn't know anything about where he was and hadn't been mixed up in it, that would . . . well, don't you see? That would narrow their circle. I thought that if I could be sort of a decoy and start out running, then whatever time it took the police to catch me would be that much time gained."

Clane merely nodded, didn't even glance at her.

"So," she said, "I spent the night with a girl friend. I drew some money out of the bank as soon as it opened and went places. I tried to fix it so the police couldn't find me, and then when they did, they couldn't prove a single darn thing on me. I was upset and just wanted to get away from everything. I thought of the amnesia racket for a while and then decided that

I couldn't get away with that. I thought I could do better by pulling the old stuff about something snapping inside my brain."

"That's a pretty tough alibi to put across with the police," Clane said.

"Don't kid yourself. Women kill their husbands every day and stand up in front of a jury and tearfully tell them about how something snapped in their brains. And doctors get on the stand and give it some scientific name with a lot of Latin embellishments, and the jury go out, and that's all there is to it. If you can kill a husband because of something snapping in your brain, why shouldn't I be able to just go out and wander around?"

"Suppose the police aren't as easily influenced as the jury?"

"Then I was going to look them right straight in the eyes and tell them, so what? I decided to go out and wander around the country. I didn't see Edward, I didn't know where he was, and there's certainly nothing you can do to a citizen for just getting out and wandering around."

"Then how did you know he . . . ?"

"No, don't, Owl," she interrupted. "I'll lie to you just as sure as shooting."

Clane grinned. "If you have any good lie, you can trot it right out. It might be a good plan to sort of warm it up and get it ready for action, because you may have to be using it soon."

"The police?"

"Yes."

"I think I'd rather tell the truth instead."

"That suits me."

She was silent for a moment. Then, as though having reached a decision, she spoke swiftly, trying to get the words out before she might change her mind. "You know, Owl, I have been doing a little commercial painting lately. Not the sort of stuff that Alma would approve of. It was commercial, pot-boiling, mail-order stuff, and I didn't want to do it under my name. So I took the name of Vera Windsor. It was sort of a pen name and I needed an address for it; so I got a post-office box. No one knew anything at all about Vera Windsor's being Cynthia Renton. Alma didn't know it."

"Edward Harold know it?"

"Yes."

"And he got in touch with you that way?"

"Yes. I went over to the post-office box and sure enough, yesterday afternoon there was a postcard giving me the address of the warehouse of the Eastern Art Import and Trading Company. Nothing else on it, just the printed address."

"What did you do with the card?" he asked. "You didn't leave it in your purse, did you?"

"No, I put it right back in the post-office box. I felt that it might be dangerous evidence and I wasn't at all certain but that at any moment some detective might step out and tap me on the shoulder. And then I knew they'd search me. But I felt they'd never dare to go in and search a post-office box; so I just read the card and dropped it right back in the box and left it there."

"You knew it was from Harold?"

"Yes."

"And there was just that address on it and that's all?"

"Yes."

"So what did you do?"

"So I knew you were coming in on the boat and I wanted to ask you what to do. I didn't know whether I dared to see him or what to do. And I wasn't at all certain that I wasn't being shadowed. So I went down to the boat and I saw them nab you. And then I was pretty much in a pickle. So I came back and waited around."

"Why didn't you tell me right away?"

"I had to sort of sound you out first to . . . Oh, I don't know, Owl. I'm just not built that way. I can't throw myself wide open without any preliminaries. I care so much for you that it hurts. But even you can't open the door and walk right in."

"But you intended to tell me?"

"Yes. I was stalling around. I wanted to find out how important your errand was and—well, I wanted to suggest that you go down there and see Edward with me."

"You don't think he'd have liked that, do you?"

"I don't know. I . . . I . . . I *don't* know, Owl."

"But why did you want me with you?"

"I don't even know that."

"You knew it was dangerous to see him?"

"Yes."

"You knew he was in love with you and wanted to see you alone?"

"I suppose so."

"But you wanted to drag me along?"

"Yes."

"Why didn't you tell me? Not right away, but after we had been talking a while?"

"I don't know, Owl. It was sort of delicate. I thought you might not like to go and I felt that Edward might not like to have you there and—but *I* wanted you there. And if you ask me why, all I can tell you is, I don't know, and if you keep on asking me why, I'll tell you one of the most marvelous hand-embroidered lies you ever heard in your life."

Clane ground out the end of his cigarette. "I still don't get it."

"Neither do I."

"You must have had some reason, something in the back of your mind."

"Well, I'll tell you what it may have been, Owl. I have always wondered about Edward and whether . . . well, I think perhaps I wanted to find out just how far things were going to go. I . . . Owl, stop it, you're making me lie to you and I don't like it."

"And that was a lie?"

"That was the beginnings of a peach of a lie," she said, "a gee-whillikens of a lie. I was making it up as I went along, but I was just a paragraph or two ahead and it sounded fine to me. What was coming would have really been a razzle-dazzle. Stop asking me questions about it."

"If you didn't arrange for Harold's escape, then who did?"

"It must have been Bill Hendrum. I can't think of anyone

98

else. Hendrum is just the type who would have gone through with it."

"But you don't *know* it was Hendrum?"

"No, I'm just guessing."

"Tell me something about Hendrum."

"He's a big, tall, raw-boned chap, reckless as they come. It would be just like him to do something like that."

"But you haven't talked with him about it?"

"No."

"Have you had *any* communication with him?"

"No."

"Why?"

"Hendrum was the last man in the world I would have tried to talk to. You see I didn't *want* to know. I didn't want to have any knowledge that would be dangerous. And then, of course, I knew that the police would be keeping an eye on me, so I thought I'd just run around in circles and—well, you know, that would be a help."

"And then you dropped your purse."

"And then I dropped the purse," she said bitterly.

Terry Clane thought things over.

"Well?" she asked after a few moments.

"I think," Clane said, "we have to find out about Hendrum."

"Why?"

Clane said, "I'm not certain but that this escape plays into the hands of the police rather than otherwise. Of course, the police are irritated at the ease with which it was accomplished. At least they pretend they are."

"But you think it may be some sort of a police trap?"

"No, not that. But the point is that Harold is playing right into the hands of the police now."

"What do you think he should do?"

Clane said instantly, "I think he should surrender himself into custody, then go ahead with his appeal."

"It would be pretty difficult to convince him."

"But I think we have to do just that—difficult or not."

"Well," she said, "in order to do that, we've got to find him and we've got to talk to him. That isn't the sort of thing you can do without personal contact—you know, you couldn't just put an ad in the personal column of the paper, and say, 'Dear Ed—Terry C. thinks you should go to nearest police station and surrender.' "

Clane poured Cynthia another cup of coffee, filled his own cup, said, "There's one way you could bring him out into the open."

"How?"

"Let the police catch you and charge you with aiding and abetting in his escape. Then he'd come forward."

"I don't like that way, Owl."

"I don't either."

"Any other suggestions?"

Clane said, "I think we should talk with this man Hendrum. If you'll give me his address, I'll get in touch with him."

"And what do I do in the meantime?"

Clane said, with emphasis, "There are only two things that you can do. One of them is to stay here without even going near a window, keeping yourself absolutely out of sight."

"And what's the other thing?"

"You can try to be smart and pull something and get your picture in the paper."

Cynthia said, "You do think of the most wonderful things, Owl." Then she started to hum, "Oh, what a beautiful morning, oh, what a beautiful day."

Clane took a pencil from his pocket and on the tablecloth traced a circle about the size of a half-dollar. Within that he placed a circle the size of a dime, and within that second circle a dot.

Cynthia gave him her undivided attention, watching him as he put the pencil away, then watched his eyes come to a focus on that dot in the center of the tablecloth.

For some six or seven seconds Clane sat absolutely motionless; then he took a long breath, pulled the cigarette case from his pocket and opened it.

"I'll have one now, Owl," she said.

He handed her a cigarette, took one for himself, and snapped a match into flame with a quick motion of his thumb. When they were both smoking, Cynthia indicated the circles on the tablecloth. "Something new?" she asked.

"Just a device," he said, "to assist the mind to bring itself to a sharp focus."

"What did you think out, Owl?"

Clane said positively, "You can't stay here. Sooner or later the police are going to be looking for you here."

"But I can't leave, Owl. They're watching the place. They'd nab me as soon as I left."

"They're watching the place," Clane conceded. "That doesn't mean you can't leave. It means we must take precautions so that when you do leave you aren't picked up."

"But how can you do that?"

Clane walked over to the telephone, dialed Chinatown exchange and spoke to the operator in Chinese. Shortly afterwards he heard the voice of Sou Ha on the line.

"Hello, Embroidered Halo," he said, translating her name into English and thus letting her know who was at the other end of the line.

"Hello yourself. Did you sleep last night?"

Clane went at once into Chinese. "My sleep was filled with dreams of you," he said, and then added abruptly, "Sou Ha, I have one mouth; there are many ears."

"Speak, then, for one ear alone."

Clane said, "It would be a great favor to me if you and your father should come to visit me."

"When?"

"Any time. But I can hardly wait to see you."

"Are there any suggestions?"

"Dress warmly."

Sou Ha thought that over for a moment, then she said, "Your desires have been communicated. They will be obeyed. Is there anything else?"

"That," Clane said, "is all. Tell your father how much I regret having to inconvenience him."

"It will be a privilege," she said. "We will see you within four characters of the clock," and hung up.

Clane dropped the receiver into place, returned to the breakfast table.

Cynthia was watching him with speculative eyes. "I always get suspicious of you when you go into that Chinese stuff, Owl. Was that Sou Ha?"

"Yes."

"What did you ask her to do?"

"I asked her for her help and her father's."

Cynthia said abruptly, "I suppose you know, Terry, that she loves you?"

"Sou Ha loves me? Nonsense!"

Cynthia shook her head. "You are wise in the ways of the Orient, Terry, but you are but a man in the ways of a woman. I do not know the Orient, but as a woman I know women."

"Don't further complicate the situation," Clane said.

"It is not I who complicate it."

They were silent for a moment.

Abruptly Cynthia asked, "Owl, tell me again just what is the meaning of that figure on the back of a mule, the one that you gave me before you left for China, the one who rides the mule backwards?"

"It is the story of Chinese fatalism," Clane said. "Which in reality is not fatalism at all."

"Are the Chinese fatalists?"

"Not in the sense that we understand fatalism. They have a doctrine of nonresistance, which is something entirely different."

"Is Sou Ha coming here?" she asked abruptly.

"Yes."

"Alone?"

"No, with her father."

"How soon?"

"She said within four characters of the clock."

"Which means how much, Owl?"

"I have told you that before," he said.

"I've forgotten."

"Each character represents five minutes. Four characters is twenty minutes."

"Oh yes, I remember now. Tell me some more about the Chinese philosophy of nonresistance, Owl."

"Why do you want to know that now?"

THE CASE OF THE BACKWARD MULE

"Because you have brought Sou Ha into the picture and ... and I want to have you talking to me so I can listen."

"And think of some good lie?" Clane asked.

"Perhaps," she said, "that is the way a woman concentrates. In place of drawing circles and putting a dot inside, she ... Go ahead, Owl, tell me about the Chinese philosophy of nonresistance."

Terry said, "Chow Kok Koh, the little carved figure which I gave you, is an old man and a wise man. You need only to look at the lines on his face to see that he has lived a full, rich life. And he is happy. He is filled with a zest for life and for life's adventures."

"And he rides his mule backwards," Cynthia said. "Why does he do that, Owl?"

"Chow Kok Koh," Clane said, "believes that the various vicissitudes of life are but the tools with which the divine architect shapes one's character. He believes mortals are placed here on earth to develop character.

"Whether a man has good fortune or whether he has bad fortune is relatively unimportant. It is only his reaction to the good or the bad fortune that counts.

"A man who suffers adversity and reacts in the proper way to that adversity has developed his character in such a way that he has achieved a net asset, so that in the long run he has been fully as benefited as though he had good fortune. A man should not be swollen with pride at triumph, nor should he be despondent over defeat. He should cooperate with Destiny to strengthen his character by whatever experience life has to offer.

"And because Chow Kok Koh recognizes these things he rides his mule backwards, because he says it makes no difference where he is going. A destination in life is unimportant. It is only what one does along the way that counts."

Cynthia Renton thought that over. "I like it," she said at length. "It makes me feel sort of quiet and calm. Is there any more?"

"Lots more," Clane said. "Man, journeying along the road which cannot be traveled, the way which cannot be walked, must never regard wealth as his goal. Only as triumph or de-

103

feat affect his character, are they important. One who learns to be truly indifferent to wealth and fame has gone far toward becoming superior to failure.

"The Chinese recognize this principle. That is why position or wealth entitles a man to material comforts in China, but only the development of character entitles him to respect.

"We North Americans are too prone to judge a man by his wealth and social position. Yet with all the wealth and social position in the world a man may still have the character of a rotten egg. Many do. Such men have used wealth not as a step on the path, but as a destination.

"Chow Kok Koh knows better. Wealth and Poverty are but two forces by which character is shaped. If they are otherwise regarded, then the journey through life is a failure. So ride your mule backwards, pay no attention to the things that happen to you, pay attention only to your reaction to those things, the effect they have on your character. I have told you these things before," Clane concluded.

"I know," she admitted. "And at the time I was sort of riding the crest of the wave and I'm afraid it didn't register so much. I remembered some of it. I tried to tell Edward about it. He seemed terribly interested."

"Edward Harold?"

"Yes."

"Did you at any time let him have your figure, the little wooden image which I gave you?" Clane asked.

"What makes you ask that, Owl?"

"Never mind the reason back of the question. The question calls for an answer, and the answer is the important thing. Did you ever let him have the figure?"

"Yes."

"When?"

"Do I have to answer that?"

"I want you to."

"I'll lie."

"Don't do it, Cynthia. This is one thing you can't lie about. Look at me."

She met his eyes.

"Did you ever lend him the figure?"

"Yes."

"When?"

"The day . . ."

"Go on."

"The day Horace Farnsworth was murdered. That afternoon."

"How long did he have it?"

"Just that day. He brought it back the next day."

"Where is it now?"

"In my apartment."

"You're sure?"

"It should be."

Clane shook his head and said, "The police have it, Cynthia, and there are some spots of blood on it. They've been asking me questions about it."

Her exclamation of startled surprise was almost a gasp.

"What did you tell them?"

He smiled reassuringly at her. "Nothing."

## 12

IN EXACTLY eighteen minutes after Terry Clane had telephoned, the buzzer in the apartment rang.

Clane waved Yat T'oy aside and opened the door.

Chu Kee stood on the threshold, his face bland and expressionless. He was wearing a light topcoat, his hat and gloves in his left hand. He shook hands with Terry Clane, American fashion.

A step behind him, Sou Ha was bundled up in a fur coat with a high collar which reached above her ears. She wore a brimless hat with a red feather trailing out at a jaunty angle. The hat was bright blue and the feather of vivid, conspicuous crimson.

"How'm I doing, Terry?" she asked.

"That's fine," he told her.

"I had to do a little mind-reading over the telephone."

"You made a fine job of it. Come in."

Cynthia Renton dropped a little curtsy to Chu Kee, then went over to give Sou Ha her hand. Yat T'oy, his aged eyes sparkling with pride in his race, took their hats and coats, brought in pots of hot tea, little plates of dried melon seed, cigarettes and shavings of fresh coconut boiled in sugar, and thin crisp wafers made from rice flour; saw that cigarettes and ashtrays were in place, and then discreetly withdrew.

Clane got down to business at once. "Cynthia is wanted by the police," he said.

"For what reason?" asked Chu Kee.

"They aren't sure."

"Ignorance breeds uncertainty," Chu Kee remarked.

"The police," Clane explained, "are investigating."

"Only the lucky dare to hurry," Chu Kee observed, his graceful fingers picking up a dried melon seed.

"Don't beat around the bush, First-Born," Sou Ha said. "You want her out of here and the place is watched, isn't that right?"

Clane nodded.

Sou Ha said, "I thought that was it. I wore a coat with a collar that conceals most of my face. The natural target for the police gaze would be the blue hat with the conspicuous red feather."

"You mean I'm to dress in her clothes and go out?" Cynthia Renton asked.

Clane nodded.

"And then what?" Cynthia Renton asked.

Chu Kee spoke almost instantly, as though the speech had been rehearsed. "I am no longer young," he said. "Some day I shall join my ancestors. Perhaps it will be sooner than I think. I desire that I leave behind some likeness of myself. I wish a portrait painted. You are the portrait painter I have selected. Would it, perhaps, be possible for you to live in my humble dwelling for a time and paint the portrait which I desire?"

"Dark in tone," Sou Ha said eagerly. "A rather dark background and then my father's face illuminated so that it shows the expression of the eyes, the kindly lines about the mouth. You could make a wonderful portrait, Cynthia."

Chu Kee regarded her with resignation. "Oh, that I might but capture the wisdom of youth," he said.

Sou Ha abruptly became quiet.

Terry Clane said, "It would have to be a good job, Cynthia. You'd have to make it convincing. It should be pretty well finished by the time anyone finds you long enough to ask questions."

"But, Owl, I haven't anything with me. I haven't my paints. I've lost my purse. I haven't even lipstick."

"Things which can be bought will be provided," Chu Kee said.

"Paints, they are available, are they not?" Sou Ha asked. "Canvas may be purchased in the stores which deal in artists' supplies, and lipstick is in every drugstore."

"Wouldn't questions be asked about the *new* paints?" Cynthia inquired of Terry Clane.

Sou Ha said with dignity, "My father is a man of distinction. Paints that are used for his portrait must be used once and only once. It is unfitting that the paints which have been used to paint the portrait of my father should thereafter be used to paint the likeness of a man of less importance."

Chu Kee thought that over, then slowly nodded in grave approval. "There are times," he said, "when one may become conceited without seeming arrogant."

Sou Ha was on her feet almost at once. She said to Cynthia Renton, "It is cold out. You have a heavy coat?"

"Yes. I . . ."

"Not heavy enough for this chill wind which I think is apt to come up a little later on," Clane said.

"That is fine," Sou Ha observed. "I will lend you my fur coat, and would you mind putting on the hat? I want to see how it looks."

Terry Clane clapped his hands. Yat T'oy appeared at once carrying hats and coats.

Sou Ha fitted the distinctive blue hat with the red feather on Cynthia's head. "Oh, it's delightful on you," she said. "Please accept it as a gift. It is *so* much more becoming to you than it is to me. You must take it and wear it."

"Well," Cynthia said, hesitating, and then laughed a little

nervously, "I suppose you'd be willing to accept mine by way of a swap?"

"Oh, but that's wonderful of you," Sou Ha said.

"And I hope you'll take my coat. It's rather a distinctive plaid and—you know, in case you should want to go out before I get back with your coat."

"You are kind," Sou Ha said.

There were tears in Cynthia Renton's eyes. She took the Chinese girl in her arms, kissed her on the cheek. "You are wonderful, Sou Ha."

Sou Ha's face was without expression. "Thank you."

"And now," Chu Kee said, "it is time to depart. Posing for a portrait is very tiresome. I am no longer young and I wish to have the freshness of morning upon me when my features are placed upon canvas."

Clane said in Chinese, "You will, perhaps, be followed by those who are interested in seeing where you go."

"There is no secret about where I go," Chu Kee said benignly. "I will go to a door which is at the foot of a flight of stairs. After I have climbed those stairs, the eyes of a spy will not know what becomes of me; and if he should wait for me to emerge from that same door, he would be a very old man before he again saw me."

Clane nodded approvingly.

Chu Kee bowed and shook hands, this time after the Chinese fashion, with his hands clasped over his heart. He turned to Cynthia Renton. "If you are now ready?" he asked.

She laughed nervously. "I am now ready."

Clane watched them down the corridor, then went back to where Sou Ha was sitting, her silken legs crossed at the knees, her fingers languidly picking up dried melon seeds which she cracked with her teeth, deftly extracting the kernel with the tip of her tongue, performing the whole operation as neatly as a canary bird cracking hemp seeds.

"I didn't like to ask it," Clane said, "but there seemed to be no other way out."

"Don't feel like that, First-Born," she said with some feeling. "My father is your friend. It is a privilege when he can do things for you."

"And you?"

Her eyes went to his face. "You know how I feel," she said. Then suddenly her eyes moved away and she added, in almost an undertone, "Or *do* you?"

"Smoke?" Clane asked.

"No, thanks. I will follow the custom of my race and sip tea and eat melon seeds. I feel very Oriental today, not an American at all."

"Why?" he asked.

"I don't know. I am fighting a tendency to retire within myself."

"Why fight it?"

"Because I want to, I suppose."

"And why do you want to?"

She smiled at him and said, "Because I think I will have more fun if I don't."

"Are you," Clane asked, "leading up to something?"

"Yes."

"Go ahead."

"You know that in China we have an expression—you've probably heard it: *tie doh hahk hay*."

Clane nodded. "Meaning 'too much of a guest.' "

"Exactly," she said. "It is a rebuke that a hostess some-times gives to a person who is on sufficient terms of intimacy to be accepted as one of the family, but who is acting with the formal restraint of a guest."

"And what is the application in this instance?" Clane asked. "Do you think you are being too much of a guest?"

"No, you are."

"I am the host."

"You know what I mean."

"Suppose," Clane said, "I ask for a bill of particulars?"

"Whenever you wish us to do something, you are too diffi-dent."

"This particular thing may be rather tricky and dangerous, Sou Ha."

"It's a pleasure to feel that what one does is important. Tell me, First-Born, is it only when things concern the Painter Woman that you become so self-conscious and embarrassed

109

about asking our aid? Is it because you feel that your friends are not our friends, particularly the friends who are closest to you?"

Clane faced the steady, inscrutable eyes. "What are you getting at, Sou Ha?"

"It would be embarrassing, if she were to become your wife and thereafter felt that there was any reason why she should not avail herself of our friendship—*any* reason."

"She is not my wife."

"She may become your wife."

"Is not that crossing a bridge before one comes to it?"

She said, "I do not like your proverbs. I prefer the proverbs of China. You say that one should not cross a bridge before one comes to it. In China we say that the wise man does not follow the road which is known to be infested with bandits. In both instances it is a case of looking ahead. We consider it a wisdom, you consider it a vice."

Clane said, "But there is a difference between following a road on which there are bandits and following one on which there is a bridge. One should not cross the bridge before one comes to it."

"Is it not unwise to follow a road where a bridge is out?"

Clane nodded.

"And unless one looks ahead far enough to see if the bridge is there, how is one to know when it is not there?"

Clane smiled.

"No, no, First-Born, do not smile. We are talking of Chinese proverbs, but what we have in the back of our minds goes far deeper."

Clane said, "Look here, Sou Ha, this is no ordinary matter. This is a murder. And yet, it is much more than a murder. A man has been convicted of murder and he has escaped. Those who aid him in that escape are guilty of a very serious crime."

"I know no man who has been convicted of murder," Sou Ha said with a wooden face. "I know only that I have lent my coat and hat to a friend."

"Try telling the police that in case you're caught at it," Clane said.

She looked at him, wooden-faced. "I will."

"And probably get away with it at that," Clane said. "Look here, Sou Ha, you can't leave here now. You've got to wait until it gets warmer. Then you can carry your coat over your arm and—and we'll just pray they don't notice the discrepancy about the hat."

"I am in no hurry."

"But in the meantime, I have to go out."

"I will be happy here with Yat T'oy. He and I will converse about the Chinese classics. He thinks that I am deplorably lacking in the knowledge of my fathers. How long will you be gone?"

"Perhaps an hour."

She said, musingly, "The police will think the apartment is vacant. They have seen a man and a young woman enter. They have seen a man and a young woman leave. Now then, when you leave . . ."

"They will know that Yat T'oy is here."

"Very well," she said. "I will wait."

"You will, of course, keep away from the windows."

"Am I a fool?" she asked. "Or have you grown accustomed to women who lack responsibility?"

## 13

THE man who opened the door in response to Terry Clane's ring was tall, rawboned, and flat-waisted. He had long arms, huge hands, big features and bushy eyebrows from underneath which dark intense eyes, that could easily become angry, surveyed his visitor with curiosity but no welcoming friendliness.

"My name is Clane. I am a friend of Cynthia Renton and I wanted to talk with you."

Bill Hendrum stood to one side. "Come in," he said. "I've heard of you."

Clane entered the apartment. The place had the litter of masculine occupancy about it. There was a desk in the center of the room, a typewriter on the desk, several sheets of type-written manuscript, the morning newspaper open and dropped carelessly by the side of a chair. Within convenient reaching distance were a humidor of tobacco, a crusted brier pipe, matches, an ashtray. Hendrum's coat was draped over the back of the chair in front of the desk. The long sleeves dangled down, awkward in their emphasis on the length of the man's arms.

Hendrum kicked a chair around with his foot. "Sit down."

Clane seated himself. Hendrum looked at him for a second or two, then picked up the pipe, pushed tobacco into it, tamped it into place with his powerful forefinger, lit the pipe and settled back in the chair without seeming in the least to relax.

"What's on your mind?"

Clane said, "Because of my friendship with Cynthia, I want to help Edward Harold."

"Frankly," Hendrum said, "I don't see that that necessarily follows."

"What doesn't?"

"Because of your friendship for Cynthia, you want to help Edward. One's a woman, one's a man. It could be just the opposite, you know."

"You mean that because of my friendship for Cynthia, I *wouldn't* want to help Edward?"

"It could be."

"It happens that isn't the case."

"I just mentioned it," Hendrum said, puffing on his pipe.

"In order to accomplish what I have in mind, it becomes necessary for me to get in touch with Edward Harold."

"The police feel the same way."

"This morning," Clane said, "the Attorney General is moving the Supreme Court to dismiss the appeal of Edward Harold on the ground that the man is a fugitive from justice."

"So what?"

"When the appeal is dismissed, he loses his opportunity to have the Supreme Court review his case."

"Courts and lawyers!" Hendrum exclaimed in a deep, rum-

112

bling voice that indicated gathering anger. "They make me damn sick!"

"It happens that that's the way our lives are regulated," Clane said. "It's the procedure by which we administer justice."

"When you say 'justice'," Hendrum told him bitterly, "put it in quotes."

"All right, I'll put it in quotes, but it's still our way of getting justice."

"It's not the only way."

"It's the only effective way."

"It wasn't very effective so far as Ed Harold was concerned."

"He doesn't know," Clane said. "He didn't try it. He quit when he was halfway through. So far, he has only the verdict of a jury."

"And a sentence of death," Hendrum mumbled. "Don't forget that."

"Have you," Clane asked abruptly, "seen the newspaper?"

"What are you trying to do, trap me?" Hendrum asked and motioned as he spoke, almost contemptuously, toward the newspaper lying on the floor.

"George Gloster was murdered last night."

"So I notice."

"And when the police took fingerprints of the room in which the murder was committed, they found so many of Edward Harold's fingerprints that the only logical conclusion is Harold has used that room as a hideout."

"I read all that."

"Naturally, the police are pinning this other murder on Harold."

"Sure," Hendrum said. "Pick on a guy when he's down. They'll use him for a scapegoat now. Pin every murder in the city on him. Damn it, I hope he stands up on his two feet and shoots it out with them. And I'd just as soon be . . ."

"Yes?" Clane asked as he ceased speaking abruptly.

"Nothing," Hendrum said.

Clane said, "The Supreme Court justices are not supposed to be influenced by what they read in the newspapers, but just the same, any person who is human can't . . . well, he can't refrain from being human. I think it would be an excellent thing if the newspapers within the next day or two could contain some evidence which would at least throw doubt on the police theory."

"Oh, you do, do you?"

"I do. I also think it would be a good thing if Edward Harold surrendered into police custody before his appeal gets dismissed."

"So that's it," Hendrum said. "That's what you've been getting at. That's the real reason for your visit here."

"That," Clane told him, meeting his eyes, "is the real reason for my visit here."

"Make it rather nice for you, wouldn't it?" Hendrum said, his eyes suddenly angry. "You come back from China all nice and snug. *Your* neck isn't at stake. *You* aren't on the dodge. *You* can take Cynthia out to dinner and the show and all that sort of stuff while Ed Harold is slinking around through the alleys. The best he can expect is an opportunity to shoot it out with the police in some dark deserted lot somewhere. Pretty soft for you."

Clane said, "I'm trying to help your friend."

"That's what you say."

Clane went on patiently, "What the newspaper doesn't say is that there's another clue they discovered. When they searched the place, they found a woman's purse. And in that purse was Cynthia Renton's driving license, cards, address book, lipstick, compact, and about twenty-five hundred dollars in currency."

Hendrum's eyes narrowed. "Where did they find that?"

"On a packing case in the warehouse."

"Well," Hendrum said, "you should know. You were there."

"And Cynthia was there," Clane said.

Hendrum thought that over.

"I'd like to find something that would help Harold," Clane went on. "*I* think there is something in the evidence that might help him."

"What, for instance?"

Clane said, "There's a diagram of the room where the body was found, in the newspaper."

"All right. So what?"

"There was an open window on the south. Police found footprints under that window where someone had apparently jumped out. Then that person ran across some moist ground and left the footprints which the police lost on pavement about fifty or sixty feet on beyond. The footprints all went directly away from the building."

"All right."

"On the other hand," Clane said, "when I went to the place, the building was all dark."

"Yeah, when *you* went to it," Hendrum said. "Funny that *you* happened to be there at just that time."

"I had an appointment with Gloster."

"I understand that's your story."

Clane said, "Cynthia Renton was with me. I couldn't very well account for her presence, so I just didn't tell the officers about her being there. Now they've found her purse and that complicates the situation."

"You mean Cynthia was with you all the time?"

"Yes."

"That gives you an alibi, doesn't it?"

"If I wanted to use it."

"Well, why don't you?"

"Because I didn't tell the officers about her being along. I neglected to mention it. If I should change my story at this date, it would make things a little difficult."

"For whom?"

"For me."

"For Cynthia?"

"Probably not. She's in as deep as she can get right now."

"I see," Hendrum said with heavy sarcasm. "You want me, as a friend of Ed's, to get him to surrender to the police so it will put you off the spot."

"Don't be silly. Whether he surrenders will have nothing to do with what I tell the police. The point I'm getting at is that the place was dark when I arrived. The footprints out of the open window were probably Edward Harold's. The only light switch in the place is at the north end of the room. Gloster was shot with a very well-placed bullet. Obviously, the person who shot that bullet had to see what he was shooting at. There is every evidence that the bullet was fired from the north side of the room.

"The person who turned out the lights *had* to be standing at the north side of the room. Therefore, if Ed Harold killed Gloster while standing at the north side of the room when the bullet was fired, he had to turn out the lights, then go across the room in the dark, jump out of the open window and run away. That's hardly the natural or the logical thing for him to have done."

"Don't talk to me about Ed Harold's killing him. He didn't."

"I'm simply reconstructing what happened and showing you how the police theory simply can't hold together."

"Don't you suppose the police have sense enough to know that?"

"Yes."

"What's their idea in advancing such a theory, then?"

"It might be bait for a trap."

"To trap whom?"

"The murderer."

"You?" Hendrum asked.

"The police probably aren't worrying about who walks into their trap. They're busy baiting it."

Hendrum was interested now. "Go ahead. Let's hear the rest of it."

"Of course," Clane said, "Ed Harold could have shot Gloster from the north side of the room. Then he ran down to the south side, jumped out of the open window, and made his escape. If it had happened that way, it would have been because there was someone outside whom he didn't want to meet, someone who was on the north side of the building."

"Then how did the lights get turned off?"

"Someone must have entered the building, seen what had happened, turned out the lights, and driven away."

"You?"

"Don't be silly. I stayed there after I found the body and called the police. There was nothing to prevent my walking away."

"Unless the police knew of your appointment."

"They didn't."

Hendrum was watching Clane intently, his big bushy eyebrows drawn together. "Keep talking."

"Edward Harold," Clane said, "was hiding in that warehouse. He wrote a postcard to Cynthia Renton, letting her know where he was so that she could get in touch with him. It occurs to me that he might have written you a similar message."

"Oh, it does, does it?"

"It does."

"And so what?"

"And so perhaps you went down to see Edward Harold and see if you could do something for him."

"Nice theory," Hendrum said. "Try and make it stick. I suppose you'd like to drag me into it as the murderer."

"Take that diagram and, in connection with the position of the body, figure it out any way you want to," Clane said. "The most logical solution is that none of the partners had been down to that warehouse for some little time, and Edward Harold had reason to believe they weren't going to be coming down there. He established a hideout there in the warehouse. Then Gloster, in making an appointment with me and trying to get some place that would be relatively isolated, selected the warehouse. When he unlocked the front door and switched on the lights, Harold knew he was trapped. He sprinted across the room and jumped out of the window. Gloster ran over to the telephone to notify the police. Perhaps he'd recognized Harold. Perhaps he thought merely some burglar was in the place. While he was rushing to the telephone, someone who had entered the room with him stood at the door and shot him in the back, then deliberately turned out the lights and drove away."

"Why do you say it was someone who had entered the room with him?" Hendrum asked.

"The evidence indicates it."

"What evidence?"

"Gloster was evidently shot as he was moving over toward the telephone. He was shot by someone who was standing near the door on the north side. If my theory is correct,

117

ERLE STANLEY GARDNER

Gloster must have gone to the telephone just as soon as he entered the room, switched on the lights, and saw Edward Harold just going through the window. That would mean that the person who shot him had entered the room at about the same time Gloster did."

"At exactly the same time?"

"Perhaps just a step or two behind him."

"You mean then this person must have driven down there with Gloster?"

"Or he might have been someone whom Gloster was to meet there, some third party who was to furnish some information which Gloster wanted me to have. Or perhaps confront me with something which Gloster wanted to have me confronted with. He might have arrived there a few minutes before Gloster and then waited."

"Well?" Hendrum asked.

"And," Clane said, "if Edward Harold had sent you a postal card, letting you know where he was, and you had gone down to see him, there is a chance you might have noticed something which would be of some help."

Hendrum stretched his feet out in front of him, pushed his hands down deep into his trousers pockets.

"So you see," Clane said, "that I . . ."

"Shut up!" Hendrum said. "Let me think a minute."

For some seconds the men sat there. Hendrum, his pipe in the corner of his mouth, its curved stem letting it rest on his coat lapel, puffed nervously, emitting little intermittent wisps of curled smoke. His feet were out in front of him and his eyes were looking at the toes of his shoes; his hands were thrust deep in his pockets.

Clane sat silent, doing nothing to distract the other's attention.

At length Hendrum spoke with the care of one who is examining and testing each word before he puts it into circulation. "I can tell you *one thing,* and only one thing, which may help. Ricardo Taonon was driving his automobile in the vicinity of that warehouse about thirty minutes before the time the police think the murder was committed."

"How do you know?" Clane asked as the other ceased speaking.

Hendrum shook his head.

"Could I say that you saw him?" Clane asked.

"You could not."

Abruptly Hendrum took the pipe from his mouth, placed it on the pipe rack and got to his feet. "I've said all I care to say."

He walked over to the door, held it open. "I'm sorry, Clane. I've gone farther than I intended to. I thought you were something of a heel. I guess you're all right. But I still wish you'd stayed in China. Good-by."

Clane took the man's hand. "Good-by," he said.

The door of the apartment banged shut.

# 14

TERRY CLANE, emerging from the apartment house where he had been in conference with Bill Hendrum noticed a police car turn the corner and park.

Moving instinctively, Clane walked rapidly down the steep sidewalk and entered the first open door he found, that of a small neighborhood grocery store of the type so frequent in San Francisco.

Walking directly back to the shelves in the rear, Clane looked over the merchandise as though trying to find some particular brand he wanted.

The door pushed open and Clane saw outlined against the outer daylight the familiar figure of Inspector Malloy.

Malloy stood in the doorway, his broad shoulders hulking over the counter, his eyes surveying the interior of the store. Resignedly Clane moved forward, but somewhat to his surprise saw Inspector Malloy turn to the proprietor and beckon him over to the counter.

Clane, thinking this was perhaps a trap, moved up to the fruit-juice section and selected two cans of pineapple juice.

Inspector Malloy had pushed a typewritten list across the counter toward the proprietor.

"Within the last few days have you sold that list of groceries or a substantial part of it to some one person?" he asked.

Clane veered off, but it was too late. Inspector Malloy cocked an eyebrow, then suddenly snapped to surprised attention. "Well, well, well," he boomed. "If it isn't Mr. Clane. And what are you doing *here*, Mr. Clane?"

"Oh, just picking up a couple of cans of fruit juice," Clane said.

"Well, well, well. Now isn't that interesting? Quite a way from your own flat, aren't you?"

"Oh, not too far. Within walking distance."

"And you do your shopping here, Mr. Clane?"

Clane said, "Oh, no, I . . ."

"You mean did we sell this entire order to some one person?" the proprietor demanded.

"Never mind that now," Malloy said and, facing Clane, said, "Go right on, Mr. Clane, don't let us interrupt you. You were mentioning something about buying some fruit juice here. May I ask why you didn't select a nearer store?"

"Oh, I was just taking a walk and happened to remember I wanted some fruit juice."

"Rather heavy," Inspector Malloy said.

"Oh, I can carry them all right," Clane said smiling.

"I didn't mean that. I meant that it's rather unusual for a man to carry canned fruit juices some eight or ten blocks. There are stores right in your block, aren't there?"

"I suppose so. Yes. But I happened to think of it now as I was passing."

Malloy whirled to the proprietor. "Take a good look at this man," he invited. "Did you ever see him before?"

The proprietor shook his head.

"No, I haven't seen him before," the proprietor said. "And I didn't sell anyone an order like this within the last two or three days." And he indicated the typewritten list Malloy had pushed over the counter.

Malloy's face showed he was disappointed. "All right," he said, "if you're sure. Say nothing about my having been here.

Don't mention it to any of your customers. Understand? Any of them."

"Okay. I guess I can keep my lip buttoned up."

"That's fine."

Malloy turned to Clane. "Now isn't it remarkable," he said, "that you should happen to be in *this* neighborhood doing your shopping?"

"I told you, I just happened to drop in."

"Yes, I understand that. But what caused you to happen to drop in?"

"I wanted some fruit juice."

Malloy sighed. "Well, I was just making a routine investigation. I thought I'd run up and have a little talk with you some time this morning. Since you're here, we may just as well take a few minutes to chat. Tell you what I'll do. Get in my car and I'll deliver you and your fruit juice right to your own flat."

"I'd prefer to walk," Clane said. "I like the feeling of having dry land instead of the deck of a ship under me. I want to prowl around, looking in store windows where there is actually some merchandise and . . ."

"Yes, yes, I know. But you may just as well get in the car with me and we can kill two birds with one stone. Perhaps I'll drive you away from the neighborhood and then after I've talked with you, you can go and take a walk somewhere else."

"What's the matter with the neighborhood?" Clane asked. "Is there smallpox in it?"

"Well, now *that's* an idea," Inspector Malloy said. "There may be. I'm intending to quarantine it."

"To quarantine the whole neighborhood?"

Inspector Malloy's deep chuckle showed he was enjoying the situation. He said, "That's right, Clane. Sort of a quarantine. It's unhealthful."

"For whom?"

"For you."

"Here?"

"Yes."

"I don't see why."

"Well now, that's one of the things we can't always explain. But if you'll just get in this car. Here, let me take the package. Two cans of pineapple juice, eh? Now isn't that interesting? Right in the car here, if you will, Mr. Clane. Now don't hesitate. I *could* make it formal and official, you know."

Clane accompanied Inspector Malloy to the police automobile, climbed in beside the Inspector.

"Now then," Malloy said sternly, "I want to give you a word of warning. It's chaps like you, playing at cops and robbers, that make trouble."

"Just what do you mean?" Clane asked.

"You know what I mean, snooping around these stores and trying to find out where Edward Harold bought the provisions that were in that hideout."

Clane said, "I hadn't asked a question in that store."

"I know, you were laying the foundation for a casual inquiry by buying a couple of cans of fruit juice. Don't try it, Mr. Clane. I know what I'm talking about. It just makes trouble. Leave all that stuff to the police."

Clane, willing to let Inspector Malloy accept that excuse for his being in the neighborhood, said meekly, "Yes, I suppose so."

Malloy drove the car slowly and conservatively. "This Cynthia Renton," he said, "must be a very nice girl."

"She is."

"Now do I understand you haven't seen her since you got back?"

Clane said, "I don't see what that has to do with it."

"Well, the police are sort of looking for her, want to ask her a few questions."

"The police have my permission," Clane said gravely.

Malloy shot him a swift glance, then moved his eyes back to the road. "She was engaged to Edward Harold. Everyone seems to think so."

"I see."

"If that's the case, she must know where he is."

"Or was," Clane said.

"We know where he was. He was there in that warehouse

and he was provisioned up for a regular siege. Someone bought quite a bunch of groceries, apparently all in one order. Took them down and stocked the place up so he could stay there for a month or so without ever needing to stick his head outdoors."

"Did you think that person was Miss Renton?"

"In our business, we don't do too much speculative thinking, Mr. Clane. We investigate. And when we investigate we make it a point to cover *all* of the possibilities."

"I see," Clane said.

"Even," Malloy went on, "including that poker-faced Chinese servant of yours, Yat T'oy."

"I see."

"One of these days, we'll stumble on a live lead. That's the way it is in police investigation."

"Yes, I can imagine it takes what might be termed infinite patience."

"Well, we don't have too much time to be patient. We have to hit the high spots and get the job done. Now take in your own case, Mr. Clane. Are you certain you went down there last night in a taxicab?"

"Why?"

"Well now, I'm going to be frank with you. There's some evidence that we haven't given to the newspapers."

"You mean in addition to Miss Renton's purse?" Clane asked casually.

Malloy's face became wooden. "We don't always tell everything we know."

Clane said, "I have been wondering if, perhaps, Gloster hadn't found Miss Renton's purse in the warehouse and that was what he wanted to see me about. Thought he could return the purse to her through me."

"And what makes you think he had found the purse?"

"If Miss Renton had left it in the warehouse, Gloster might well have found it."

Malloy slowed the car almost to a crawl, then as angry horns blared into a demand for the road to be cleared, Malloy swung over to the curb and parked in the open space directly in front of a fire hydrant. He shut off the motor and turned

123

to Clane. "Now let's get this straight," he said. "Did Gloster say anything to you about having Miss Renton's purse?"

"He didn't *say* anything," Clane said significantly.

"But you thought that's what he wanted?"

"I'm wondering now, if . . . well, to tell you the truth, Inspector, I don't know *what* he wanted."

"But you were able to formulate an idea?"

"Only on what we might call a hunch, or perhaps mental telepathy."

"We don't go for mental telepathy," Malloy said.

"If you knew more about it, you might."

"Perhaps, but the Chief doesn't like it."

"I see."

Malloy sat silent for several minutes. Then he said suddenly, "There's one possibility."

"What's that?" Clane asked.

"I'll tell you about that in about two minutes," Malloy said, and switching on the motor, he swung out into traffic.

This time there was no hesitancy, no crawling along. Now he switched on the official red police spotlight and started making time for Clane's apartment.

"You seem to be in a hurry all of a sudden," Clane said.

"Well, you know how it is, Mr. Clane. In this business ideas strike you, and when they do, you don't have all day to think them over. I'll take you right to your apartment and then start investigating another phase of the case."

"Mind if I ask what that is?" Clane asked.

"No, not at all," Malloy said, "not a-tall, Mr. Clane. In fact, I wanted to discuss it with you."

"Go right ahead."

Malloy said, "We sort of stole a march on you last night, Mr. Clane. We searched your flat."

"The deuce you did."

"Yes. One of our men posed as a gas man, searching for a leak in the line."

"Find anything?" Clane asked.

"Not a thing, Mr. Clane. But on the other hand, it wasn't what you'd call a thorough search. It was sort of an inspection. And we *may* have overlooked something. Your place has been under surveillance ever since, but . . . Well, I think, if you don't mind, we'll go look the place over again, and this time we'll make a more thorough job of it."

"And if I do mind?" Clane asked.

"In that case, I have a search warrant."

"In that case, I don't suppose there's anything I can do about it if I do mind, is there?" Clane asked.

"Now that's spoken like a true philosopher," Malloy said. "You're quite right, Mr. Clane, there isn't a single damn thing you can do about it."

Malloy made the run in swift time, parked his car in front of Clane's flat and directly across the street.

Clane deliberately fumbled around with the car door, taking the longest possible time getting out of the car and praying that Yat T'oy would be watching from behind the curtains of the windows in the flat above.

"Come on, come on," Malloy said impatiently. "After all, it's like a cold shower. You have to do it and get it over with, and the quicker you jump in, the quicker it's over."

Clane glancing upward could see no faintest silhouette behind the lace curtains of the windows.

"I don't think I'm going," he said.

"Now, don't be like that," Malloy said. "After all, Mr. Clane, you're in a rather precarious position. The police could be just a little tough with you, you know—if they wanted to be."

Clane said, "If you have a warrant to search the place, go ahead and search it. I don't have to be there."

He turned and started to walk down the street.

Malloy was at his side before he had taken five steps. "If I have to get rough, Mr. Clane, I can do that too. You're coming with me. Are you coming—shall we say, under your own power, or are you going to come in tow?"

Clane, feeling that this byplay was as far as he dared go and that the pantomime would convey to any watcher in the upper windows the knowledge that he was virtually under arrest, said sullenly, "Oh, if you put it that way, I'll go."

"I'm putting it that way," Malloy said, and his big-knuckled hand rested on Clane's shoulder, slid down the shoulder until the muscular fingers were digging into Clane's arm. "Come on, Mr. Clane, let's go."

Clane accompanied Inspector Malloy back to the entrance to the flat, up the half-dozen cement stairs which led up from the sidewalk. "I think you have the key," Malloy said.

Clane fumbled around getting the right key, then inserted it in the door and said politely, "You first, Inspector."

Malloy laughed. "No, no, Mr. Clane, you have the wrong book of etiquette. In times like this, the host goes first and the guest comes along behind. Right up the stairs with you."

Clane climbed the stairs slowly.

"And now the key to this door," Malloy said.

Clane once more took as long as he dared getting the door open and then Malloy pushed past him into the apartment.

"Oh, Yat T'oy," Clane called and added in Chinese, "the police search . . ."

"None of that," Malloy interrupted him sharply. "We'll talk English if you please, Mr. Clane."

"My servant understands Chinese better."

"That's too bad, that's really too bad. You should teach him to understand English because, you see, things are sort of in the balance here, Mr. Clane. And if you don't talk English, you're going to find yourself in something of a mess. To be perfectly frank with you, my instructions are to arrest you and charge you with the murder of George Gloster in case your actions are suspicious."

"Charge *me* with the murder?" Clane said, raising his voice.

"Well, of course, I don't make the formal charge, but I'd arrest you on suspicion of murder and—there'd be a few technicalities. The charge would probably be as an accessory after the fact or something of that sort. Come on, now let's get this over with. We'll discuss the other part later."

There was no sign of Yat T'oy or of Sou Ha.

Clane walked from the living room through the dining room toward the kitchen, Malloy on his heels, his eyes darting around in lightning-swift scrutiny, missing no detail.

"I can't imagine where Yat T'oy is," Clane said irritably.

"And I'd like to look in the bedrooms, if you don't mind, Mr. Clane. And don't try to smuggle anyone out through another door into the corridor. I warn you that this place is sewed up tighter than a flour sack."

Clane said, "I'm not trying to get anybody out, I'm trying to find where my man is."

He pushed open the door to the kitchen.

Yat T'oy was standing by the sink, wooden-faced in his stupidity, chopping onions with a large, sharp butcher knife, using that flexible wrist motion which is the sign of a professional cook and making the knife move so fast that the blade was little more than a blur, the point resting on the chopping board, the blade being elevated and lowered by the rapid wrist motion.

On her hands and knees, Sou Ha was scrubbing the linoleum of the kitchen floor, a bucket of dirty, soapy water at her left, her hands clasped over the back of a scrubbing brush as she swayed back and forth.

Her hair was loose and stringy, hanging down around her face. She was barefooted and her skirt was pulled down tightly between her legs and pinned in back. She didn't even glance up as the two men entered the room.

Clane, taking in the situation, said angrily to Yat T'oy, "I told you not to have this woman around any more. She didn't come the day she was supposed to. You're fired," Clane said, turning angrily to Sou Ha.

She looked up at him with blank countenance.

"Alle same you go home, no come back," Clane said. "My man say you no come work day you promise come."

"I work now," Sou Ha said in a flat expressionless voice.

"If you don't mind my butting in, Clane," Malloy said, "it might be well for you to remember that you're not in the Orient any more. You can't hardly get anyone to do housework at all, let alone . . ."

"I'm running this," Clane interrupted angrily. "At least I guess the police will let me have charge of my own household. As a matter of fact, there's nothing here that one man can't do. But you know the Chinese—they like companionship and my bills show that Yat T'oy has been having this woman come in regularly."

"Rather old for a Lothario," Malloy said.

"You can't tell about these Chinese," Clane told him. "They're deep, and the old men like the young girls."

"Same as every place else," Malloy said. "I want to look in the bedroom, Mr. Clane."

"All right, we'll go in the bedroom. Yat T'oy, you get that woman out of here. You savvy?"

"Me savvy. She nice woman. Make floor very clean."

"You can make floor very clean," Clane said. "This job one-man job. You savvy?"

"Me savvy," Yat T'oy said angrily and slammed the butcher knife down on the chopping board. Then turning to Sou Ha he said angrily in Chinese, apparently addressing his remarks entirely to her, "Have no fear of the bedrooms, they have been carefully gone over."

Clane, with the manner of a man whose day has been subject to a series of exasperating annoyances, said to Malloy, "All right, let's go look in the bedrooms. Gosh, how I wish I were back in China!"

Inspector Malloy's manner showed that this search had been the result of some sudden idea which, while it seemed good at the time, was, in view of recent developments, seeming less sound with each passing minute. He looked through the bedrooms in the more or less perfunctory manner of one who is convinced, even before a door is open, that the room is empty.

"All right, Clane," he said, "just checking up, that's all."

"I hope you're satisfied."

"I am, and I'm sorry I disturbed you. No hard feelings, I hope?"

"No hard feelings," Clane said. "Have a cigar. There are some Yat T'oy picked up through some of his Chinese connections. They're very good."

"Chinese cigars?"

"Heavens no, they're a pure Havana cigar. Try one."

"Thank you, I will. Been a little difficult to get any lately."

Malloy took a cigar from the box Clane extended, smelled of the wrapper and his face instantly softened into a smile of approval.

"Put some in your pocket," Clane urged. "I don't smoke

them myself. Just keep them for guests and Yat T'oy laid in a good supply."

"Thank you, I will."

"Yat T'oy," Clane called, "get that woman out of here. If you'll pardon me a moment," he said to Inspector Malloy, "I'm going to break up this romance."

"Don't be such a spoilsport," Malloy said chuckling.

"It's the idea," Clane said. "An old man and a young girl like that. I suppose if the truth were known, she's his slave girl and he owns her just as you or I would own a dog. But just the same . . ."

Clane said in Chinese, "It is well that Sou Ha should leave at the moment Malloy leaves so that watchers will see them emerge from the door together."

Yat T'oy answered from the other side of the door, "She is ready."

"Well," Clane said to Malloy, "I suppose you're satisfied."

"Entirely satisfied. I'm sorry having to be a little rough with you, Mr. Clane, but you will admit you do get around and get into peculiar situations now and then. Well, I'll run along. It's too bad I had to make a checkup on this place but—well, you know how it is, it's all in a day's work with me. No hard feelings."

"No hard feelings," Clane said and escorted Malloy to the door.

From the back entrance leading to the hallway, Sou Ha made a dispirited exit from the kitchen. She was carrying a bundle of laundry tied up in a sheet, a bundle which Clane knew contained her expensive shoes and stockings, and Cynthia Renton's coat and hat. Sou Ha's bare feet were thrust in a pair of oversized Chinese slippers which doubtless belonged to Yat T'oy. Her shoulders were stooped as befitted a young woman whose body had already been sold in the slave market and who could not, at this late date, increase the purchase price thereof nor benefit therefrom if she could. Her slow shuffling gait spoke of dreary hours spent in menial tasks with only the prospect of more weary hours ahead wherever she was going.

Inspector Malloy said genially, "Well, I'll be on my way,

Clane. Try to be a little more discreet in the future. You're getting mixed up in this thing pretty deep. Sorry about that search, no hard feelings."

"No hard feelings," Clane said and closed the door.

From the window he watched to see Sou Ha emerge on the sidewalk to make sure that she was not stopped or questioned.

Inspector Malloy was first out. Sou Ha followed him only a second or two later. She turned and started down the steep hill, keeping perfectly in character, walking with stiff-backed shuffling steps.

Clane nodded approvingly, then saw Inspector Malloy gain Sou Ha's side in three or four swift steps. He was, Clane realized from his gestures, apparently offering her a lift.

Sou Ha shook her head, moved on. Inspector Malloy insisted, pointed to his automobile and then in the general direction of Chinatown. Sou Ha wearily turned and, with the air of one who is too tired to be grateful, climbed into Inspector Malloy's automobile.

Clane, watching Malloy drive away, felt an uneasy disquiet as he noticed the manner in which the Inspector's car gathered speed. There was something purposeful about the manner in which Malloy piloted the automobile on down the street. The Inspector was driving fast, shooting across the street intersections. It was as though he knew exactly where he was going and was in a hurry to get there.

Clane frowningly watched the car until it turned a corner in the direction of Chinatown.

Inspector Malloy could pump Sou Ha until the cows came home without getting anything out of her. He could deliver her to any address in Chinatown and she would blend into the background and promptly disappear as effectively as a young quail in a patch of dead leaves.

Nevertheless, Terry Clane was considerably concerned. There was, after all, a possibility Inspector Malloy had not been as innocent as he seemed and that, after all, Sou Ha was not being taken to Chinatown but to police headquarters.

## 15

CLANE, with a map of the city to aid him, was patiently plodding along, putting himself in the place of Edward Harold, trying to anticipate Harold's next move.

Some hundred yards behind him was the warehouse where the murder had been committed. Assuming that Harold had jumped from that window in a panic and had raced across the strip of soft ground where his footprints had been found, he had hit the pavement and then had started walking. Where would he walk and what would he do?

Clane plodded along through the drab warehouse district until he came to a small hole-in-the-wall restaurant.

Clane ordered a cup of coffee. "How late are you open?" he asked.

"Nine o'clock. Used to stay open until midnight when there was a lot of draying down here. Things are quieter now, costs are up and you can't get help, so I'm closing early."

"Any place around here that's open all night?" Clane asked.

"Don't know of any."

"Until after midnight?"

"No, I don't think so. Wait a minute, there's a place up the street, two blocks up over on the right. Sid Melrose runs the joint. I think he's been staying up lately. Used to close but I think he's been open now."

"Thanks," Clane said. "I may be on night shift down here and wanted to know where I could come for a cup of coffee."

"Most satisfactory way is to carry a thermos bottle."

Clane thanked the man, paid for the coffee, and walked up to the restaurant operated by Sid Melrose.

There was a sign over the door, *Open until 11:00* P.M.

Clane seated himself at the counter, ordered coffee, toast and eggs.

The waitress who served him eyed the dollar bill which Clane pushed across the counter. "What's this for?"

"Information."

Her fingers rested on the edge of the dollar bill. "About what?"

"I want to find out something that happened here last night around closing time. Who was on shift?"

"I was."

"And you're on again this morning?"

"Uh-huh, we stagger shifts. Today is my change-over from night shift. I worked until eleven last night and then came on again at eight this morning and work until one. Then I come back at four and work until seven. What did you want to know?"

"Some time around closing time," Clane said, "I think a man came in here and wanted to use the telephone. He didn't have a hat or an overcoat. He was rather tall and had dark hair which he combed straight back, the eyes were dark and . . ."

"Sure, I remember him. What do you want to know about him?"

"What did he do?"

"He came in here and wanted the telephone. Then he asked for some coffee. He seemed sort of nervous. What about him?"

"Just trying to check up on him," Clane said. "It's all right. Just a personal matter."

"Well, he got some nickels and went over to the telephone and dialed a number. He didn't get any answer, came back and had another cup of coffee, then went over and dialed the same number again . . ."

"The same number?" Clane asked.

"I think so. The first two calls were to the same number. At least the first two or three numbers were the same. I happened to notice him when he was working the dial on the telephone. Business was slack and . . . well, you know how it is, you just sometimes notice people like that. He seemed . . . well, there was something funny about him. I don't know exactly what it was but he seemed sort of all on edge."

"All right, what happened then?"

"He didn't get any answer either time. He came back and had another cup of coffee and then went over and dialed another number. That time he got an answer. He talked on the telephone for a minute or two and then came back and sat down. He seemed more quiet then. About ten minutes later a car drove up outside and the driver tapped the horn. The man got up, shoved a quarter across the counter at me and almost ran out of the place."

"Could you see the driver of the car?" Clane asked.

"Not very plain. It was a woman. She was a young woman, but that's about all I know."

"Blonde or brunette?"

"I really couldn't say."

"Could you tell me anything about the car?"

"Yes. It was a convertible, a sporty job. I'm trying to think of what it was about the man that made me watch him, something that wasn't just . . . well, it was something that made you think he was in trouble or something."

"Something in the way he looked?"

"Well, not exactly. Something in his manner."

"Can't think what it was?"

"I'm trying to."

Clane watched her intently. "Something in the way he was breathing?" he asked after a moment.

"*That's* it," she said. "Why didn't I think of it in the first place? He was breathing as though he was excited about something when he came in."

"Or as though he'd been running?"

"Well, not just before he came in here, but he might have been running earlier and . . . you know, he was breathing short and quick-like. You're wrong on one thing, though. It wasn't just before we closed up. It was just about ten-thirty when he came in here, and he was out by quarter of eleven."

Clane thought that over. "You're certain?"

"Absolutely. I was sort of keeping an eye on the clock. I had a date."

"You'd know him if you saw him again?"

"Sure."

"I don't suppose you could give me any clue as to the number he called?"

"Gosh, no, except that the exchange number was down by the bottom of the dial and the number was up near the top.

The exchange number might have been—oh say, Twin Oaks or something like that and he was dialing the T and then the W."

Clane pushed the dollar bill across to her and then extracted a five-dollar bill from his billfold and pushed that over to keep the one company. "Thanks a lot," he told her.

"Oh, I'm sure you're welcome. Could I . . . do you want to leave a number and in case he should come in again, I . . ."

"No, that's all right," Clane said. "I think I know everything that I need to know. You're sure the car was a convertible?"

"Yes. I know that, a dark convertible."

"And it was driven by a woman?"

"I'm pretty certain she was a young woman, but I didn't get a good look at her—through the doors you know, and looking out into the night. It was foggy and . . ."

"Yes, I know. Thanks."

Outside of the restaurant, Terry Clane paused for a moment to take into consideration the various aspects of the problem which confronted him.

Edward Harold had left the warehouse in something of a panic. He had been running. And the time element indicated the facts were not as the police had reconstructed the murder of George Gloster. In fact Edward Harold had, perhaps, a perfect alibi if he had only remained long enough in the company of this mysterious woman.

This woman had not been the party to whom he had first appealed for aid. That party had not answered. So then as a last resort Harold had called an alternate number and that number had responded. A woman in a convertible automobile had come to meet him. That woman could hardly have been Cynthia. Could it have been her sister, Alma?

Clane gave that matter consideration and called Alma by telephone. "Let's try being casual," he warned. "I didn't get you up, did I?"

"Of course not, I'm a working woman."

"Working on a portrait?"

"Uh-huh."

"Anyone I know?"

"No. Some rich nabob wants his wife portrayed on canvas. She admits she isn't looking quite her best right now but next summer she intends to take off ten pounds and those lines on her face are because she's been under quite a strain lately and hasn't been sleeping well. She's quite certain they'll disappear."

"In other words, she wants you to paint her the way she'll be next summer and she thinks that will be the way she looked ten years ago."

"Exactly."

"Nice going," Terry said.

"Oh, it isn't so bad. After all, art deals with composition and lighting and character. The envelope of flesh in which that character is contained is not quite as important as many people think. You know, Terry, I sometimes think that a really good portrait painter could paint a subject at any age from ten to seventy and if the portrayal were really faithful, there shouldn't be a great deal of difference in the eyes, the pose of the head, the set of the mouth. That isn't as absurd as it sounds. It's just expressing a principle of character. What have you heard from Cynthia?"

"I think she's all right, Alma. I'm not in touch with her right at the moment. Say, how about borrowing a car?"

"Why, certainly, you may have mine."

"What is it? Roadster, coupé, or . . ."

"It's a nice conservative, quiet sedan."

"Not a convertible?"

"No."

"I'm trying to find a convertible automobile," Clane said. "I want to drive past a building and take some movies of the lines of almost perpendicular perspective. You don't know anyone that has a convertible, do you?"

"Gosh, no. Not unless you feel on friendly terms with Daphne."

"Who's Daphne?"

"Daphne Taonon. Ricardo Taonon's wife."

"Eurasian?"

"Heavens, no! She's a blond showgirl with a figure like an art calendar. And she likes to show it."

"She has a convertible?"

"Uh-huh."

"Is it hers or her husband's?"

"Hers individually. No one else ever drives it. Not that I've seen. That is, her husband doesn't."

"You don't know her well enough to borrow it?"

"Heavens, no. Tell me about Cynthia, Terry. What's she doing? Have you heard anything . . . ?"

"I don't know where she is," Terry said, "and even if I did . . . well, you know, the walls have ears and telephone lines have feelers."

"You don't think they'd tap *my* line, do you?"

"Can't tell what they'd do," Clane said. "But don't worry about Cynthia. She's thoroughly able to take care of herse'f. I understand, incidentally, the police have some clues that weren't given to the press. You've read the papers?"

"You mean about Gloster?"

"Yes."

"I've read them. They say someone was hiding in the warehouse and that police think it was Edward Harold. If he was there, well, that should let Cynthia out of it, shouldn't it? *She* couldn't have put him *there*."

"I should think that's right," Clane said, "but let's wait to talk about that."

"When will I see you, Terry?"

"I'll be dropping by later on in the day."

"Do, Terry, and . . . well, you know."

"I know," Clane said and hung up.

So Ricardo Taonon's wife had a convertible and it was her own property and no one else ever drove it and Edward Harold had called her not as his first choice but as his second. A woman with a superb figure who liked to show it. Edward Harold's *second* choice.

Terry Clane, standing in the doorway of the telephone booth at the service station from which he had placed his call, began to breathe regularly and deeply, filling his blood with oxygen, letting the rhythm of his breathing furnish the preliminary foundation for concentration. Then when he had properly readied himself, he threw his mind completely into pin-point focus on the problem which confronted him.

Edward Harold had an alibi—or did he? When had he jumped from that window? Why had he jumped? Had it been because Gloster had walked in? If that were so, then Gloster had been in the warehouse probably as early as ten-thirty. Yet he had telephoned Clane shortly after eleven. And what of Edward Harold? That man at the time he had jumped through that window was already being sought by the police, a fugitive from justice with a death sentence hanging over his head. Routed unexpectedly from the hide-out where he had established himself for a long stay, fleeing out into the city without hat or coat . . . The police, already hot on his trail, would redouble their efforts to find him. Every new occupant of a hotel would be subject to suspicion. A man who would try to find a room without baggage at eleven o'clock at night . . . Airports watched, train terminals under surveillance . . . What would a man do under those circumstances? Where would he go? How would he hide?

A few seconds later, Clane became conscious of the service station attendant watching him.

Clane smiled and started walking away.

"Hey," the attendant called, "you all right?"

"Yes, why?"

"I don't know. I thought something had happened. All of a sudden you stood still and looked as though . . . looked as though you were sleeping with your eyes open."

"I was thinking of something," Clane said and hurried away.

He now had the answer that he wanted.

Clane couldn't be certain that he was right because he hadn't had all the facts on which to predicate a solution. But he felt that he knew what Edward Harold would try to do, the only thing that was left for him to do, if the facts were as Terry Clane understood them.

Discreet inquiry of the night man at the garage of the apartment house where Ricardo Taonon lived, plus a ten-dollar bill, gave Clane additional information as well as a look at Daphne Taonon's convertible.

The car was a dark, low-slung, sleek convertible. It had been returned to the garage at about eight-thirty in the morning.

The man didn't know when it had been taken out. He came on duty at seven o'clock.

There was no evidence that the car had been off the main-traveled highway, no dust on the inner rims of the wheel. The windshield was now clean and polished. The day man said he had done that. When the car had been brought in, the windshield had been streaked with the evidences of moisture which had collected from fog drippings. There had been two clear semicircular spaces where the windshield wipers had fought back the moisture. The sides of the automobile were still streaked with stain where water, dripping down from the windshield, had been thrown back by the wind. The day man had suggested to Mrs. Taonon that he would "clean it up a little bit." He just hadn't got at it yet. He had polished the windshield, checked the radiator, and was about ready to wipe off the car with a damp cloth. It didn't need a general wash, just a good wiping.

Clane made note of the license number.

The garage man volunteered more information. The night switchboard operator had told him long distance had been calling Mrs. Taonon at intervals all night. There had been no answer; apparently both Mr. and Mrs. Taonon had been out since midnight at least.

In a rented "drive-yourself" car, Terry Clane started exploring the possibilities.

Time, he knew, was running out. Yet he had to play a lone hand; to hurry would be fatal. His course of action called for self-discipline as rigorous as that inflicted upon himself by a race-track habitué who must discipline himself to a predetermined manner of betting over a period of weeks in order to play a consistent system.

Simply because he did not have the time to cover all of the territory, and because he knew that according to the law of probabilities, the better class of auto courts would have been completely filled up long before midnight, Clane decided on only the smaller, less pretentious courts.

He had four routes to choose from—one over the Golden Gate Bridge up through Marin County, another across the bay bridge up the Sacramento Road, another down through the Altamont Pass to the San Joaquin, and, last of all, the peninsular road down to San José. And it was this last road that Clane took, merely because it would have been difficult to guard. The other roads involved crossing toll bridges, and plain-clothes officers unobtrusively stationed at the toll gates could have scrutinized closely the occupants of each automobile as toll was collected.

Clane sped on down the wide road, passed up all stops until he had left San José behind. Then he started his inquiries.

It was quite conceivable that Daphne Taonon would have written down a wrong license number on the register of an auto court, but she was not so apt to have misrepresented the type of car she was driving since that would have been a glaring discrepancy too easy to check.

Painstakingly Clane covered all of the smaller auto courts until at length a growing doubt turned to the bitter taste of defeat. He had quite evidently failed to duplicate Edward Harold's process of reasoning. Or else they had taken a chance in crossing on one of the toll bridges.

Clane drove on, confident that he had now passed the last remote point of probability at which the parties would have stopped. He was now persevering only because he could, for the moment, think of nothing better.

An auto court of the cheaper sort was ahead on the right and because it offered a good place to turn around, Clane drove up to it. His inquiries were made merely from force of habit. Had a convertible containing a man and a woman registered at about—and Clane, doing quick mental arithmetic as to driving time, fixed the hour as one o'clock in the morning.

The woman who ran the place was in the aggressive forties, a woman who had been kicked around enough by life to learn to fight back. Her combat with life had given her a "what's-in-it-for-me" attitude and a theory that if you didn't grab what you wanted out of life the minute you saw it someone else was going to snatch it first.

Obviously she didn't want any trouble with the law, but Terry would get no real cooperation from her until she knew more of what was in the wind.

"We rent cabins pretty late sometimes."

139

"My question was specific," Clane said, and paved the way with a ten-dollar bill, his pulse surging with sudden hope.

"Well, yes. We did rent a cabin. What's *your* interest in it?"

"I am trying to find the woman," Clane said. "I believe she drove away."

"Yes, she's working in town. The husband's got the flu. He's staying here in bed."

"That's too bad," Clane said. "You don't know where I could locate the woman?"

"She's some sort of a saleswoman, I think. They're selling stockings or something. Maybe cosmetics. She said she'd be out early in the morning, I don't know just what time she left. She was gone when I got up. The husband's still there, feeling pretty much under the weather. Maybe if you wanted to go into town, you could spot the car, a nice convertible."

"I'll talk with the husband," Clane said. "He may know. What cabin's he in?"

"Just a minute," the woman said. "Let's have an understanding. I don't want any rough stuff."

"There won't be."

"Sometimes a married woman runs away from a husband she don't like."

"That's her privilege."

"And the husband lots of times thinks he should follow her up and get nasty."

"I wouldn't feel that way. If a woman didn't want me, I certainly wouldn't want her. What cabin did this couple take?"

"You a friend of the man or the woman?"

"I've never seen either one of them in my life."

"You ain't a paid detective?"

Clane, meeting the hesitancy in her eyes, was conscious of a red light.

He turned to look over her shoulder. A high-powered sedan of the type driven by county sheriffs was slowing down at the entrance of the driveway.

"Quick," Clane said. "Where's your register, what's the cabin?"

"I don't know . . ."

Clane pointed toward the red spotlight. "You fool," he said,

140

"do you want your place advertised as a gangster hide-out?"

She gave the car a quick look. "Number three," she said.

Clane sprinted for the cabin she had indicated, noticing as he did so that the big sedan had stopped, blocking the driveway, apparently waiting for other cars which were behind to catch up before turning into the court.

The door of the cabin was locked from the inside.

"Who is it?" a man's voice called.

Clane said gruffly, "This is your landlord. There's a long-distance call from San Francisco for you. A woman wants to talk to the occupant of cabin three. She won't give her name. Think you can take it?"

"Sure."

There were quick steps on the thin carpet behind the door, then the door opened.

Clane, lowering his shoulder, charged against the door.

The occupant of the cabin was not caught entirely by surprise. He spun back, somewhat off balance for a moment, but quickly caught himself, and Clane found he was looking into a round black hole at the business end of a .38 caliber revolver. Back of the weapon were eyes that were hard with desperation and a species of insane defiance. The man circled, keeping behind the gun, kicked the door shut.

"You're Edward Harold," Clane said. "I'm Terry Clane, you may have heard of me."

"So *you're* back."

"I'm back."

"How did you trace me here?"

"The same way that the police did," Clane said, "only I had to leave a back trail."

"What do you mean, the police did?"

"Just what I say. Take a look out through that curtain and you'll find the sheriff's car blocking the road out. He's probably waiting for an automobile driven by Inspector Malloy of the San Francisco Homicide Squad to make a rendezvous with him."

"I see. You want me to look out the window so you can jump me."

141

Clane said, "What I want you to do is to walk out and give yourself up."

Harold's laugh was derisive.

Clane said, "I have a theory on this thing. I think I can help you but I can't do a thing if you don't surrender."

"I know. You want me to surrender. You'd like to have me out of the way. You came back from China at a very opportune time, at a *very opportune* time, didn't you? You walked out on Cynthia and now you'd like to have her back. For a while I was in the way, then you heard . . ."

"Don't be foolish," Clane said.

"I'm not being foolish, I'm just telling you facts. If you're telling the truth and there's a sheriff's car out there, I'm not going out of here alive. I'll fight it out right here. I've got the guns and the ammunition. Personally, I think you're lying to me."

"I'm telling you the truth."

"All right, I'm going to go out feet first and you're going out the same way. Don't kid yourself, Clane. The minute the first shot is fired, I'm going to see that you get a dose of lead poisoning."

Clane said, "You fool, I think you stand a chance. If . . ."

There were hard pounding steps on the porch, knuckles banged on the door. "Open up," a gruff voice said.

Harold motioned Clane to silence as he tiptoed stealthily back toward a corner.

"Come on, Harold," a voice said, "the jig is up. This is the sheriff. I'm taking you into custody as an escapee."

Harold said nothing.

"Come on, don't be a fool. We've got the place surrounded," a new voice said, the voice of Inspector James Malloy of San Francisco.

"Come and get me," Harold shouted as the doorknob rattled and the door bent under the weight of a burly shoulder. "Stay away from that door if you value your life. I'm going to start putting lead through it."

There was that in his voice that carried conviction. There was a sound of motion outside the door, then sudden silence.

Seconds became minutes. Nothing from the outside disturbed the calm tranquillity of the afternoon. Inside the shabby cabin the curtains were drawn. The afternoon sunlight which turned the curtains into oblongs of gold beat against the western side of the flimsy board cabin and warmed the close air in the place until it seemed stifling.

The cabin contained the usual cheap furniture: an iron bedstead with a thin mattress, a worn carpet, a cheap dressing table, a dark-finished pine rocking chair, two cane-bottomed straight-backed chairs, a cement shower with a faucet which wouldn't quite shut off.

In the tense, hot silence of the cabin, Clane could hear the drip, drip, drip of water from the leaky shower and the lazy buzz of a big fly which circled around the room, striking against the warmth of the window shades at intervals in an attempt to follow the source of sunlight to a means of egress.

Clane noticed the tenseness of the skin over Harold's knuckles, saw the sheen of small beads of perspiration across the skin of his forehead.

Clane said evenly, "If you surrender, you stand a chance. The minute you pull the trigger on that gun for the first shot, you've sealed your fate. That's assault with a deadly weapon with intent to commit murder. It's resisting an officer. They'll throw the book at you even if you could fight free on the other charge."

Harold said grimly, his eyes still on the door, "Don't kid yourself, the first shot isn't going to be any assault with a deadly weapon with intent to commit murder. It's going to be a dead-center shot right in the middle of your yellow guts."

Clane said, "Whoever engineered your escape wasn't doing you a favor. It was putting your neck in a noose."

"Keep talking," Harold said. "If you can talk your way out of this, you'll be a world's champion. You . . ."

A slight scraping sound from the front porch caused him to jerk the gun half toward the door.

Abruptly and without warning the glass of the window crashed explosively. The window shade billowed inward from the force of a solid body which had been hurled through the glass, then snapped upward as the impact released the catch which was holding the shade down.

A tear-gas bomb from which the plug had been pulled rolled free of the broken glass; from the nozzle came a hissing sound as the gas spewed out into the room.

"Don't reach for it," Clane yelled as Harold started forward. "They'll be waiting to machine-gun you."

The first whiff of the tear gas stung Clane's nostrils. He saw Harold brace himself for a leap to grab the tear-gas bomb and throw it back out through the window.

At that moment Clane went forward in a football tackle.

He felt his shoulders smash against Harold's body, heard the rattle of a sub-machine-gun, then a voice yelling, "Hold everything."

Clane's eyes and nostrils caught a full undiluted whiff of the tear gas and he went blind, the tears streaming down his face; but his hands were busy getting a wrestler's lock on Harold's arms.

They were threshing blindly about the floor, Clane holding on with dogged persistence, trying to get a scissors hold on Harold's legs, Harold kicking and pummeling with his knees, trying to break free.

Clane could hear the sound of Harold's labored breathing, felt the cold perspiration of Harold's skin against his cheek, heard the hissing of the tear gas; and then suddenly Harold's arms were jerked back. The struggling ceased.

From the vague realm of space above him, which he could not see because of his blinded eyes, Clane heard Inspector Jim Malloy's voice saying in shocked surprise, "Well, I'll be damned! It's Terry Clane!"

## 16

CLANE felt the bite of handcuffs on his wrists. He was guided to a chair out in the open air away from the sting of the tear gas.

Jim Malloy did the talking. "You certainly do get around, Mr. Clane. You certainly do get around."

"I was trying to get Edward Harold to surrender to the police."

"And we got here just in time to upset your plans."

"That's right."

"Now ain't that too bad?" Malloy said sympathetically. "That's just a lousy, rotten break, because the way it's going to look to the D.A. is that you had been hiding Harold all along. First you get down to the warehouse where he's hiding and then blessed if you don't take right off in an automobile and pick him up in the auto camp where he's hiding. I suppose you'd call it sort of an intuition. Maybe you're like a bird dog and can just locate him by scent."

Clane said, "I located him the same way you did."

"And how did we locate him?"

"I suppose by using your head."

"Well, now, isn't that interesting? Do you mean a man could just sit down and think and find out what particular auto court this man happened to be hidden in?"

"Don't be foolish," Clane said wearily. "I decided an auto court was the only place for him to go, an auto court that was pretty well outside of the city. If you'll check back you'll find that I've been stopping all the way between San José and here asking at every one of the less pretentious auto courts."

"Well now, if you have," Malloy said, "that might be . . . No, I guess it wouldn't either. The D.A. would laugh at me. He'd say, 'Don't be silly, Jim, that's an easy way to make an alibi. It's something the guy did himself and it didn't take him over half an hour or an hour at the outside to do. If word got around that we were pushovers for stuff like that, why everybody would be doing it.'"

"Have it your own way," Clane said.

"You're something of a mystery to me," Malloy went on. "I mean you really are, Clane. I just can't figure it out. Now here you are, back from China, sitting on top of the world, and you start right in mixing in with this thing, which is after all really none of your business. Now take that Chinese scrub woman you have, for instance. You know, you almost had me fooled there. I thought I'd better give her a lift down to China-town and talk to her a little bit, and then she fooled me. I was all ready to let her go but I thought I'd better take a look in that laundry package. And what do you think I found in there?"

Clane said nothing.

"A woman's plaid coat and a hat, an expensive pair of shoes that fit the Chinese girl's feet like a glove, a pair of real genuine nylon stockings and an expensive silk blouse. Now I leave it to you, Clane, if that ain't a mighty funny package of laundry for a woman to be taking away from a man's apartment. Now, the funny thing about that coat is that it seems to be Cynthia Renton's coat. There's a tailor's label on the inside and the tailor says it's a coat he made for Cynthia Renton."

"And what does the Chinese girl say?"

"Well, the Chinese girl doesn't say anything much. She sort of intimates that the clothes are cast-off things that had been given to her by some Chinese charitable outfit, but she was carrying a purse with over five hundred dollars in it and a driving license in the name of Sou Ha, and she can't tell us the name of the charitable agency that gave her the clothes. And then I got to thinking around about that case we had years ago and darned if there wasn't a Chinese girl mixed up in that case. I think *her* name was Sou Ha. You know how it is with these Chinese, Mr. Clane, it's hard to remember their faces, particularly the women. One looks exactly like another."

"And so you arrested her?" Clane asked.

"Well, we didn't exactly arrest her. We're holding her for questioning. She's what you might call the guest of the city, if you know what I mean."

"I guess I know what you mean."

"Perhaps *you* can explain how it happens that she had Cynthia Renton's coat?"

"I don't feel much like making explanations right now."

"Well, now, that's too bad. And you were the one who could concentrate so readily, too. You could concentrate regardless of distractions and all that stuff."

Clane said nothing.

"I was hoping perhaps you could concentrate on some of this stuff. After all, Clane, I hate to take you along and charge you with being an accessory after the fact. Now suppose you tell us just how you knew Harold was at this place."

"If you've been sleuthing around, locating him here, you certainly must have crossed my back trail."

There was a moment's silence and Clane would have given much if he could have seen the expression on Malloy's face. But after a moment Malloy said, almost too casually, "Suppose you tell us just how you went about it, Clane."

Clane told him of the survey of the places from which Harold could have placed a call, the trail he had uncovered, his patient work in running it down.

Malloy listened without interruption. How much of it was news to him, Clane had no means of knowing.

When Clane had finished, Malloy said, "I've been looking into the whereabouts of the two Taonons. Around eight-thirty this morning Mrs. Taonon rang up police headquarters to see if there had been any news of her husband—said he hadn't been home all night and she was afraid there might have been a traffic accident or something. She said he got a phone call around ten o'clock and rushed out as though he was in quite a hurry. He told her he'd be back in thirty minutes—but he never came back. And now it seems that *she's* disappeared, too. The man that went to their apartment reports that she isn't there.

"Now then," Malloy went on, "I saw you in that grocery store up near Hendrum's place. I suppose you were making inquiries trying to find out where those groceries came from. Now that's police routine. An amateur just can't do that sort of stuff. In the first place, you don't have any standing. You make the grocers suspicious and you're talking about a good customer of theirs.

"You can see what's bound to happen. You go into a store and start asking questions about whether Bill Hendrum, let us say, bought an order of groceries in the last few days consisting of about forty or fifty dollars' worth of canned goods and stuff. The manager of the store won't tell you whether he did or didn't. Then, before you're out of the store good, the proprietor rings up Bill Hendrum in case Hendrum happens to be a customer of his and tells him all about the conversation."

Clane looked properly contrite.

"So you see," Malloy went on, "that's where you amateurs mess things up. Now the police move in, take over the inquiry and have some official status. They can warn the grocer not to say anything and then start questioning him. In that way, they don't alarm the suspect."

"Yes, I see your point, now that you make it," Clane said apologetically.

"So, you see," Malloy went on, "by ten o'clock this morning, we knew where those groceries came from—something you wouldn't have been able to find out in a week, even if you'd done nothing but leg work."

"Where did they come from?" Clane asked.

"Well, now," Malloy said, "I don't know as there's any harm in telling you, the way things are right now. They were purchased by Mrs. Ricardo Taonon."

Clane was silent, thinking that over.

"And," Inspector Malloy went on musingly, "Taonon was a pretty good husband in some ways."

"You say 'was,' " Clane observed.

"Well, now, I did, didn't I?" Malloy said. "That's funny— just some sort of a subconscious trick, I guess."

"You mean he's dead?"

"He's disappeared, was the way I expressed it."

"That was the way you expressed it, and then you started referring to him in the past tense."

"Well, I don't know why I did that," Malloy said. "What I started out to say was that he was a good husband. He has a lot of businesses that are more or less tangled up, but I understand he's fixed things so that in case anything happens to him his wife won't have any trouble raising money to meet taxes and all that stuff. He carries quite a slug of insurance."

"And you think something's happened to him?"

"Well, now, I wouldn't want you to quote me as saying he'd been killed."

"But you think he has?"

"I'm not thinking. I'm asking questions. You don't know anything about him, do you?"

"In what way?"

"Oh, about his not being—shall we say available?"

"No. I wish you'd tell me what you found out about him. How did he die?"

"I didn't say he was dead."

"You intimated it."

"I'm just commenting about what we found out," Malloy said. "You see, we're trying to find out about that call that sent Taonon rushing out last night. So we asked his partner in this Oriental company—chap by the name of Stacey Nevis. You know him?"

"Yes."

"Well, Nevis hadn't called him, but he thought Gloster had."

"Indeed?"

"That's right. Nevis had a call himself from Gloster. You see, Stacey Nevis was out with some friends playing cards— a sociable little poker game—and Nevis was winning. So naturally the boys didn't want him to leave and take the winnings with him—just human nature."

"Go on," Clane said, fighting to keep the eagerness out of his voice.

"Well, now," Malloy said, "that's just about all there was to it. Nevis got to winning early in the evening, and it seems he began to get telephone calls wanting him to go places, and naturally the boys didn't want him to go. He had a call from Gloster, who seemed very much excited—said that he'd gone down to the warehouse for something or other and found that someone was living in the warehouse, and he wanted Nevis to come down there right away. Said he had already called Ricardo Taonon and got him to come down. Said he'd been trying to call Nevis for half an hour. Wasn't until Taonon gave him the number of the place where the poker game was on that Gloster knew where he could reach Nevis."

"And what did Nevis do?" Clane asked.

"What could he do? The minute he started to talk about getting away, the boys got up in arms. They could hear his conversation on the telephone. He was in an adjoining room, but the door was open and they started shouting at Nevis that if he left the game before midnight, it would mean a fifty-dollar fine. Well, Nevis was in something of a quandary. First he told

Gloster he'd come down there; then he explained the situation to him and they talked for a minute, and then Gloster said that he'd tell Taonon to wait for him and he'd make a quick run up to where Nevis was playing poker and talk with Nevis up there. So Nevis finally agreed to that."

"And Gloster came up?" Clane asked.

"That's right. Gloster drove up outside and honked his horn. Nevis went down and talked with him. Then Nevis went back to the game and Gloster went back to the warehouse. And that, as nearly as the time can be fixed, was about ten or fifteen minutes before Gloster telephoned to you. Gloster must have had that talk with Nevis and then driven back to the warehouse, met Ricardo Taonon, talked with you, and then got himself murdered when he was trying to put through a telephone call to somebody."

"And who do you claim murdered him? Who's the official suspect now?"

"Either you and Cynthia Renton did it," Malloy said, "or Edward Harold came back and pulled the trigger to keep Gloster from calling the police. My associates pick Harold. Me, I'm not so sure."

"I suppose," Clane said somewhat wearily, "Nevis has witnesses to all these facts you're giving me?"

"Witnesses?" Malloy said. "My gosh, what are you trying to get at now, Mr. Clane?"

"I was just asking a question."

"Well, it sounded suspicious. Like a little more of your amateur getting the cart before the horse. Witnesses, bless my soul, yes! I guess you never tried to get away from a poker game when you were a heavy winner. Has he got witnesses? He's got a whole tableful of witnesses, six men in that poker game and five of them out money to Stacey Nevis! Has he got witnesses? I'll say he has."

"And what time did this poker game finally break up?"

"About three o'clock in the morning."

"Nevis still winner?"

Malloy chuckled. "Nevis lost his shirt. So you see, Mr. Clane, why it's a bad thing to have you running around with this amateurish enthusiasm of yours. You mess things up—although I will admit you probably saved us some shooting when we picked up Harold here. But I'm afraid I've got to put you out of circulation for a while."

Clane said, "Tell me one thing, Inspector."

"What's that?"

"Down in that warehouse, there were four fresh fingerprints on the desk blotter—apparently the prints of dusty fingers. Whose prints were they? Taonon's? Harold's?"

"No, they were Gloster's."

"Gloster's!"

"That's right, the dead man's. The prints of four fingers on the left hand, spread out so each was about an inch apart."

Clane said, almost musingly, "As I remember it, the prints of the first and second fingers were broad, that of the little finger hardly more than a dot."

"That's right."

"Indicating that Gloster was standing at the desk—probably bent over it, his weight resting on his left hand which was turned so that most of the weight was on the first two fingers and on the thumb."

"That's right, only there was no thumb print."

"It's almost impossible to put weight on the first two fingers without touching the thumb to the same surface," Clane said.

"I didn't say he didn't *touch* the thumb," Malloy said. "I said there was no thumb *print*. The prints were made from dust. The thumb simply didn't have any dust on it, therefore it left no print."

"And why was there dust on the fingers but none on the thumb?" Clane asked.

"Lord bless you, Mr. Clane, *I* wouldn't know! That's the sort of thing we leave to you bright amateurs. And now, Mr. Clane, if you're ready, I'm afraid I've got to arrest you as being an accessory after the fact. It's too bad, but I have to do it. No hard feelings, Mr. Clane."

But Terry Clane made no answer. For the moment his face was an expressionless mask as though he were in a hypnotic trance.

## 17

THE sweetish smell of jail disinfectant filled the air, permeated Terry Clane's clothing, clung to his hands until it seemed a sticky tangible something from which there was no escape. The corridors reeked with an aura of discouragement, of human oppression. Under the veneer of men's enforced acquiescence in the will of their captors lay a vicious resentment that lurked in the corners of the jail as an intangible psychic force evaporating wherever one looked, only to form in a miasmic menace behind one's back.

Terry Clane and Edward Harold occupied the cell together, a cell which contained two wooden stools, an unscreened toilet, a washbasin and two steel bunks, hinged to the wall and let down by a chain into a level position. Each had a thin straw mattress and one blanket.

Harold said to Clane, "They have no right to put you in here. They haven't even put a charge against you yet."

Clane said, "Right or not, I'm here."

"Aren't you going to do anything about it?"

"Perhaps."

Harold, seated on the stool, his elbows resting on his spread knees, his back humped in an attitude of dejection, said, "I'd ten times rather be dead."

Clane said nothing.

"I'd made up my mind to go out fighting. I don't want to be cooped up like a rat watching the days trickle away until they drag me out of my cell and shove me into a gas chamber."

Clane said, "On the contrary, this is the best thing that's happened to you for a long time."

Harold raised his eyebrows.

"Now," Clane said, "we're going to go ahead with your appeal. You would have been in a stronger position if you had surrendered to the police, but even as it is you have a chance. The Supreme Court is going to look over the case pretty carefully. It won't have the emotional instability of a jury. The

152

only thing that convicted you was lying about going back to Farnsworth's house that second time. But that doesn't necessarily mean you committed a murder. It merely means that you falsified your testimony."

Harold's head drooped down until his eyes were fixed in unwinking scrutiny on the floor of the cell.

There was a long period of silence, a period which would have been awkward under any other circumstances. But in the jail there was no criterion for the passing of time. Here human beings were frozen into a static existence which left them divorced from life itself. They had the semblance of free and independent agencies but there was no place for them to go, nothing to do. Time moved on, but time ceased to have any significance because time would lead to no change. It was as though some motion-picture machine had suddenly broken down, leaving the images of men projected upon a screen. The attitude was one of action. The external manifestation of the figures was that of animation, but that appearance was only an arbitrary illusion. The figures remained stationary on the screen. The figure that was walking kept his leg advanced, his foot upraised, but the step he was about to take never materialized.

Already the grip of the jail had impressed itself upon these men so that the long minutes of silence seemed to call for no attempt at alleviating the conversational inactivity. There in the jail cell, silence and inaction were normal. One could resist them with spasmodic bits of conversation, with an occasional physical motion, but those were gestures of futility. In the end, the silence and the inaction were destined to dominate the scene.

"You know," Harold said at length, "for a while I thought . . . I thought you were sort of a god. Then, after I had started to worship you, I came to hate you."

Clane sat silent.

Harold kept his head down, his chin on his chest. "Hell," he said, "what's the use? I'm finished. My race is run. I worshiped you and then I came to hate you because you were standing between Cynthia and me. You have done something to Cynthia that can never be undone. You have impressed your personality so indelibly upon her that you have made her a part of you. You can separate, you can even fight, but you can't resist that peculiar blending. You're welded together in some way."

"In other words," Clane said, "you're jealous. And your jealousy has distorted your perspective."

"Of course I'm jealous. I was jealous. I've nothing to be jealous of any more. A dead man can't have a wife."

"You're not dead yet."

"I'm legally dead."

"Nonsense."

Once more silence dominated the scene, a silence steeped in the sticky sweet smell of jail antiseptic. Night had fallen and this wing of the big jail was silent save for an occasional rumbling of noise which came from one of the tanks up near the front. A big incandescent blazed down from the ceiling. Soon it would be switched out and only a small night light would furnish dim illumination, the forces of darkness allying themselves with those of silence to finish their work of crushing the human initiative of the inmates.

"I suppose I did make a mistake," Harold said. "I certainly got my defense all messed up. I lied to my lawyer and that's always bad. After all, it was really you that did it."

"I did?" Clane asked in surprise.

"You remember that figure you gave Cynthia, the figure of the man on the mule?"

"Yes."

"I don't know how much of the real philosophy of that Cynthia ever got. She's a spontaneous creature. You don't associate her with philosophy. She's an opportunist, an extravert."

"I know," Clane said.

"Lovable because she has no need for philosophy. She lives her philosophy. She's keyed to the universe in some way. She is life. What I'm trying to say is that life manifests itself through her and life is immortal. Life is spontaneous. Life is perpetual youth. And Cynthia is a priestess of that ... Oh, hell, I'm getting all balled up trying to tell you something that you can't express in words."

"I know what you mean," Clane said.

Harold was silent again, then after a minute or two went on as though there had been no break in the conversation. "She told me something about the philosophy of that figure on the mule. You'd told her about it and she'd remembered just enough of it to make it impress itself on my mind. I kept thinking over what she'd told me, adding to it. Perhaps building up something of my own ideas in connection with it until it seemed . . . Well, it seemed something of a philosophy of life that was completely satisfying, a soul food which contained all the vitamins. Damned if I know why I'm talking to you this way, but you're probably the last man I will ever see who will have the ability to understand what I'm trying to say. Despite the fact that I hate your guts."

"You don't need to hate me," Clane said.

"I do, and don't come back with any of that sop about having no hatred for me, only pity. You stepped in and succeeded where I've failed. I thought I had Cynthia's love before I learned that she didn't have any love left to give. Her heart was yours. She thought she had taken it back from you, but she hadn't. She couldn't."

Clane said, "As to that, I'm quite sure you're wrong."

"And I'm sure I'm right."

"I know Cynthia pretty well."

"You knew her pretty well. How much have you seen of her in the last three years?"

"Nothing."

"There you are," Harold said. "You planted a seed. It germinated and grew—just as a man could stick a seed in a flower pot and walk away and say, 'See, there's nothing but barren soil in that flower pot.' But three months later he'd come back and find that it had sprouted a rose bush which had come into blossom. I tell you I've been with Cynthia. I studied her. I've seen her and I know."

Clane sat silent and the other seemed to have no feeling of resentment for that silence, to consider it as purely normal.

"You can believe it or not," Harold went on, "but I liked Farnsworth. Farnsworth was an interesting chap. He had a lot on the ball. And he had a lot of thoughts that many people don't have. The day Farnsworth was killed I went to see him, and there was something on Horace Farnsworth's mind. He tried to talk to me and couldn't. He bogged down. It was something that had him on the ropes. I asked him if it was about Cynthia's dough, asked him if he'd lost it. He said, no, that her money was all right. And then he told me that he'd got himself in a jam where there was no way out. He said he was licked. I couldn't get out of him what it was. But I did learn that he was right on the ragged edge. He was . . . hell, Clane, the guy was getting ready to commit suicide."

"So what did you do?" Clane asked.

"I told him to wait right there, that I was going to be back, and I went out to Cynthia's and got that figure of the man on the mule. I wanted to go back and talk to Horace Farnsworth about it. That philosophy has steadied me down in many a tight spot. The figure got to mean a lot to me. The old guy was a friend of mind, an adviser, a father-confessor. I was hoping that I could talk to Horace Farnsworth and make him understand something of what I saw in the figure."

Harold ceased talking, and the silence of the cell enveloped them.

Clane shifted his position on the stool. Harold sat with his elbows on his knees, motionless, brooding, dreaming of the past and of the strange whim of fate which had trapped him in the meshes of a first-degree murder charge, left him an outcast among his fellows, a man condemned to death.

"Funny thing," Harold said, musingly, after a while, "the way Fate has tricked things around. There I was wanting to go to Farnsworth to give him some sort of a philosophical life, and as a result I have to die."

"You're not at the end of your rope yet," Clane said.

Harold might not have heard him. "It's not that I am afraid to die. I want to live, but that doesn't mean I'm afraid to die . . . only to the extent that man fears the unknown. After all, what *is* death?"

"A name," Clane said.

"How's that?"

"I said death was nothing but a name, a label. When man encounters something he can't understand and doesn't know how to study, he puts a label on it and then dismisses it. Just so a thing has a tag . . ."

"How could you study death?" Harold interrupted.

"By studying life."

"Death is different from life."

"Who said so?"

Harold thought that over, then laughed, a short, nervous laugh. "Well, of course, it's always taken for granted that it has to be different from life. It's the absence of life. It's the antithesis of life."

"How about birth?" Clane asked.

"That's life."

Clane said, "What we call life is merely a segment. It's a narrow band stretching from birth to death. Granted the phenomenon of birth, we necessarily have the corollary of death. It's all a part of life. The trouble is that we don't have enough confidence in the Divine Architect. We think of Him as being able to plan the universe and control the heavens, but we're not entirely certain He knows what He's doing when it comes to *our* lives. We're just a bit uneasy that the divine scheme of things may be unjust, unpleasant, and inefficient. Therefore, we regard death as something which may have intruded upon the scheme of things when the Divine Architect had his back turned. We should realize that it's a part of life because it has to be and that if the Divine Architect planned it, it should be beneficent. . . . However, as you were saying, you intended to go back and see Farnsworth. I presume you took the image along?"

Harold nodded. "I went to Cynthia's, got the image, took it over to show Horace Farnsworth. I thought the story of that man on the mule might help him. Somehow I didn't feel his trouble was as big as he thought it was."

Harold ceased talking again; then after a moment said, "I suppose that when a man really faces death he becomes somewhat detached from life. I can see things now more as a bystander."

Clane waited. Harold remained silent.

"You were talking about going back to Farnsworth's," Clane prompted.

ERLE STANLEY GARDNER

"That's right. I wanted him to see that figure. I thought it might help him to get a grip on himself."

"Did it?" Clane asked.

"It was too late. I went up to the front door and rang the bell. There was no answer. I pounded on the door, still no answer. I was worried. When I left him, I had an idea he was ready to do something desperate. So I walked around the house. When I came to the back door, I tried it. It was unlocked. I opened it and went in.

"The house was quiet. I called out Farnsworth's name. There was no answer. I went on through the kitchen, into the study. He was there—dead.

"He was in his chair, his head over on the desk. There was a bullet wound in the head and blood was dripping down to the floor. I thought at the time that he'd killed himself. I ran over and took hold of his shoulders, trying to straighten him up. When I did that, the body slumped down to the floor, overturning the swivel chair in which he was sitting.

"Well, of course, I intended to notify the authorities. But before I did so, I looked around for the gun with which he'd killed himself and . . . well, there wasn't any gun. It took a minute or two for it to dawn on me what *that* meant. And then I realized I was in a spot. I'd gone around the house and got in the back door. That would take a lot of explaining. . . . I had an overpowering desire to get away. It was a blind urge to run. I grabbed up the image and got out of there. Of course, I was foolish, which is bad; and I was also unlucky, which is worse. People saw me leaving . . . there was blood on my trousers. I've been thinking afterwards that there may have been a spatter of blood on the image. . . . I returned it to Cynthia later and was too rattled to look and see. You just can't explain the things I did so they sound logical. Anyway, I took the easy way out and that was that."

"Do you have any idea who murdered him?"

"Of course not. If I had, I'd have done something about it."

"Any enemies?"

"I don't know of any. He was a good egg."

158

"Look here, when you went into the kitchen, what did you find?"

"What do you mean?"

"You went in through the back door?"

"That second trip I made, yes."

"And when you entered the kitchen, did you notice a pot of water on the stove?"

Harold thought for a moment. "I remember that at the trial there was evidence of a teakettle boiling on the stove. My best recollection is that the teakettle was on the stove but was *not* boiling when I entered the kitchen."

"You're certain the teakettle was on the stove?"

"Yes. And I suppose the wrist watch must have been in the oven. Of course I didn't look to see. I just walked on in through the kitchen. I've tried a hundred times to figure out why Farnsworth would have put on that water and put his wrist watch in the oven to dry out. The only explanation for the water, of course, is that Farnsworth wanted to steam open the flap of an envelope. As soon as I left, he went out to fill the kettle and was so nervous he must have got his wrist under the faucet. That got water in his watch, so he turned on the oven to dry it out while he was waiting for the water to heat."

Clane nodded thoughtfully. "No idea of what that envelope could have contained—the one he wanted to steam open?"

"No," Harold said, curtly.

Clane waited but Harold relapsed once more into silence.

Abruptly Clane broke the silence. "What happened down there at the warehouse?" he asked.

"Why should I tell you?"

"Is there any reason why you shouldn't?"

"Yes."

"What?"

"I can't betray the person who helped me."

"Don't mention that person. Just tell me what happened."

"I was being given sanctuary there in that warehouse. There was every reason to believe that it was a safe place, that no one would come there. I had been assured that things would

. . . well, that they'd be arranged so that I'd have the place all to myself.

"Then out of a clear sky something happened. I heard an automobile drive up, a key in the door, and someone was coming in. I couldn't get out through the door. I ran to the window and jumped out and ran. The lights came on just as I was climbing out of the window. I looked back and saw Gloster standing there in the doorway. He was absolutely flabbergasted. I think he saw and recognized me. I don't know."

"And he walked over to telephone?"

"I don't know what he did. I didn't stop to find out. I got out of there."

"What time was this?"

"A little after ten, about ten minutes after ten I think it was."

"And you went directly to that restaurant and telephoned?"

"Yes."

"To whom did you telephone?"

"That is something I'm not going to answer."

"Someone came and got you?"

"Yes."

"Who was it?"

"Try and find out."

"The police know."

"Then you'd better ask the police. They can tell you; I can't."

"You mean you won't."

"All right, it's the same thing."

"Gloster wasn't one of the persons who helped you escape when you were taken from the automobile?"

"Don't be silly."

"Was Bill Hendrum one of the . . ."

"Damn it, Clane, don't go flinging names around that way. Leave Bill out of this."

Clane said, "You had quite a stock of groceries there. Who bought those for you? The same person who established you in the warehouse in the first place?"

"What do *you* think?"

"I'm trying to find out what to think."

"Find out some place else then."

Clane was starting to say something when he heard the sound of echoing steps in the corridor. A key rattled in the lock. A burly, thick-necked man said, "Which one is Terry Clane?"

"I am," Clane said, stepping forward.

"Out," the man said.

"I knew they'd spring you," Harold said. "*You* haven't any hard luck."

Clane extended his hand. "Good luck," he said. "I'm probably merely being transferred. But here's luck."

After a moment Edward Harold reached out and took Clane's hand. Clane noticed that the fingers which circled his hand, the palm which pressed against his, were wet with perspiration.

"If you see God's blue sky again," Edward Harold said, "tell it hello for me," and then deliberately turned his back on Clane and the turnkey.

## 18

"**W**HAT is it?" Clane asked as they walked down the corridor.

"You are being sprung," the turnkey said.

"How?"

"Some Chinese girl and a lawyer. That's one thing about the Chinese. When they get lawyers, they get good ones. Long as I've been here, I don't think I've ever seen a Chinese show up with a cheap lawyer. He either has none at all, or else he gets the best, regardless of what it costs. Don't ever kid yourself the Chinese ain't shrewd. Cripes! I've seen lots of fellows that thought they were wise guys show up with mouthpieces that we knew all about. Damn ambulance chasers. The guys were just throwing their money away, falling for a line of bull some cheap shyster passed out. But you take the Chinese. Boy, when they show up, they really have lawyers. And you've got one this time that's the best."

"Who?" Clane asked.

"Carl Marcell."

"Never heard of him," Clane said.

"Where you been the last few years, buddy?"

"I've been in the Orient."

"I guess that accounts for it. Right this way."

The turnkey unlocked the door at the end of the corridor, flung back the heavy steel casement, and Clane found himself in a waiting room near the entrance corridor of the jail. Chu Kee and Sou Ha were there, and a tall impressive man with a profile of granite, and silver-gray hair which swept back in well-kept waves from a high forehead.

"Clane?" the man asked.

Terry nodded.

Chu Kee beamed at Clane.

The tall man put out his hand, enveloped Clane's in a muscular grip. "I'm Carl Marcell," he said. "I've been retained to act for you. I've threatened a writ of habeas corpus, and they've turned you loose rather than put a charge against you."

"And how about Sou Ha?"

"I sprang her an hour ago," Marcell said. "I had a little more trouble with you. They tried to hang on to you until the last minute. They really hated to let you go."

A door opened. Inspector Malloy appeared, his face positively beaming. "Well, well, well. You're leaving us, Mr. Clane. That's fine. That's really splendid. I'm sorry we had to detain you. It was just one of those things. But you have Mr. Marcell in your camp, and he'll take care of you. Yes, indeed, Mr. Clane, he'll take care of you."

"No hard feelings," Clane said, smiling.

Carl Marcell said, "You were only holding him. There was no charge booked against him. You had no right to put him in a cell with a convicted felon."

"Well, now, of course," Malloy beamed, "accommodations are pretty hard to get in even the best hotels. And you take a hotel such as we run, on short notice that way it's sometimes difficult to provide just the accommodations we want. But it's all right now. We didn't intend to keep your client too long."

"No longer than it took a lawyer to threaten you with a habeas corpus."

Malloy merely grinned.

The jail doors swung open and the little party debouched into the night, meeting the stares of some curious pedestrians who gazed first casually then with eager curiosity as someone pointed out the tall figure of Marcell, the famous criminal lawyer, flanked by the Chinese man and woman on the one side and a Caucasian on the other.

Clane heard one of the men say in a low voice, "Probably opium. He . . ." And then Sou Ha was opening the door of Chu Kee's big limousine and Clane was helping her into the car, then getting in beside her.

Carl Marcell gravely shook hands.

"You're not coming with us?" Clane asked.

"No," the lawyer said, "I have my own car. I don't think you'll have any more trouble, Mr. Clane; if you do, call me. Here's a card which has my office number on it, and that number up in the right-hand corner is my night number, a private phone where you can get me at any hour of the day or night. Just don't give it out to anyone. It's a number I reserve for my important clients."

"And your fees?" Clane asked.

Chu Kee said in Chinese, "What has been done is a matter of friendship."

Marcell was more explicit. "I don't suppose your friend cares about telling you all of the details, but . . . well, there is no charge."

Sou Ha added by way of explanation, "Father keeps Mr. Marcell retained by the year."

Clane showed his surprise.

"For situations of just this sort," Sou Ha said.

Then Marcell was moving back toward his car, walking with the grace of a man whose business it is to impress spectators; and Sou Ha, behind the wheel of the limousine, was warming up the motor. A moment later they glided smoothly away from the curb and out into the traffic of the city; and Terry Clane, watching the life flowing past him, could not but contrast his lot with the plight of the man whom he had left in the jail cell to be subjected to the final indignity of being stripped of his outer clothing and pushed into a small circular chamber in which presently there would be the hiss of escaping gas.

Clane's thoughts were interrupted by Sou Ha's penitent voice. "I am clumsy, O First-Born. I am so slow in my mind as to be unworthy of your teachings. I failed to outwit this police person."

"That police person," Clane said, "is plenty hard to outwit. Just what happened?"

"I do not know when he first became suspicious," Sou Ha said. "Perhaps it was almost immediately. But he took me to where I wished to go. It was only as I was getting out of the car that he suggested he had better inspect the bundle. To have protested would have made him only the more suspicious; so I pretended that it was only the outside of the bundle he wished to see, and I held it for his inspection, then pushed his hand against it so that he could see that only clothes were on the inside. I said, 'Dirty clothes. Me wash.' But it didn't fool him. He said, 'Well, let's take a look at the dirty clothes,' and right then I knew the jig was up."

"Was it bad?" Clane asked.

"Not bad. Only they wouldn't let me telephone unless I talked in English."

"Wouldn't they let you phone your father?"

"I suppose so, but that I dared not do because of the Painter Woman. The officer was smart enough to know that I must have taken the place of the Painter Woman."

"Then how did your father know where you were?" Clane asked.

Sou Ha said, "When the hours passed and I did not return, my father communicated with the lawyer."

Chu Kee sat with his hands folded in his lap, beaming out through the windshield, his alert little eyes missing no detail of the traffic, his ears taking in the conversation. But there was nothing in the expression of his countenance to indicate that he understood what was being said.

"And what about Cynthia Renton?" Clane asked.

"The Painter Woman is safe."

"Has she been able to communicate with her sister?"

"A messenger has told her sister she is all right."

Clane settled back against the cushions.

Chu Kee said blandly, as though merely pointing out a bit of scenery, "A car follows us."

"Did you think I hadn't noticed *that?*" Sou Ha asked, almost petulantly.

Chu Kee said in Chinese, "It is an ambitious fountain that seeks to be higher than the stream which feeds it."

Sou Ha said contritely and also in Chinese, "I am sorry, Father. The words slipped past my tongue."

"The wise man develops a slow tongue."

"I am afraid that today I am not wise. But," she added artfully, "I did not want you to think your daughter was unworthy of you. I expected of course we would be followed, and remember that I have the benefit of the rear-view mirror."

There were several moments of silence. "Are you going to try to ditch the following car?" Clane asked, seeing that Sou Ha was driving directly toward Chinatown with no attempt whatever to take advantage of traffic signals or crowded intersections.

"To ditch them would but make them suspicious that we had something to conceal," Sou Ha said. "We will be so innocent that we flaunt our virtue in their faces." And then she laughed.

"But we must not take them to Cynthia's place of concealment," Clane said.

"We won't," Sou Ha told him, and then almost angrily said, "I know I have done everything wrong today, but at least give me credit for *some* sense."

Chu Kee shifted his eyes in silent rebuke to his daughter's petulance, then turned his attention back to grave contemplation of the road.

"Where we are going," Sou Ha said hastily, attempting to atone for her fault, "is to see the wife of Ricardo Taonon."

"You know where she is?" Clane asked in surprise. "The police have tried to locate her without success."

"She made the mistake of going to Chinatown," Sou Ha said.

"Why a mistake?" Clane asked.

"My father," Sou Ha said with pride, "knows everything which goes on in Chinatown."

"Pride," Chu Kee said, "is the club by which Misfortune beats the virtuous into submission."

"I speak but the truth," Sou Ha pointed out.

"Ever the truth is humble," Chu Kee retorted.

"What is Mrs. Taonon doing?" Clane asked, anxious to save Sou Ha from further rebuke.

"She is attempting to hide."

"From the police?"

"From the police and others."

"What others?"

"That remains to be ascertained," Sou Ha said. "My father thought *you* would like to ask the questions."

Clane bowed his head in acknowledgment of the compliment.

Sou Ha deftly piloted the car through the traffic, entered the streets of Chinatown, turned with no attempt at concealment into a side street, and stopped the car, switched off the lights, and turned off the motor.

Another car paused at the corner to disgorge two men who seemed particularly naïve tourists, desiring to explore the streets of Chinatown.

Sou Ha did not even deign to glance at them. She stepped forward and opened the door of a small Chinese store.

A man who was seated behind the counter glanced up and then lowered his eyes to the book in which he was writing Chinese characters with a camel's hair brush held rigidly perpendicular between thumb and forefinger.

Sou Ha led the way. Her father followed, and Clane brought up the rear.

There was an arched doorway near the rear of the store. Two faded green curtains hung down to shield this doorway. Sou Ha parted the curtains and went through. They moved down a narrow passageway, came to a large room where a dozen Chinese were grouped around a circular table, playing

Chinese dominoes. They did not even glance up as the little party filed through the room and entered another passageway, then a smaller room, where there was furniture stored—apparently merely a storeroom for odds and ends, though shrewd eyes would have noticed that this furniture collected no dust, and that there were no cobwebs.

Sou Ha's fingers pressed a hidden catch, a panel of wood slid smoothly back, operated by an electrical mechanism which betrayed its presence only by a faint whirring noise. The moment Clane had stepped through the sliding panel it closed behind them and they were in darkness. A small flashlight in Sou Ha's hands disclosed steps which went down into a passageway where there was the smell of dampness. They followed this passageway for some fifty yards, then dipped down another flight of stairs, and Clane knew they were going beneath a street. Another hundred feet and they were climbing again and once more came to what seemed to be a solid wall. Again Sou Ha pressed a catch and a door opened. Another passageway led them into a small Chinese apothecary shop which fronted on a dimly lit side street.

Sou Ha glanced questioningly at her father. Chu Kee stepped forward and opened a door near the back of the store which disclosed a short corridor.

"At the end of this corridor," he said in Chinese, "there is a place, the sign on the street proclaiming it to be the Green Dragon Hotel. It rents rooms to people who sign names which are fictitious upon the register. The woman you wish is in room twenty-three. We will go there without letting her know that we come."

From here on Chu Kee took the lead, marching through the door at the end of the corridor into a narrow, dingy room which was large enough to hold half a dozen chairs and a small partitioned-off space in which were a desk, a rack for keys, a small telephone switchboard and an emaciated Chinese clerk.

The clerk barely glanced up, gave an all but imperceptible nod, then returned to a perusal of the columns of a Chinese newspaper.

Chu Kee led the way upstairs.

167

There were sounds of revelry in the first room at the head of the stairs, the laughter of a woman, too loud, too shrill and too harsh, a man's blatant boastful voice. . . . The stealthy, shadowy figure of a Chinese moved noiselessly through the dim shadows near the end of the corridor, opened a door, entered a room and quietly closed the door behind him. Another door opened. A woman dressed for the street flashed past them, leaving behind her a smell of perfume so heavy that it reminded Clane of the banked flowers at a funeral. She was still young, but her face beneath the veneer of makeup was hard; the eyes had the look of brazen defiance which is born of an inner fear. She glanced at Clane, started to smile, then saw Sou Ha and walked on past them.

Chu Kee seemed not even to notice.

The room they sought was near the end of the corridor. Chu Kee glanced questioningly at Clane.

Clane nodded and Chu Kee tapped gently on the door.

There was no sound from within.

Chu Kee knocked again, then tried the knob of the door. It was locked.

A woman's voice from behind the door called out, "Whatdyawant?"

Chu Kee signified by a sign that Sou Ha was to answer.

"I wish to talk with you," Sou Ha said politely.

The words which came from behind the door were slurred together with a coarse, careless diction. "I ain't dressed and I don't wanna talk to anybody. Get out."

"It is on account of the register," Sou Ha said, her voice subtly accenting the peculiar lilt which branded her unmistakably as being Chinese. "The last name cannot be read. It is necessary that it be written legibly so that the police will not question."

"The name's Brown. Write it any way you damn please."

"But it is necessary that you should write it, otherwise sometimes there is trouble."

"You got the book with you?"

"Yes."

The room gave forth the sounds of motion. A bolt shot back, the door opened a crack.

Clane put his weight against the door.

"Say, what the hell is this?" the woman demanded.

Clane pushed his way into the room. Chu Kee and Sou Ha followed.

Clane gently closed the door.

The woman who stood in the middle of the floor was barefooted. She was wearing a slip and apparently nothing else. Her blond hair was uncombed. A cigarette dangled from her lower lip and her face had the sullen expression of surly defiance which comes to those who have refused to conform to the conventions of life and mask their doubts behind a pose.

On the dilapidated dresser with its cheap mirror which gave a distorted reflection of the room was a square bottle of gin half full. A streaked water tumbler on the dresser was partially filled with gin and an empty gin bottle lay on its side near the edge of the dresser.

"Say listen," the woman said, "I'm respectable. I come here when I want to go on a bat. My old man don't like me to hit the booze. I've paid my rent and I'm living alone and liking it. All I want is a chance to finish off this bottle of gin, twelve hours' sleep, and then I'll walk out of here and go back to listening to his line of chatter and washing dishes and ironing his shirts. Now what the hell do *you* want?"

Clane noticed that, while the room itself was impregnated with the odor of gin, the smell of alcohol was that of fresh liquor, not the stale smell which comes from the breath of a heavy drinker.

"I'm sorry, Mrs. Taonon," he said, "but in this particular instance, the disguise won't work."

Her eyes were quick with startled fear.

"So," Clane said, "we may as well dispense with the alcoholic subterfuge and get down to brass tacks."

For a moment she regarded him dubiously, then her eyes shifted to Sou Ha and Chu Kee. They were shrewd, calculating eyes now which studied facial expressions with quick appraisal.

Abruptly she crossed to a closet, took out a smart, well-tailored dress, slipped it on over her head, opened a drawer, took out well-made, expensive alligator shoes and nylon stockings. She put on both shoes and stockings, opened her handbag, took out a comb, and combed back the tangled mass of her hair. Abruptly she had transformed herself from a blowsy blonde into a smartly tailored, quick-thinking, dangerous antagonist.

"Won't you sit down?" she asked. "I think there aren't any bugs. That's about all I can say for the place. Two of you will have to sit on the bed. The girl can take the rocking chair. I wouldn't advise that straight-backed chair. It's treacherous. Now what is it you want?"

"What are you running away from?" Clane asked.

"From people who want to ask me questions—perhaps."

"Why?"

"Because I'm tired of answering questions."

"Whose questions?"

"Yours, for one. Suppose we start with you. Let's find out who you are. What authority do you have to question me?"

"I'm looking for information."

"So I gathered," she said somewhat scornfully.

She was calm, poised, and wary—very much in command of herself and rapidly ready to assume command of the situation.

"I'm Terry Clane. I know your husband."

"Oh, so *you're* Terry Clane."

"Right."

"And who are these people?"

"Friends of mine."

"And why should you ask questions?"

"Because I'm trying to clear up a mystery. Because if you don't choose to answer my questions, I'll ring up a friend, Inspector Malloy, tell him where you are and let him ask the questions."

That shot told. She said, "Go ahead and ask your questions."

"What are you running away from?"

"I'm afraid."

"Of what?"

"It might be any number of things."

"Such as what?"

"My husband, perhaps."

"What have you done that would make you afraid of him?"

"Nothing."

"Where is he now?"

"You'll have to ask him."

"Where were you last night?"

"Looking for someone."

"Who?"

"Perhaps it was my husband."

"Was it?"

"I'm not saying."

"Where did you go?"

"Places."

Clane sighed. "This isn't getting us anywhere. I guess we'll have to let the police do the questioning."

Once more she showed fear. "Tell me specifically what you want to know. I'll answer."

"Do you know Edward Harold?"

She hesitated, then said, "Yes."

"You met him last night. Did your husband ask you to meet him?"

"What makes you think I saw Edward Harold last night?"

"A witness says you did, a waitress in a restaurant."

"That's nonsense."

"Are you hiding from the police or from your husband?"

"What do you think?"

"I don't know. I'm asking because I want to find out."

She faced him, took a quick breath, then said, "All right, if you're going to drag it out of me, here it is. So far as Edward Harold is concerned, he means nothing to me. He's friendly with my husband. We were both sorry to hear of his arrest for murder and I for one was glad to hear of his escape.

"But there's another matter where Ricardo and I aren't so . . . well, there's another man, a business associate of my husband's. He thinks he's in love with me, and he wants to have a showdown with Ricardo. . . . I'm in the clear. I've done nothing. But Ricardo is insanely jealous at times. I don't know how much he thinks he knows or what he'd do. And he's disappeared and I'm hiding out until I see what's happened—or whether anything's going to happen. I'm scared."

"Who is this business associate of your husband who is infatuated with you? Is it Nevis?"

"Don't be silly."

"Was it Gloster?"

"Now aren't you smart!"

Clane said, "Your husband carries quite a bit of insurance. It's payable to you. Your husband is dead."

She stiffened into frozen attention. "Ricardo dead?"

"You know he is."

"Then if you know that, you must know why he was hiding."

Clane said nothing.

"And why I was hiding," she added.

"You were hiding for the same reason he was?"

"Of course. He got me on the phone, told me to get under cover where I couldn't be traced. The fat was in the fire."

"Do you mean," Clane asked, "that he had murdered Gloster?"

She said, "If you know so much why don't you know more?"

"I'm asking you."

"Ricardo is dead?"

"So I understand from the police."

"How?"

"I don't know the details. A police inspector inadvertently let the cat out of the bag."

"That Ricardo was dead?"

"Yes."

"When did he die?"

"I don't know."

For a long moment she studied him with thought-narrowed eyes. Then she said suddenly, "That's different. Let's go."

"Where?"

"Back home."

Clane said, "You don't seem to show any grief."

Her manner was scornful. "I thought I was dealing with someone of intelligence. You know as well as I do there's no use showing any grief over something that has happened. Furthermore, the women who have hysterics and sob and shriek and whoop and want to be comforted are the ones who are putting on an act. I know the way I feel and that's all that counts."

Clane said dryly, "The position of the police is that you stand to profit by your husband's death. You can't expect them to overlook that."

"What are you getting at?"

"Surely you can put two and two together?"

"Meaning that I killed him?"

Clane met her eyes. "You could hardly expect the police to overlook the obvious."

She took the half-filled glass of gin, poured it into the slop-jar, took a hat out of the closet, adjusted it in front of the cheap wavy mirror, put on her coat, and said, "Let's go."

"After all," Clane said, "before you . . ."

"Let's go. Let's face the police. Let's get it over with. Surely you weren't bluffing, Mr. Clane?"

Chu Kee blandly held the door open. Clane stood to one side to let the women precede him.

Her head held high, Mrs. Ricardo Taonon sailed through the door and marched down the corridor, no longer the blowsy blonde who had retired for a gin binge in a cheap Chinese hotel, but a trim, smartly clothed woman, keeping her own counsel and playing her own cards.

"I think," Clane said, "we'll call Inspector Malloy first."

"Call anyone you damn please," Mrs. Ricardo Taonon snapped at him. "I'm going home. And if you don't call the police, I will."

# 19

THE eight-room apartment of Ricardo Taonon was furnished with objects of Oriental art. Some of these were museum pieces, carved ivories, and polished jades. The place might well have been the residence of a wealthy Hong Kong merchant. And in this setting, Daphne Taonon assumed an assurance of manner which held just a trace of condescension. Apparently Inspector Malloy was impressed despite himself.

Mrs. Taonon said to Inspector Malloy, "Let's understand each other right at the start. Mr. Clane told me you were looking for me, that you wanted to question me."

"That's right."

"He came to me and started to ask questions. These two friends of his, the Chinese man and, I understand, his daughter, were with him."

"Very interesting," Malloy said. "How did he know where to find you?"

"I don't know."

Malloy turned to Clane and raised his eyebrows.

"Deductive reasoning," Clane said.

"Very, very interesting," Inspector Malloy observed. "I'll ask you more about that after a while. In the meantime I want to talk with Mrs. Taonon. By the way, did Mr. Clane say what the police wanted to ask you about?"

"My husband's death."

"Well, well, well," Malloy said. "And how did Mr. Clane know that your husband was dead?"

"I don't know. He told me that my husband had been— killed."

"Murdered?"

"I gathered that was what he meant."

"Well, now," Malloy said, "perhaps that deductive reasoning of Mr. Clane's has gone a lot farther than I had thought at the time. You see, Mr. Clane himself had been under suspicion and we gave him a clean bill of health only a short time ago because we thought he'd told us all he knew. But it seems he knew that your husband had been murdered and he knew where to go to find you to tell you about it."

"Isn't that the truth?"

"What?"

"About my husband?"

"I wouldn't know, ma'am. When was the last time you saw him?"

"Last night."

"Perhaps you can fix it a little closer than that as to time?"

"About ten o'clock. He was called to the telephone."

"Know who was talking?"

"No."

"And what happened?"

"My husband seemed very much excited, very much put out about something. He also seemed a little alarmed. He put on his hat and coat and went out."

"And didn't come back?"

"Not to my knowledge."

"By the way, where were you?"

"I went out."

"Where?"

She said, "A friend of my husband's telephoned and was very anxious to see him. He asked me to drive him to a place where I thought my husband might be. I drove him there."

"Find your husband?"

"No."

"Who was this friend of your husband's?"

"I prefer not to answer that question."

"Not some friend of yours?"

"I said that he was a friend of my husband. His friendship for me was incidental."

"And how long were you gone?"

"Well, after I left that friend, I did some things on my own."

"What?"

She shook her head.

"What time did you get back?"

"Some time this morning."

"Left your car here and then you yourself left almost immediately?"

"Yes."

"Where?"

"Where this gentleman found me."

"And where was that?"

She met Inspector Malloy's eyes. "It was in a cheap Chinese hotel," she said. "I was registered under the name of Mrs. George L. Brown and I had used the best disguise I could on a moment's notice. I tried to make myself look like one of the women who frequent places of that sort."

"Why?"

"Because I was afraid."

"Of what?"

"I can't tell you that."

Malloy said, "You came back to this apartment in the morning?"

"Yes."

"And how soon did you leave?"

"Within five minutes."

"Not in your car?"

"No."

"Why?"

"Because I had no place to leave my car. I wanted to go where I couldn't be traced."

"Again why?"

"Because I tell you I was frightened."

"You weren't frightened until you came back here and found your husband wasn't here?"

"Well . . . perhaps so, yes."

"How long was it after your husband left before you left?"

"Not very long."

"I'm afraid I've got to know what frightened you," Malloy said.

"That is a personal matter."

"And it wasn't until Mr. Clane told you your husband was dead that you were willing to come back?"

"I don't see that that follows."

"But after you heard he was dead, you came back."

"You can, of course, put it that way if you want to."

Malloy turned back to Clane and said, "Now every time I run into a blind alley, you seem to be lurking in the shadows. You and this Chinese girl. Now suppose you tell me . . ."

The telephone rang.

Mrs. Taonon answered it. "It's for you, Inspector."

Malloy sighed wearily, postponed his questioning, got up and lumbered across the room to the telephone, picked up the receiver, said, "Yeah, this is Malloy."

He listened for several seconds while the party at the other end of the line apparently poured out a steady stream of conversation. Then Malloy said, "Uh-huh," and then after a moment asked, "Where?"

Again there was a period of silence, broken at length by Malloy, who said, "All right, I'm up here. Bring your party up here . . . Yeah, I'll do it here. G'by."

He hung up the receiver, walked back to his chair, settled himself comfortably, bit the tip off the end of a cigar and said, quite casually, "All of this stuff interests me. How Clane knew where he could go and find you right away. You any idea how he knew where you were, Mrs. Taonon?"

"No, I had never met him before. To the best of my knowledge I had never seen him in my life."

"Him and this Chinese girl," Malloy said, shaking his head. "They certainly do get around." Then he added, all in the same breath, "That call was from police headquarters. They found your husband."

"His body?"

"Your husband. Seems he was hiding too."

"Where?"

"San José, in an auto court. You see, we thought we might find Edward Harold located in an auto court somewhere so we put out a dragnet. And, because we thought your husband might have driven him down to the auto court, we broadcast a description of your husband. Your husband didn't drive Harold down to an auto court."

"No?" she asked courteously.

"No."

"And you say my husband's alive?"

"Very much alive."

She whirled to Clane. "What the devil were you trying to do?" she demanded.

Clane, at a loss for an answer, sat silent.

"No," Inspector Malloy said calmly, "your husband didn't take Edward Harold down the peninsula and put him in an auto court. *You* did that."

She looked at the police inspector with the defiance of a trapped animal.

"But now," Malloy said, "I've got to find out why you hid and why your husband went down the peninsula a good half to three-quarters of an hour in advance of your trip. Couldn't have been because you stayed behind to kill George Gloster, could it?"

"Don't be absurd."

"That package of groceries that we found down there in the room at the warehouse where Edward Harold had been concealed. You wouldn't know anything about that, would you?"

"Certainly not."

Malloy's eyes were kindly but insistent. "Your grocer," he said, "tells a different story."

Color rushed to her face, then faded from it. Twice she tried to speak, but no words came out.

"So," Inspector Malloy went on, "unless you make some satisfactory explanation, we're going to have to hold you for investigation, which is just about the same in this instance as dumping a murder charge in your lap, Mrs. Taonon."

She smiled at him. "Dump a murder charge in *my* lap," she said, "and it will bounce right back and hit you in the face."

# 20

TWO officers brought in Ricardo Taonon. For a moment he stood in the doorway motionless with surprise, watchful, wary, his mind probing the situation. Evidently he had not been apprised of the fact that police were there interrogating his wife, or that Terry Clane, Chu Kee, and Sou Ha were also there, held in a species of unofficial custody.

Taonon stood there in the doorway for the fractional part of a second and in that brief period of time adjusted himself to the situation as he saw it. He was slender, dark, high of cheekbone, with just a slight slant to his eyes. And there was about him the reaction so characteristic of the Japanese, of smiling broadly when he found himself cornered. While he had always claimed a Chinese-Italian ancestry, rumor had it that his mother had been a young Japanese girl who had met a suave Italian on the Street of the Wild Chicken in Shanghai.

Daphne Taonon gave her husband his conversational lead. "My *darling!*" she exclaimed and moved toward him, face tilted.

Taonon stepped forward to take her in his arms and the period during which they clung in a passionate embrace gave her an opportunity for one swiftly whispered word.

Then Daphne moved back from the embrace. "Darling," she said, "do you know what they told me? They told me you were dead. And do you know what this man Clane said? He said that *I* had killed you for the insurance."

For a brief moment there was a flicker of dark anger on Taonon's face and then he threw back his head and laughed, that nervous, staccato Japanese laughter. "Well, well, well," he said. "Mr. Clane's vaunted powers of concentration seem to have led him far afield."

Malloy said, "I guess I'll do the questioning. Come over here and sit down. Where have you been, Taonon?"

"I took a little trip."

"Went down the peninsula, headed for Salinas, registered in an auto camp under an assumed name, and hid out for a while, didn't you?"

"Frankly," Taonon said, "I'm given to fits of nervous depression. When I have those, I want to get away from everyone. I want to be quiet. I want to be undisturbed. I don't want to think any business and I don't want to have anyone talk any business to me."

"So you got a telephone call from George Gloster and suddenly decided you wanted to go on one of these trips of retirement. Is that right?"

"I fail to see the significance of connecting up the two events," Taonon said with dignity. "You might as well say, 'So you opened the bathroom door and suddenly decided you wanted to get away on one of these trips.'"

"But you did get a call from Gloster?"

Taonon hesitated.

"Come, come," Malloy said. "You did get a call from Gloster. We know that."

"All right," Taonon said, "I got a call from Gloster."

"And he told you he was at the warehouse?"

179

"If it's any of your business, yes."

"It's plenty of my business," Malloy said. "You went down to the warehouse to see him?"

"I did."

"What time?"

"I don't know. It was around ten-thirty, I guess, when I arrived."

"And Gloster was there?"

"That's right."

"You talked with him?"

"Not very long."

"Why not?"

"Because I didn't have much to say."

"Why did Gloster want you to come down to the warehouse?"

"He had gone down on some business or other and found evidence that someone had been living there in the warehouse, someone who had evidently got in with a key. He seemed to think that this person might have been Edward Harold. A man had jumped out of the window when Gloster entered. Gloster thought it was Harold. Gloster tried to call Nevis, but Nevis wasn't at his apartment. He called me. I answered, and came down to see what the trouble was."

"Any words?"

"Frankly I was irritated that Gloster hadn't called the police. I saw no reason for him to call Nevis and me."

"What did you tell him?"

"I told him that I knew nothing about it and didn't want to know anything about it. I demanded that he call the police. He didn't want to do it until he had first found out whether this party, whoever he was, had been staying there in the warehouse with the consent of one of the partners."

"So what did you do?"

"So I told him where I thought Nevis could be reached at a poker game."

"And what happened?"

"I don't know. I walked out. I gave him to understand that if he wasn't going to call the police I didn't want to have anything to do with the entire affair.

"He was calling Nevis as I went out of the door. I was angry and nervous. I drove around for a few minutes, stopped in at a bar for a brandy, and then decided I didn't want to inflict myself on my wife; so I drove for a couple of hours to steady my nerves, found an auto camp that had a vacancy and went to bed."

"I see," Inspector Malloy said dryly. "You drove aimlessly, found an auto court, registered under an assumed name, and were within five miles of the auto camp where Edward Harold had also registered under an assumed name."

The surprise which showed on Taonon's face could hardly have been simulated. "What?" he cried.

"Five miles farther down the road, Edward Harold was staying, also under an assumed name in an auto camp. He must have followed you!"

"Is this a joke? Or some weird third degree?"

"It's neither," Malloy said. "It's the truth, and the woman who drove Harold down to that auto camp was your devoted wife. And in case you're also interested, the person who established Harold there in the warehouse was also your devoted wife."

"What are you talking about?" Taonon demanded.

"The grocer down in the market on the corner says that the groceries supplied to Harold in his hide-out were purchased by your wife."

Taonon turned to his wife.

"So," he said.

And before anyone divined his purpose, he sent his fist lashing out to crash into the point of her jaw.

There was a moment of motionless surprise on the part of Inspector Malloy as he watched the woman's figure crumple. Then his big hand caught a fistful of Taonon's shirt, twisted it into a hold that gave him purchase, and shook the Eurasian as a big dog might shake some street cur.

Abruptly, he steadied the man. His free hand slapped Taonon hard across the face. "Resist me," he begged. "Kick at me. Give me a chance to smash your face in."

Taonon, the red imprint of Malloy's hand on his face, merely grinned his nervous grin.

"I'm not *that* easy," he said.

Inspector Malloy turned to the officers who had brought Taonon in. "Take them down to Headquarters—both of them. I'll be right down."

"Do you want to take me back into custody?" Clane asked Malloy.

"Bless you, no," Malloy said. "I wouldn't think of it. You're ever so much more valuable out here running around and playing bird dog. You do flush the damnedest game. How did you know where to go to find Mrs. Taonon?"

"A matter of deduction, I guess."

"Well, keep on deducing," Malloy said. "Go ahead, flush some more of them. The way you've been doing, I wouldn't doubt a bit if the next person you dug up would turn out to be Cynthia Renton. I just have an idea that you'll lead us to her if we give you a little rope. Go right ahead, Mr. Clane."

Clane smiled at him. "Good night, Inspector."

"Good night, Mr. Clane. And do try to get some sleep. I imagine I'll be seeing you somewhere along the line. And you, young lady, don't you take in any more washing."

"I won't," Sou Ha assured him.

"Of course, if you're *really* looking for housework," Malloy said, "I can give you a job."

"Thank you, I'll keep it in mind," Sou Ha promised.

# 21

CYNTHIA RENTON rushed toward Terry Clane impulsively, "Oh, Owl," she exclaimed. "I'm so glad you're back. Tell me, what happened?"

"Lots of things," Clane said. "Ricardo Taonon disappeared and was found. His wife disappeared and was found. I have been in jail. I have seen Edward Harold and . . ."

"How is he, Owl? Tell me, how is he?"

"Naturally," Clane said, "he's pretty blue and discouraged. He's resentful. He didn't feel particularly cordial toward me. If it hadn't been for Chu Kee here, I'd still have been . . ."

Clane broke off abruptly as he realized Chu Kee was not

there. The Chinese and his daughter had quietly slipped away.

"They came in with you," Cynthia said, looking around. "Where did they go?"

Clane said, "Probably thought we wanted to be alone."

"Don't we?"

"Not now, Cynthia. I have some work to do. I'm going to have to take some chances."

"All right, Owl. I'm going to take chances with you."

"*You* are going to stay right here."

She laughed. "That shows all you know about it. I'm going with you. I've got you into a mess and I'm going to be with you from now on, helping you if I can. If I can't help, I'll at least walk into the arms of the police and take the responsibility for what's been done. I've been sitting here hating myself for the way I've let you run risks on my account. You've always been a refuge for me when times got tough, and it seemed natural to run to you for help. Only in the last few hours did I realize how unfair it was . . . Owl, *please* let me go with you."

Clane saw the pleading desperation on her face. "All right," he said at length, and then added, "Perhaps Harold will feel better about it if you clear the mystery up instead of me."

"Don't be silly, Owl. Ed Harold thinks you're one of the grandest men on earth. I've told him so much about you that I . . ."

"Have made him hate me," Clane said.

She made a little grimace. "He'll get over that. When do we go?"

"Now."

"Where do we go?"

"We're going down to the warehouse of the Eastern Art Import and Trading Company," Clane said. "We're going to hope that police don't have it under guard and that we can find some way of getting in. It will be a felonious entry at best, and may be something a lot more serious."

"And what are we going to do when we get in there?"

"If we don't get caught," Clane said, "we're going to try and determine why George Gloster's dust-covered fingerprints were left on a desk blotter."

"Why, Owl? What does that have to do with it?"

Clane said, "It may be the solution of the whole business."

"Owl, do you know how to get out of here? Coming in we went through tunnels and down staircases and . . ."

"I think so," Clane said and, raising his voice, called out, "Embroidered Halo!"

She appeared almost instantly, moving through embroidered silk curtains which concealed a doorway. She had changed from her American clothes into Chinese garb, and with the change she seemed to have renounced everything about her which was of the Occident. She was completely Chinese as she looked up at Clane with an inscrutable countenance; and, recognized her mood, Clane instinctively addressed her in Chinese. "Embroidered Halo, I have to leave upon a mission of some danger. The Painter Woman wishes to go with me. She is not accustomed to inaction. It is not wise that she go with me; but I am going to try to clear up the murder which was committed in the warehouse. If the man she loves is to be cleared of murder, it would be better that Cynthia herself did it."

"The man she loves?" Sou Ha asked in Chinese, her face expressionless.

"Yes."

"The man she loves is standing beside her."

Clane flushed. "Don't be silly, Sou Ha. She is going to marry Edward Harold."

"And you wish to leave here undetected?"

Clane nodded.

"It will be arranged," Sou Ha said. "Will you come with me, please?"

She led them through a corridor, paused before a door of carved and inlaid wood. Clane knew that the other side of this door was of steel with a veneer of varnished pine.

Sou Ha stopped, her hand on the catch which controlled the door. Her face, without expression, was raised to Terry Clane. "Will you always remember," she asked in Chinese, "that in the abode of my father there is a refuge for you and your friends? that such things as we can do for you are yours to command? Anything. Everything."

"You are a dear girl," Clane said. "I am indebted to you both more than I can ever repay."

Her face flushed. "Never speak of repayment to Chinese," she flared and pressed a catch which caused the door to swing open. A Chinese stood on guard in the dingy, grimy corridor which was disclosed beyond the door.

"Will you see that these people are escorted to the street and that they are undetected?" Sou Ha asked in Chinese.

He bowed acquiescence.

Clane turned with outstretched hand, "Good-by, Embroidered Halo, and . . ."

He paused as he realized he was addressing a blank wall. Some pressure of her foot had caused a partition to slide into place, leaving only the open door and what seemed to be a solid wall.

"Don't you see, Owl," Cynthia said softly, "that is why she changed to Chinese clothes, to tell you that there is between you the gulf of racial difference. Let's get out of here, Owl, before I start bawling."

## 22

AT THE warehouse of the Eastern Art Import and Trading Company Clane dismissed the Chinese driver. "Do not wait," he said. "It may be dangerous."

"I was instructed to be at your service."

"You've done a splendid job. You're certain we were not followed?"

"You were not followed," the Chinese driver assured him positively.

"That is all I ask," Clane said. "You may report to your master that you have done all that I wished."

The Chinese inclined his head, the motor whirred into activity, and the car glided smoothly away through the poorly lighted streets.

Terry Clane and Cynthia Renton stood there in the darkness,

waiting until the taillight had vanished around a corner, until the sound of the motor was no longer audible.

"Owl," Cynthia whispered, "I'm scared."

"Want to go back?"

"Gosh, no! I wouldn't miss it for a million dollars. I'm just telling you I'm scared. That makes it all the more thrilling. What do we do next?"

Clane tried the door. It was locked. Like two furtive shadows, they moved around the building until they came to the window through which police claimed Edward Harold had made his escape the night of the murder, only to return later and kill the man who had discovered him.

Not only was this window unlocked, but it had not been entirely closed. There was an opening of an inch and a half at the bottom.

"Gosh, that's luck," Cynthia whispered.

Clane frowningly contemplated the window for several seconds.

"What's the matter?"

"It's almost too inviting," Clane said. "It may be a trap. If you hear a noise when we raise the window, Cynthia—the sound of a burglar alarm or anything—just get moving. Don't wait for me."

Clane slipped on light gloves so his fingers would leave no print, and raised the window.

The sash slid up smoothly and noiselessly.

"You'd better wait here, Cynthia, and . . ."

"Don't be a sap, Owl. I'm coming in. You give me a boost and I can help you up."

Without a word, Clane lifted her in his arms, boosted her through the window, then followed her into the silence of the office.

"Now what?" Cynthia whispered.

Clane said, "I want to find the paper which Gloster must have found before he was killed."

"How do you know he found a paper, Owl?"

Clane said, "I don't *know*. I'm guessing, but we have pretty good grounds for guessing. Gloster came to the warehouse for something. He found Edward Harold here. That must have started him looking around. His hands got in some deep dust somewhere. Then he must have found something. Whatever it was, he took it to the desk here and put it on the desk. The fingerprints of his left hand were outlined in dust on the blotter. The nature of the prints showed he was putting pressure on the first and second fingers of his hand. That means he was leaning over the desk in the position a man would assume in studying a paper. In that position his thumb must have also borne part of the weight he was resting on his hand. But there is no thumb print."

"Why, Owl?"

"Malloy says it's because there was no dust on his thumb."

"You don't think so?"

"No. I think he had found a rolled paper in a dusty place. He went to the desk, unrolled the paper and held it with his left hand, the fingers on the blotter, the thumb on the top of the paper. So put your feminine mind to work and tell me where a rolled paper could have been concealed in a place where dust must have been a quarter of an inch thick."

"There's only one place, Owl, that I can think of."

"Where?"

"That picture molding around the top of the wall. After all, this is a warehouse and they don't do too much housekeeping."

Clane moved a chair over to the wall, put a box on top of the chair. While Cynthia steadied the chair, he climbed up to the box. The beam of his flashlight slid along the edge of the picture molding.

"Dust enough, Cynthia," he said, "but nothing here."

"Let's try the other wall."

The second wall also yielded a blank, but midway along the third wall, Clane saw where the dust had been disturbed. There was something which could have been a rolled piece of paper reposing in the dust.

Clane marked the place, said excitedly, "I think we've got it, Cynthia! We'll have to move the chair."

Too excited now to bother about being cautious, they dragged the chair midway along the wall, and Clane climbed up on the chair, then on the box and possessed himself of two sheets of paper which were held in a tight roll with two small elastic bands.

Clane slipped off the elastic bands, unrolled the papers. They were covered with fine pen-and-ink writing.

Clane held the flashlight. He and Cynthia put their heads together reading.

"It's Farnsworth's handwriting," Cynthia said, "and the date . . . Owl! It's the date he was murdered."

Clane nodded, gave himself to a perusal of the document.

To Whom It May Concern:

I have lost the desire to live. There is no atonement I can make, save to confess. And after I have made that confession, I do not care to go on living. I was trustee for money for Cynthia Renton. I invested this money in gold-mining properties near Baguio in the Philippines, gold-mining properties which I had carefully investigated and which looked good to me. At that time all of my personal money was invested in a partnership enterprise for Oriental trade, a partnership consisting of George Gloster, Ricardo Taonon, and Stacey Nevis as my associates. We all held an equal interest. We had an opportunity to plunge heavily and we plunged and lost. In the meantime, the mining enterprise in which I had invested the trust moneys proved to be immensely rich. I had an opportunity to sell out at an enormous profit. It was then that Ricardo Taonon pointed out to me that no one knew the gold mine had been an investment of trust funds since it had all been in my name. I had only to take some money from that to recoup the partnership business, and there would still be enough left to yield Cynthia a handsome profit; and the money would only be in the nature of a loan to the partnership.

Ricardo Taonon made the thing sound so convincing that I felt certain taking twenty-five thousand dollars of the profits on the gold mine and investing it temporarily in the partnership business would give us just the added capital we needed to get over the hump and would enable us to turn what would otherwise have been a hundred-thousand-dollar loss into a half-million-dollar profit.

Either the man hypnotized me or I was crazy. I did as he suggested. That involved signing papers. I signed them—papers showing the whole gold mine was a partnership investment. Then I asked Taonon for an accounting. It was then he told me I could draw out any sum of money I wished to reimburse Miss

Renton for her trust funds but that the documents I had signed were to the effect I had acted for the partnership in the mining deal. I was trapped in my own duplicity. True, Cynthia would sustain no impairment of her trust funds, but she had lost enormous profits. I decided to try again. I put five thousand in an oil deal for her. This oil proposition looked better than the mining deal ever had. I convinced myself Taonon's treachery had all been for the best. And then the oil deal failed to be profitable. It gives every sign of simply dying on the vine. But Cynthia Renton is asking for an accounting. I am satisfied that Edward Harold, to whom she is engaged and who has just called on me, is suspicious and intends to make a detailed investigation.

The only way I can really make atonement is by a full confession. Cynthia Renton is the real owner of all of my interest in the Eastern Art Import and Trading Company. Moreover, she is entitled to all the assets of that company. She is also the real owner of the contents of the envelope which I am leaving in plain sight on the desk. There is nothing I can add to this statement. I only wish to God that I could subtract from it. I have loved Cynthia Renton. I have been entrusted with her confidence. I have failed her, and I have failed myself. The only thing I can say by way of justification is that Ricardo Taonon is unspeakably evil. The man has a hypnotic influence upon those with whom he comes in contact. Under his suave, persuasive influence I have done that which has robbed me of the desire to live. I am taking the easy way out. I only hope that Cynthia will forgive me.

On the other hand, however, I have received money from the partnership. Taonon is evil, but the other partners are blameless. I leave a fair sum in insurance and no immediate relatives. I therefore give, devise and bequeath all of my individual estate, share and share alike, to George Gloster, Stacey Nevis, and Ricardo Taonon as copartners transacting business under the firm name and style of Eastern Art Import and Trading Company.

HORACE FARNSWORTH

"He killed himself," Cynthia said breathlessly.

"I felt certain that he did," Clane told her. "Edward Harold told me what had happened. I think that was the first time he ever told anyone the true story of what had occurred. He found Farnsworth very dejected, hinting at some dark secret. He went back to get that image I had given you. He wanted to use

189

it to cheer Farnsworth up. Harold said it had helped him and
. . . well, you can see what happened. All that the picture
needed to be a complete case of suicide was this letter on the
desk and the presence of a gun. Someone slipped into the room,
removed the gun, and took this letter and the envelope of
papers. That made it look like murder."

"You mean Ricardo Taonon had . . ."

"No, no," Clane said impatiently. "Don't you see? There's
only one person. Once you look at the evidence properly, it
points to— What's that?" he asked, stopping abruptly.

"What?"

"I thought I heard a noise, a . . ."

A switch clicked, lights blazed into brilliance—a blinding
illumination which left them dazed and blinking. Their eyes,
having accustomed themselves to the darkness and the faint
illumination of the fountain-pen flashlight which Clane had
been using, failed for a moment to adjust themselves to the
sudden burst of light.

Inspector Malloy's voice was booming and genial. "Well,
well, well, Clane. You did it again. You really did! I told you
that you were more value to us running around loose and playing bird dog. You flushed some real game this time. Cynthia
Renton! We've certainly been looking for you. I rather expected Clane would come back here and start snooping around;
but to think that you . . . And what have we here, Mr. Clane?
What's this paper you were talking about?"

Wordlessly Clane handed him the paper.

Inspector Malloy glanced at it, then gave it intense study.
"A plant?" he asked suspiciously.

Clane shook his head.

Malloy said, "This could be serious, you know, Clane. This
will be subjected to scrutiny by the best handwriting experts in
the country."

"Scrutinize it all you want," Clane said. "You can see now
what happened. It's the only thing that *could* have happened.
Gloster found something that startled him, something that
made it imperative that he meet with the others immediately.
He couldn't reach Nevis at once because Nevis was in a poker

190

game. But he called Taonon and told him to come to the warehouse at once."

"Go on," Malloy said.

"Gloster had to get something here in the warehouse," Clane went on. "He drove here. Harold was hiding here. He jumped out of the window as Gloster came in. Gloster phoned Taonon. While he was waiting for Ricardo Taonon, something made him decide to look around. He found this note.

"The note speaks for itself. Farnsworth committed suicide. Let's examine the evidence in the light of that hypothesis. Farnsworth was despondent, trapped. He took the easy way out.

"Now let's look at what happened after that—the only thing that *could* have happened. When the police arrived at Farnsworth's house, they found a kettle of water on the electric stove, the water boiling rapidly. They found the oven hot, and Farnsworth's wrist watch, bearing evidences of having been wet, drying in the oven. When Harold returned to the house, the back door was unlocked.

"Figure it out. Sam Kenyon must have returned from his afternoon off. He let himself in through the back door. He put on a kettle of water, turned on the oven, and then went in to see what Farnsworth wanted for supper. He found Farnsworth dead, this document on the desk, the gun lying where it had dropped from Farnsworth's nerveless fingers.

"Kenyon evidently is an opportunist. He saw a chance to get rich. He took the gun, the envelope, the document, and he went to Ricardo Taonon or to Stacey Nevis. He made his demands. Whatever they were, they were met. He was instructed to return to the house and call the police.

"When he went back to the house he let himself in through the front door. He called the police, and then just before they arrived he went back to the kitchen. The water was boiling merrily away. The oven had been turned on and was now smoking hot—evidence that he had previously been to the house. Even if he had dumped out the water, he couldn't have cooled off the oven. The police were driving up to the place even then. He thought fast. He rushed in, took Farnsworth's wrist watch, snapped off the back, put water in it, put it in the

191

oven, and then let the police in. Later on, when police looked around and found the boiling water and the wrist watch, it looked as though Farnsworth had put the water on the stove, had got water in his watch in the process and had put the watch in the oven to dry.

"The police never did explain that kettle of boiling water and the wrist watch. Because of the way Harold messed up his case, they didn't have to. But when you put the whole thing together, there's only one explanation."

Malloy frowned as he studied the paper. "It sounds logical the way you outline it—and *if* this is genuine. But right now it looks like a plant to me. It smells fishy."

"It's genuine. It has to be. It can't be a plant. Once Farnsworth had killed himself, once Kenyon had seen the body and this note . . . it's so obvious there's no use wasting time talking."

"And so they let Harold take the rap?"

"At the time, they didn't know anything about Harold, or about Harold's visit. They were merely turning a suicide into a murder so as to save their own skins. It probably never occurred to them someone would be convicted of that murder."

Malloy thought things over, pursing his lips as he fitted this new evidence into the picture.

"Everyone agrees Gloster was honest as the day is long," Clane went on. "He was a grouch, but he was on the square. So he wasn't in on it at all. Taonon simply told Gloster that Farnsworth had been working for the partnership in locating those Philippine investments. Gloster believed him. Then came Harold's trial and conviction. Taonon and Nevis were in a quandary. To let Harold be executed for a murder he hadn't committed was beyond the scope of their plans. They didn't dare to speak up and tell the truth. . . . So they did the next best thing. They arranged for Harold to escape."

"And what of this paper?" Malloy asked.

"They concealed it here. They didn't dare destroy it because if the worst ever came to the worst, this was a will. They could plant it in some place where it could be found. If the cat got out of the bag and there was other evidence Farnsworth had left which would strip the partnership of the mining properties, then Farnsworth's estate would be a consolation prize. So they concealed the paper here. After Gloster was killed, the paper was reconcealed in its original hiding place."

"Go on," Malloy said.

"Gloster couldn't get Nevis on the phone because Nevis was at a poker game," Clane said. "But he got Taonon, and Taonon came down here."

"And killed him?"

"No. He told him where Nevis could be reached, and then Taonon ducked out. He crawled in a hole and pulled the hole in after him. He would probably have tried to leave the country if the newspapers next day hadn't carried the story of Gloster's death. So Taonon hid out to wait and see what the next developments were, and he phoned his wife and told her to do the same thing. That's the only consistent way of explaining what happened."

"Then who the devil killed Gloster?" Malloy asked.

"Let's reconstruct what must have happened," Clane said. "Gloster got Taonon down here. Taonon told him to call Nevis. Then Taonon skipped out. That made Gloster mad. He called Nevis at the number Taonon had given him, and he called me later on."

"I'm listening," Malloy said. "So far this is your baby."

Clane said, "Nevis came down here and . . ."

"No, he didn't," Malloy interrupted. "He didn't come down here. Gloster went to see him."

Clane shook his head. "Nevis came down here."

"Clane, you're crazy. There are half a dozen witnesses to . . ."

"To what?" Clane interrupted.

"The telephone conversation when Nevis and Gloster agreed to meet—to the meeting itself."

"How many witnesses saw Nevis and Gloster engaged in conversation?" Clane asked.

"Well, of course, you can't expect . . ."

"Nevis lied," Clane said. "Gloster never went to see Nevis at all. Nevis came down here to see him."

"Any evidence to prove that?" Malloy asked.

"Gloster's car."

"What about the car?"

"Did you notice anything peculiar about the car when you saw it?" Clane asked.

"In what way?"

"The windshield, for instance?"

"No."

"Notice where particles of fog moisture had condensed on the windshield?"

"Yes. There was nothing unusual about that. It was foggy. Naturally the moisture would have condensed on the windshield."

"And some of the moisture had run in little rivulets down the hood."

"Yes."

"But did you notice any fan-shaped streaks on the windshield which would have been there if the windshield wipers had been at work, or any splash stains where drops of water running down from the windshield had been blown back by wind caused by the motion of the car? You did not. The reason you didn't see those things is that they weren't there. The reason they weren't there is that the fog settled some time after ten and before eleven, and Gloster's car wasn't moved after the fog settled. The mute evidence of that car proves Nevis is a liar."

Malloy scratched his head. "Well, now, Mr. Clane, you've contributed something there. Damned if you haven't."

"So," Clane went on, "we are in a position to reconstruct what happened. As soon as Stacey Nevis arrived, Gloster must have realized his danger and started for the telephone. Perhaps to call the police. Nevis shot him."

"They both were in on the murder?" Malloy asked.

"Nevis killed him," Clane said. "If Taonon had known he was dead, he would never have gone into hiding. While Gloster was telephoning to Nevis, Taonon saw his opportunity to wash his hands of the whole mess and get out. He left it entirely up to Nevis."

"What makes you think that?"

"Because of the way Taonon skipped out, then phoned his wife to skip out.

"Nevis is a man of action, not a man of words. Gloster told

him enough over the telephone so that Nevis knew what had happened. He made up his mind right then to commit murder. He put his finger on the receiver hook to cut the connection, then raised his voice so everyone at the poker table could hear him and said he couldn't get away from the poker game, that if Gloster wanted to come up and honk the horn, he'd go down and talk with him briefly. He was gone approximately twenty minutes. He had ample time in the twenty minutes while he was out of the poker game to drive down to the warehouse, kill Gloster, turn around and come back. I have an idea that if you check back on that poker party, you'll find that no one actually heard the honking of the horn except Nevis, that Nevis made it a point to tell everyone he had to be dealt out for a hand or two while he went down to talk with his partner on a business matter. He told them he would only be away five or ten minutes. Actually he was away for twenty minutes. But because he had been careful to implant the belief in their minds that he was sitting down in an automobile talking, everyone thought that's where he was. When you stop to analyze it, Nevis has no alibi at all. And furthermore, the mute evidence of Gloster's car shows that Nevis was lying. It has to be that way."

"I began to think that it might be something like that," Malloy admitted, "after I heard Harold's story."

"*You* heard Harold's story?"

Malloy grinned. "Sure. What the hell did you think we put you two in the same cell for? We wouldn't have put you in with a convicted murderer unless we'd wanted to hear his story. We thought he might talk to you."

"And you had the room wired?"

"Sure," Malloy said. "Us professionals can't do this brilliant deductive reasoning that you amateurs do, so we have to rely on a little practical stuff now and then. Well, that's the way it goes. Anyhow, you certainly did a job on that automobile. Guess that's something we overlooked. . . . But you *must* learn not to go around breaking into buildings, Mr. Clane, and doing all those unconventional things. When you have any information in the future, you'd better go to the police and tell them frankly what you have."

"And be laughed at for my pains," Clane said.

Malloy grinned. "Well, now, Mr. Clane," he said, "just between you and me, I don't think the police are going to laugh at you any more. I really don't for a fact. And now I have an idea perhaps you and this young lady would like to get the hell out of here, because we're going to bring Mr. Nevis down here and ask him a few questions."

"And how about Edward Harold?" Clane said.

"Well, now, if the conversation with Nevis turns out the way I think it's going to, I'm going to get in touch with the district attorney and the Governor, and there's just a chance a pardon might come through for Mr. Harold."

"In which event," Clane said, "I think you will agree that it's only fair Cynthia Renton should be the one who takes the news to him."

"We'll do it together," Cynthia said.

Clane smiled. "I think you'll find two would be company and three would be a crowd. But I think you'll agree, Malloy, that Miss Renton is entitled to go to police headquarters and wait there until you have some definite information."

"She is for a fact," Malloy agreed.

"And *you?*" Cynthia asked. "Where are *you* going?"

Clane said, "As far as I'm concerned, I've got to go hunt up Yat T'oy, and I think it's only fair I should tell Chu Kee what has happened."

"That's the old Chinese party you were with?" Malloy asked. Clane nodded.

"A pretty good friend, I'd say," Malloy said. "Damn it, Clane, we sewed up Chinatown. I mean we really had men parked all around it, and damned if you didn't slip through our fingers. And also what I want to know is how it happened you went in a door at the east end of Chinatown and made your next appearance in the hotel where Mrs. Taonon had hid herself—more than two blocks away, with every street corner guarded? Will you kindly tell me how the hell you did *that?*"

"That," Clane said, "is a matter of concentration, my dear Inspector . . ."

"Yeah, I know," Malloy said. "You go into the fourth dimension and wrap yourself in a robe of invisibility or something. All right, Clane, we'll let it go this time, but you might tell this Chu Kee person that if things like that keep up, the police are apt to make a raid on Chinatown and look around a little. We may not be able to find the secret doorways, but a sledgehammer will accomplish a lot."

"Thanks," Clane said dryly, "I'll tell him."

"And in this particular instance," Malloy went on, "you might give him my thanks, and that good-looking Chinese-American girl, too."

"I'll tell her."

Cynthia Renton followed him out. "Owl," she said, "you're leaving me just when I . . . damn it, just when I want you more than I ever wanted you in my life."

Clane said, "You have a duty to perform, Cynthia. Edward Harold has lost his faith in everything. You've got to tell him the news in such a way that he feels that justice can triumph in the world."

"When you're around to help it triumph," Cynthia said, "Where would he have been if you hadn't shown up?"

"Don't put it to him that way," Clane said, "or you'll undo all the good you want to accomplish."

"What will I tell him?"

"Tell him he's been exonerated and they're rushing through a pardon for him as soon as the red tape can be unwound. That's about all you need to do."

"And you? Where will you be?"

"Oh, I'll be around."

"Owl, are you trying to . . . Owl . . . are you in love with that Chinese girl?"

Clane said, "She's just a dear friend, Cynthia."

"You play around with that stuff and you'll find out something about friendship you never knew before," she told him. "Owl—come here."

He moved closer to her. Suddenly her arms were around his neck and her lips, salty with tears, were against his. "Oh, Owl, I need you so much," she sobbed, "and you're going away."

"Not very far away."

She watched him wistfully. "One can never tell about you, Terry Clane. I . . ."

Inspector Malloy opened the door. "Men are bringing Nevis down here," he said. "You'll have to get out of sight, Miss Renton. And you, Clane, are . . ."

"Just leaving," Clane said.

Cynthia Renton stood in the doorway with Malloy, watching Clane walk away into the darkness.

Inspector Malloy said musingly, "A remarkably talented young man."

"A rank amateur," Cynthia said, so savagely that Malloy turned to her in surprise. "The things that a really smart man should know, he doesn't know a damn thing about!"

Malloy raised his eyebrows, then stepped back inside the warehouse and softly closed the door.

>>> If you've enjoyed this book and would like to discover more great vintage crime and thriller titles, as well as the most exciting crime and thriller authors writing today, visit: >>>

## The Murder Room
**Where Criminal Minds Meet**

**themurderroom.com**